Secrets of the Silver River

The Four Bridges

B. Dailey

Copyright © 2023 Brendan J. Dailey

All rights reserved.
Published by Belden Books LLC, Chicago, Illinois.
First Edition.
ISBN-13: 9798391564461

The characters and events portrayed in this book are fictitious. Any similarity to real places or persons, living or dead, is coincidental and not intended by the author.

No part of this book may be reproduced, or stored in a retrieval system, or transmitted in any form or by any means, including electronic, mechanical, photocopying, recording, or otherwise, without express written permission of the publisher.

For permission requests, contact Belden Books LLC at BeldenBooks@gmail.com.

Printed in the United States of America.

To L.M. and S.C.

Prologue

I spit tiny bits of glass out of my mouth and rolled onto my back. My eyes were open, I think, but everything was dark. Well, everything except for a bright white ring at the center of all the black. The light wasn't really there anymore; it was just a shape burned into my vision, as if I had stared at the sun for a split second.

As I spread my arms across the marble floor, my skin touched slivers of crystal and globs of warm wax. Other bodies were around me somewhere, but no one was moving. If not for the ringing in my ears, I would have assumed I was dead too, crushed under the dome or smashed by a chandelier like some of the others.

I was one of the lucky ones, though. Lying there on the floor of the council chamber, the moments leading up to the blast floated back: the flash and then the boom when Aris pulled the trigger. To this day I still can't believe he actually did it. Aris, of all people. When he picked up the crossbow and aimed it at the stained-glass ceiling, surrounded by Search & Rescue guards, I was standing right next to him. And after all these years, the hearing in my left ear hasn't fully come back.

I watched the whitefire explode, but I don't remember the dome crashing down. I must have hit the ground immediately and covered my head. Some of the others didn't react fast enough. Maybe they were in shock, or maybe they assumed the council chamber was indestructible—after all, the room was the root of their power, where the laws were both made and enforced.

Yet even I knew justice was hit or miss in there, and I was only a kid back then.

Sometime after the roof collapsed, I woke up and heard muffled voices on the other side of the dome, urgent and frightened. It took them a while to get us out.

First, they tried banging on the silver with their axes. When they realized the metal shell wouldn't crack, they tried to pry open a section from the edges. That strategy worked eventually, but it wasn't easy. The dome's panel was difficult to lift not only because it was so heavy but also because the whitefire had melted the silver where the shot burned through.

While I waited in the dark, listening to them banging on the wall, I heard someone say my name. The ringing in my ears hadn't subsided yet, so I couldn't tell if the voice was real. But then I heard him say my name again.

"Bimo, is that you? Are you alright?"

Up until that point I wasn't entirely sure. I hadn't thought to check if I was breathing or bleeding or if any bones were broken. But when I heard Aris's voice, I knew we would be alright.

"I'm okay, Aris."

"Hold still. They'll get us out of here. Sera, where are you? Are you hurt?"

At the time I didn't know Sera at all. In fact, I didn't know much of anything about the Philosopher, the council, or the library. Nevertheless, when she told us what she saw inside the Silver River earlier that evening, I knew the city needed her. So, when she answered I felt weightless for a moment, the marble floor surging beneath me, lifting me like a raft.

"I'm over here, Aris. A little dizzy but I'll be fine."

By the owl, you'll have to forgive me—and not for the last time, that's for sure. Now that I'm writing this down, I realize you may not know much about the Philosopher either, or the Grand Fireplace, or the Silver River Gorge. For all I know, you might be reading this journal somewhere on the other side of the continent, and it's possible you've never heard of the Four Bridges.

So, maybe I should begin there.

Yes, that's the perfect place to start, I think.

Chapter I

The Silver River Gorge cuts at an angle through two towering mountain ranges—the Cloudhorns on the northwest and Shoulder Ridge on the southeast. Thousands of evergreen trees dot the steep gray shelves of the Cloudhorns, sparsely at first near the cloud line and denser down below where the forest stretches its arms into the valley. At the river's edge, the crowded branches hang low with pine-needle hands holding wet, heavy snow.

Whereas the highest peaks of the Cloudhorns can only be seen on rare, cloudless mornings, the rounded hilltops of Shoulder Ridge are always visible in the distance. Tucked away in its hills are mostly white oaks and vine maples, with hemlocks and firs interspersed at higher elevations. Spread out across the valley's bottom is the City of Sterling, where farmers have taken advantage of the ridge's gradual slopes to cultivate fields that rise neatly in rows up the mountainside. Carrots, potatoes, and grapes are grown where the soil suits them best, alongside yellow-green hops for bright ales.

For centuries the patient craftsman who carved this gorge has flowed in the same direction as the wind does most days, from northeast to southwest. The Silver River earns its name from its metallic tinge, mainly due to the clouds and the gray alps reflecting off the stream of clear snowmelt.

Indeed, the natural beauty to be found in that canyon between the mountains is unlike any other across our vast continent. Even so, any recent visitor returning home from the Silver River Gorge will no doubt tell you first about the Four Bridges. Wherever you may sit as witness—at your dinner table, in your garden, at the pub—the account will always begin with a warning that words alone cannot paint a worthy picture. But I suppose I'll give it a try, nonetheless.

Spanning the Silver River at four places within Sterling are magnificent wooden structures connecting bank to bank. Each overpass is set solidly into the earth by way of two marble towers. From these supports, elegant arches built of ancient oak reach across the water in a tall curve. The wood is stained a color somewhere between orange and red that's so bold, you might think the arch itself was smoldering.

And yet, my friend, those are only the foundations. The ropes that suspend the horizontal beams are painted with a brilliant coat of silver, melted in the furnaces of the old mines. With the arrival of every new season the bridgekeepers plant fresh flowers in the railings, which are hollowed out precisely for these parallel gardens. They are busy too before each sunrise, hanging long banners from the archtops and raising flags on the towers. At nightfall these fine cloths are folded away, and the bridgekeepers light the many candles that flicker in stone bowls along the handrails.

I wish I could show you the carvings in person so you could run your fingertips across them, because these bridges were built for more than simply transport or aesthetics; the very history of our people is carved into these beams. Etched into the paneled deck of each bridge are the names of all who have ever lived and died in these neighborhoods. "Not to step on the memory of our ancestors," the folks here will tell you, "but to allow them to carry us forward." Also carved into the tall arches are accounts of notable events, like the First Fire and the Disarming, which the Philosophers have carefully chosen for public display.

When you walk across one of these platforms, all this cursive script flows past you like swirling water, and it feels like centuries are floating by, right under your feet . . .

Ah, you see? I got carried away already. My reason for starting this journal was not to share *my* views on the Four Bridges. I ended up in the council chamber mostly by chance.

So, let me tell you about Aris Harper, the boy who actually brought the Capitol's dome crashing down.

For one thing, I know Aris didn't feel some grand sense of history that day in early May when he crossed the southernmost bridge toward his house in the Low Quarter. Not once did he stop to admire the architecture, the flags, or the spring flowers that the bridgekeepers had recently planted. Instead, Aris crossed the Low Quarter Bridge the same way he always did: in a straight line with his head down, drumming a fast-paced rhythm on his chest as if that would help speed up his feet.

If there was any other route home Aris surely would have taken it, but the bridge was the only path across the Silver River at that end of town. Aris lowered his shoulders, leaned forward, and kept his feet shuffling. Usually, this strategy enabled him to reach the other side before any memories came flooding back.

On that particular afternoon, however, he wasn't so fortunate. The platform was packed with the afternoon traffic of travelers and vendors busily preparing for the inauguration festivities. About halfway across, Aris found himself trapped in the push and pull of the crowd's heavy current, bumped by fat shoulders and poked by sharp elbows. His chest tightened like the head of a snare drum. He lifted his chin to the sky to steal a breath of fresh air above the sweaty bodies jostling around him, although the relief lasted for only a moment. When he lowered his eyes back to the ground, the slow-going crowd dissolved like a fog, and Aris could see the bridge in his memory, just as it was on the day of his father's funeral.

Black tulips drooped in the railings, and black banners wobbled in the wind. In between the arches, rows of wooden chairs lined the bridge platform from end to end. All the neighbors from the Low Quarter were in attendance, including the councilman, and many guests from the other quarters too. Everyone had come to pay their respects for the tragic loss of a staff sergeant in the Silver River Search & Rescue and to witness his name carved into history during the inscription ceremony afterward.

At the bridge's far end, where a flower cart now stood, the casket had been set on stage for viewing. From a distance Aris could see his ten-year-old self standing on stage next to his mother and his brother, shaking the hands of guests in a line that stretched beyond the bridge and wound into the side streets of the Low Quarter. Though Aris had half the bridge yet to walk between them (not to mention nearly six years), he could smell his mother's perfume in his memory: a wildflower-honey mist. That's how Aris remembered it, at least. His mother hadn't worn any perfume since. She thought it was kinder to give the bottle away to someone who could use it.

Then the sounds of the funeral resurfaced too. Beneath the midday commotion of mules clicking and carts rattling along the floorboards, Aris heard the somber cadence of the eulogies.

"A devoted friend," said one of his father's crew members.

"A fearless climber," said another.

"A pain in the ass, but an honest man," the chief added.

The speakers didn't need to describe the death itself because in a city as small as Sterling, news traveled fast. Everyone at the ceremony had already heard some version of the story, which went something like this: on a solo patrol in the Cloudhorns, Amos Harper was ambushed by a sudden snowstorm that the Search & Rescue guards called "a blizzard from nowhere." When they realized their sergeant was missing, the climbers scanned the peaks, taking turns coming back down for air, until the outline of a gray uniform was found in the grip of a claw-shaped snowdrift. The S&R guards chipped away at the icy fingers until the body broke free, and then waited out the starless night at the nearest outpost. At sunup they carried Amos down to the city for a proper funeral and inscription ceremony.

As Aris crossed the bridge, replaying those speeches in his memory, the rhythm he was tapping on his ribcage unraveled. Without any cadence to follow, his feet tripped over each other like they had forgotten how to walk. Aris caught himself before he fell, but he was forced to stop in the middle of the bridge to regain his balance. In that brief pause, he considered turning around. *If I push through the crowd,* he thought, *the beam with Dad's name will be right there.* It had been years since he had seen it up close. His brother, Zeno, on the other hand, stopped on the bridge every time and traced the letters with his fingers.

But Aris's motivation quickly dissolved. "Keep moving, kid," an old man muttered, prodding Aris in the back with his walking stick. That was enough to change his mind. His skin stung a little where he had gotten poked, but seeing the words "Amos Harper" carved into the wood every day burned all over.

Aris held his breath until he reached the end of the platform. As he raced down the ramp, escaping the crowd, he heard voices calling out to him.

"Aris, we're over here!"

Aris let all the air gush out of his lungs. Next to the dirt road leading to the Low Quarter proper, his friends Kati and Kevi were waiting for him under the shade of a pine tree . . . and I was hiding behind it.

"By the owl, what took you so long?" Kevi asked.

"Sorry, I had to pick up medical supplies for my mother." Aris patted the satchel hanging over his shoulder. "How are you two holding up at school?"

"We miss you," Kati said. "We haven't found anyone else to play in our band."

"Well, have you held any auditions?" Aris joked, waving his hands in the air like a conductor. Before Kati could answer, I jumped out from behind the tree and onto Aris's back, holding on tight with my bony arms.

"Get off me, Bimo! You little silver eel!" Aris spun me around in circles while Kati and Kevi laughed. "I should throw you back into the river!"

After gently wrestling me to the ground, Aris straightened out his gray tunic and tried to reset his feather-soft brown hair, which I had managed to dishevel. With a shy smile that only showed his top row of teeth, smooth as piano keys, Aris tossed us a few apples that he had bought on the way home, knowing the three of us would be hungry.

As we headed home through the Low Quarter, I bounced ahead of the others, hopping over piles of rubbish and puddles of spring rain. Every time I failed to clear a jump, black water splattered my legs. Back then the soot that drifted in constantly from the Down Quarter covered the whole neighborhood.

Aris lifted me up on his shoulders so I wouldn't ruin my clothes. He was always looking out for us. At sixteen, Aris was the oldest of the group, while Kati and Kevi were a couple of years younger. I was only ten, not even out of primary school. In the Low Quarter children could attend school until they turned fifteen, although the building could barely hold everyone. The older kids got tired of standing in the back all day, leaning against the wall, so most of them dropped out early to help at home.

"Aris, can we hike to the clearing before it gets dark?" Kati asked, tugging his sleeve.

"Yes, let's go!" Kevi agreed, pulling his other arm. "I'll invite the Philosopher, if that's what it takes to convince you."

Several years earlier, while hiking together in the trails outside the city, we found a semi-circular clearing in the woods that resembled the concert hall in the Capitol. This secret place is where we put on plays together, and eventually concerts once Aris got his violin. The rest of us didn't have instruments—and no real audience, besides the wildlife—but that didn't stop Kevi and I from becoming percussionists with sticks and boulders while Kati conducted our ragtag orchestra from a tree stump.

"The Philosopher might be a little busy with the inauguration, don't you think?" Aris nudged Kevi with his elbow. "Anyway, you don't need to convince me; I'd love to go. But my mother was expecting me home ten minutes ago. Next week, okay?"

By then we had reached the end of Aris's street, the last row of stone houses in the Low Quarter. My memory of that evening is still vivid, so it's strange to see it again from a different angle. Down the narrow road I saw gray figures smoking cigars outside of his house, the tiny orange ends floating up and down in the shadows like fireflies.

He carefully lifted me off his shoulders. "So long, Aris," I said, walking backward with Kati and Kevi, all three of us waving goodbye, our hands sticky from the apples.

Now, I'll admit it's memories like these that make trips through the Grand Fireplace so unsettling. That night, all those years ago, Aris and I went our separate ways.

This time, with the help of the Four Bridges, I followed him down the block.

Aris approached slowly, searching for familiar faces in the cloud of smoke that hovered around his front porch.

"Is that you, Mr. Harper?" a low, gravelly voice asked from the bottom of the porch stairs. The speaker was a terribly thin man, the tallest of the group. He waved his bony arm back and forth in a vain attempt to clear the smoky air. "Ah, it is indeed. Look out, everyone, step aside. Let Mr. Harper through." The speaker hopped off the staircase while the other men and women, about four or five altogether, scampered out of the way. "Can I help you carry anything inside, Mr. Harper?"

"No, that's alright, sir, I can manage. Thank you for the offer, though . . . sir." Aris declined as politely as possible, although the second "sir" landed more awkwardly than he intended. He had tried to remember the man's name but couldn't come up with it in time. With so many visitors coming and going, it was hard to keep track; most of the guests would stay only a few nights, maybe a few weeks, which wasn't much time to get to know someone.

His mother, Zita, on the other hand, had no trouble with names. She remembered every person who shared a meal at their table—and all their stories too. Aris wasn't quite there yet, but he was trying his best.

"How are you holding up this evening, sir?"

"Holding on as best as I can," the tall man responded. His words sounded like they were wrapped in crunchy fallen leaves. The man took a long puff of his cigar and exhaled the bluish smoke with a deep sigh. "Only one direction to go from here, so at least I don't feel completely lost."

"Well, keep looking up then. Have you seen my mother? And is Zeno around?"

"Yes, Zita served a delicious soup, for which we are most grateful," rambled another stranger leaning against the porch's railing. He bowed slightly to emphasize his sincerity. Aris noticed that he was as skinny as the taller man, maybe more. His frowsy clothes hung loosely from his wiry frame. The stranger's bottom teeth had the same light-green stain as the other guests—like the underside of a new leaf.

"Zita's in the kitchen," the tall man said, "but I haven't seen your brother."

The aroma of purple carrots and pepper hit Aris as he crossed the threshold. The single-story structure consisted of only a few square rooms, but what it lacked in creativity it made up for in durability and warmth. All of the houses in the Low Quarter were built after the First Fire, constructed from enormous slates of rock carried down from the mountains. They had short chimneys that led down to broad fireplaces—the centerpieces of the modest homes. Each fireplace had an image of a snowy owl carved into the stone above the hearth, painted white like the owl above the Grand Fireplace in the Capitol. Aris walked through their common room, through a blast of warm air from the fire, and into the kitchen, where his mother was at the table writing her weekly letters to the council and humming a tune to herself.

"Hello, Mother, I'm home." Before she could look up from her writing, Aris kissed Zita on the top of her head. She had the same light-brown hair as Aris, with a few wisps of gray, and the same amber eyes. He laid his satchel on the table next to her scattered papers and started pulling out the medical supplies. "Eight vials of spiderleaf extract and three bundles of thimbleberry stems, just as you asked."

"Thank you, honey. I know it was out of your way."

"How many were here for supper? I can help you with these dishes; it seems like you had quite a crowd."

"Oh, dear, first help yourself while the soup is hot. I know I made the same stew last night, but I can't waste the basket of carrots that Mr. Marcel bought for us."

Zita moved her letters and inkwell aside to make space for Aris at the table. He sat down across from her, blowing steam from the thick lavender soup.

"Aris, I'm afraid it's getting worse. We had twenty-one today. The cellar has room to sleep five, so the others are out in the cold tonight. I'm demanding that the council do something about this, straight away."

Zita wrote to the City Council about all of the problems in the Low Quarter, chief among them the pollution, the poverty, and the need for a bigger schoolroom. But that day she was writing about the northern trillium seeds and the hold they had on the city. If you've never heard of them, the seeds grow in the pods of delicate white flowers, imported from the north by the early pioneers of the Gorge. Squirrels and chipmunks handle the seeds just fine, but then a few climbers discovered their potency. Holding a light-green seed, or "trill," in your lower lip causes a calming intoxication. When the seed's shell eventually dissolves, releasing its chemical heart into the bloodstream, the ensuing rush feels like total euphoria. Needless to say, the seeds are highly addictive.

Zita looked up from her letters when she heard Aris drop his spoon into the empty bowl.

"I'm sorry, dear; I didn't think of dessert. Would you like me to make something?" She got up and started searching through the mostly empty cupboards. "I might have some flour I could mix with—"

"No, no, thank you, this was more than enough. Let me help you with these dishes. Where's Zeno, by the way? He should help out around here once in a while too."

"Your brother is up there again, training with Erro." Zita gestured with a flip of her arm toward the Cloudhorns. "He's supposed to be back tomorrow, but you never know with him. If you see him before I do, honey, please tell him to be careful. The neighbors say the Alpinees have been spotted in the foothills. They never scared your father, I know, although I worry anyway. Everyone in the Low Quarter is on edge about it."

Zeno can take care of himself, Aris thought, tossing his bowl into the washbasin. He grabbed a wet rag and started scrubbing dried soup from the bowls with lukewarm water. He looked out the kitchen window and saw the jagged outline of the snow-covered Cloudhorns. *Zeno found his ticket out of the Low Quarter. How will I ever escape?*

When he finished the dishes, Zita was still focused on her writing. Aris kissed the top of her head.

"Thanks for dinner, I'm going to bed. The shop will be busy tomorrow with travelers arriving for the inauguration. Oh, and I promised Mr. Marcel I would stay until closing, so don't wait up for me."

"Goodnight, honey. Send Mr. Marcel my best. And be safe."

Aris whistled while he walked down the short hallway to his bedroom, which he shared with Zeno to open up more space for the homeless guests that Zita hosted in the cellar. From under his bed Aris pulled out the leather case that protected his violin. It was too late to take out the bow—he didn't want to disrupt his mother or the guests—so he lightly plucked on the strings instead, trying to replicate the tune his mother had been humming when he came home.

Aris closed his eyes to focus. The melody was simple, so it only took him a minute to find the right notes, and one more to string them together. The soft, peaceful song made his eyelids heavy. *I must be more tired than I thought.* Aris put the instrument away and curled himself under his covers on the straw mattress.

His brother's bed was empty, its wool blanket a messy blob on the floor. *How in the Gorge does he fall asleep in the bitter cold?* Aris snatched Zeno's blanket and wrapped it over his own. *I wouldn't cut it as an S&R climber. Maybe I'll open my own shop someday. The Mid Quarter could use a proper music store.*

As he pictured the shiny trumpets and trombones that would stick out from his shelves, Aris rubbed his eyes. The pressure formed tiny dots that floated around in swirling patterns on the back of his eyelids. The dots reminded him of the light show that would start the following night along the Four Bridges, officially marking Inauguration Eve and kicking off the celebrations. Better yet, whenever he stayed late to lock up, Mr. Marcel invited him to stick around for violin lessons.

Although thoughts flicker through occasionally, I can't tell you what Aris dreamed about that night—that's not really how the Grand Fireplace works—but I do know Aris never imagined we would find ourselves in the rubble of the Capitol's dome, his shy smile responsible for its collapse.

He fell asleep tapping a rhythm on his stomach with his fingers.

🏛

"Hey, Erro, toss me my pack!" Zeno shouted across the crevasse. "And the rope too!"

Erro sat on the other side of the deep gap that sliced through the glacier, sipping tea from a wooden cup. The pair had stopped to rest before making their final ascent to the top of Mt. Southspur, a minor peak in the Cloudhorns at the southern end of the range. The spring air was still cold and thin, so they had started a small fire to melt some snow and added tea leaves to their cups. The mild, minty drink did wonders to stave off altitude sickness.

"When you're ready, I'll take the lead up the next approach," Zeno said. This was their second straight day of climbing, and Erro had been slowing down a bit. Zeno wanted to set a firm pace to ensure they had sufficient time for the descent. He had been carefully monitoring the weather, and all signs indicated that the clear skies would hold, but they were running out of daylight, and the sun wasn't going to slow down just for them.

"Hold on, Z, hear me out," Erro said, tilting his head back to get the last few drops of tea out of his cup. He was strong but a bit bulkier than his climbing partner. Steam drifted up in swirls from the sweat glistening on his close-cropped black hair. "I say we head back while it's light out. Remember what your dad used to say? 'Don't forget to stop and smell the skies, lads.' Well, here's the best view on this side of the mountain. Let's catch the sunset on the way down."

The unexpected allusion to his father made Zeno's knees buckle, and his stomach flipped the same way it did the first time he looked down into a deep crevasse: the crystalline snow at the edges, the walls gradually fading from white to sky blue, from sky blue to midnight blue, and from midnight blue to black. As Zeno described it to me once, the fear of falling into that absolute darkness was paralyzing because he wasn't sure what was worse: smashing into rock at the bottom, or falling forever into the void.

Erro meant no harm by his comment, and he was right about the stunning view of the Gorge from that height. But Zeno was carrying more on that climb than his equipment. When he turned nineteen in a few months, he would finally be old enough to take the climbing test for the Silver River Search & Rescue. As the older brother, the eulogies at their father's inscription ceremony about bravery and honor hit Zeno harder than Aris. Now, climbing was etched into him. Barely two weeks after the funeral service, Zeno had his gear packed for multiple days on the mountain. His natural talent was unmistakable. Within one year he was glacier climbing. Within two, he had ascended the most challenging routes up Shoulder Ridge. In his third year he started serious training in the Cloudhorns, determined to be accepted as a Search & Rescue climber the same day that he turned nineteen.

And for the last few months, Erro had been a steadfast training partner, even if he lacked Zeno's sense of urgency. Erro lived in the Mid Quarter, where his mother was a wealthy textile merchant. If he failed the climbing test, his family's shop on Weaver's Row would be there waiting for him. Erro enjoyed alpine climbing for its adversity and for its moments of tranquility, but mostly he climbed to be with his best friend.

"No way, we can't turn back now," Zeno said when he regained his focus. "We need the practice. And if you think this view is nice, wait till we hit the summit."

Together the boys examined the path ahead. To reach the top, they needed to climb around a serac and then negotiate a near-vertical pitch to the summit. Although the peak wasn't the tallest in the range, the route was highly technical, which was exactly why Zeno had chosen it for training. Many mountaineers called that segment of Mt. Southspur the "Snake" because the line of ascent weaved back and forth in an S-shape up the impossibly steep rock face. Now that he had a chance to see it himself, Zeno noticed that not only its shape but also the surface itself was eerily reptilian. Multiple layers of ice and rock overlapped each other like scales, and the path ahead was scarred with gullies, cracks, and crevices.

"I don't know," Erro said, scratching his chin. "Maybe we should wait—"

Boots crunched in the snowpack somewhere above them. The sound startled Zeno as well; he hadn't seen any other climbers on the mountain all day. With the column of ice blocking their line of sight, they couldn't tell who was heading toward them.

If it's the Alpinees, we don't stand a chance, Zeno thought. He instinctively reached for the axe on his belt loop. Erro must have had the same fear, for he hopped over the crevasse and stood next to Zeno, his axe raised.

They both let out a sigh of relief: from behind the serac emerged two S&R guards, connected to one another at the waist by a climbing rope. The guards moved swiftly and efficiently down the bottom stretch of the Snake toward the crevasse.

"By the owl, you should've seen the look on your face," Erro said, poking Zeno in the ribs with his axe handle. "You thought it was the ice thieves, didn't you?"

Zeno didn't respond. His eyes were locked in on the S&R guards, observing how smoothly they moved down the mountain. Their steps were coordinated perfectly so that they always maintained the right amount of slack in the rope. *I need to learn that technique*, Zeno thought.

"How's the route up ahead?" Erro called out when the guards were close enough to hear him.

"Tougher than it looks," the first guard hollered back. As he approached the young climbers, he set down his pack and held up his forearm, grinning proudly. The guard's uniform was ripped from elbow to wrist, and blood stained the fabric along a gash in his skin. "Lost my footing, and the Snake bit me," the guard explained. "The view up there was worth it, though. The chief won't let us climb in this area anymore, so I'm glad we got it in."

"What about you guys?" the other guard asked, removing her cap so she could retie her short ponytail. "How was your climb?"

Zeno still couldn't put a sentence together. He was too busy admiring the guards' uniforms, which consisted of the

17

traditional gunmetal-gray jackets and tan pants, which were tailored to each guard's particular build and designed for climbing. Though the S&R's responsibilities had expanded beyond mountain patrol to include law enforcement in Sterling generally, the kit's design hadn't changed. The guards' leather gloves and boots also looked brand new, especially compared to Zeno's equipment. His outfit was cobbled together mostly from his father's old gear.

"So far, the climb has been perfect," Erro answered on behalf of them both. "But my partner here wants to push for the summit."

"At this hour?" the first guard asked. "Night will come quicker than you expect."

"And you should never climb alone," the second guard warned.

"What do you mean?" Zeno asked. "We've got plenty of daylight left."

Erro won't bail on me now, Zeno reassured himself. In fairness, his confidence was well founded. The two boys met in primary school when Zeno asked Erro if he wanted to skip class to fish in a new pond that he had discovered in the backwoods. Erro didn't hesitate, asking if he could dig for the worms. Ever since that day, he followed Zeno everywhere. The two explored old mines under Shoulder Ridge, climbed oak trees in the backwoods, and paddled every stream that fed into the Silver River. Zeno was always looking for the next challenge, and Erro never turned him down. Zita joked sometimes that Erro was Zeno's shadow, in the most positive sense of the word. "Without him you'd lose your sense of direction," she teased.

But this time, Erro was ready to call it quits. He tossed a snow chunk at Zeno, and it exploded into dust when it struck his arm. "Come on, Z, let's head back with them. We can catch the sunset on the way down."

Zeno bit the inside of his lip until it stung. On the outside he looked disappointed, but on the inside he felt completely abandoned. This was their chance to show the

S&R that they had the skill and the strength to join their ranks, and Erro was willing to throw it away for *a sunset*. There would be a million more of those.

Dad climbed alone in the Cloudhorns all the time, Zeno thought. *I can make it on my own.* He snatched the rope lying at Erro's feet and began to coil it up.

"Good call, Z. Let's pack up and—"

"I'm not turning around," Zeno said. "I'm going to give it a shot."

The two S&R guards looked at each other with their eyebrows drawn together. Erro shook his head.

"It's really not a good idea, kid," the first guard said. "If something happens, it'll be hard for us to reach you up there."

"Don't worry; I'll be quick. I climb faster when I'm on my own." Zeno's comment came out harsher than he intended. He tried not to look at Erro when he said it.

The second guard leaned on her axe, sizing Zeno up. The boy was wearing the right gear, he was in good physical condition, and if he had made it that far up Mt. Southspur, he had to be a decent climber.

"Alright, listen," she said. "If you don't reach the summit in an hour, I want you to turn around. We'll wait for you at the next shelter. Don't make us climb back up there and risk our lives to rescue you, got it?"

"See you at the outpost," Zeno replied. He pulled his hat over his wavy brown hair, which was longer than his younger brother's and swept back with a little wax. He threw on his rucksack and swung the coil of rope over his shoulder. Then he completed his routine gear check, securing the harness around his waist, tightening his bootlaces and slightly rusted crampons, and finally, as always, fastening the wrist straps of his leather gloves. The gloves had been his father's and were stamped with the S&R insignia on the back of each hand. Even with all of his gear on, including a bulky leather parka, Zeno looked tall and trim.

The group watched Zeno trudge up the Snake alone, his ice axe chipping away at the glacier's top layer of crisp snow. When he reached the serac and disappeared behind it, they began their descent to the outpost.

"I hope your friend isn't too brave for his own good," the first guard said to Erro. "The Snake can really bite."

About thirty minutes past the first serac, Zeno reached another ice column, although this one was bigger—a lot bigger. The blue ice block curled over his path like a frozen ocean wave. Zeno guessed he was more than halfway to the summit, so he stopped to examine the course ahead. The S&R guards were right; nothing about it looked inviting. Impossible angles everywhere. As he tightened the iron plates on his boots, Zeno earnestly considered turning around. *If I take one wrong step, I'm done. What in the Gorge was I thinking?* His breathing accelerated into short, shallow bursts. He tried to spot Erro and the two guards on the mountain below, but the group had already cleared the glacier.

Zeno squinted at the summit as the spring sun dipped lower in the sky. The ice block reflecting off his eyes made them look even bluer, and a full day of sun and wind had turned his cheeks red. Two sharp points of rock jutting out near the summit vaguely resembled fangs, like the Snake was smiling at him, daring him to keep going. *That settles it, then,* he thought. *I'm coming for you. Give me a minute to catch my breath.*

Zeno took his father's advice and gazed out at the city at the bottom of the Gorge, which was painted in a yellow-orange glow. Sterling appeared so tiny and delicate that it almost seemed imaginary. Zeno blew out a puff of air just to see if it would collapse. But at the same time, he could see the city's structure so well from that perspective—better, in some ways, than standing inside it.

Each neighborhood was roughly centered around one of the four great bridges. Starting near the North Gate (the farthest point Zeno could see from here) was the Up Quarter, a neighborhood consisting of lofty log houses, most of them two or three stories high, with cobblestone streets winding in between. Moving south it blended with the Mid Quarter, which was made up of cottages mixed together with fine clothing stores, jewelry shops, and bakeries. Next to that was the Down Quarter, where gray smoke rose from plain brick buildings that served as workshops for blacksmiths, carpenters, and other tradesmen. His eyes naturally followed the smoke drifting southward over the Low Quarter, where he could make out the general location of his street—the last row of stone houses at the city's edge. Beyond that it was the thick forests and fields of the backwoods all the way to the sea.

At the center of it all, nestled between the Mid and Down Quarters, was the Capitol. If the mountains were the eyes and the bridges were the heart, then the Capitol could rightfully be called the mind of the city, for it housed the council chamber, the concert hall, and the library. The base was constructed of smooth stone, with a footprint the size of a city block, that stretched over the river. The masonry was masterfully designed to form a barreled vault through which the Silver River flowed right beneath the building before dropping off into the Down Quarter as a low waterfall on the other side. The highlight, however, was the Capitol's dome, which was built of wood but had been painted a bright silver color to cover the charring from the First Fire.

From Zeno's vantage point, he could practically see how history had shaped the city. The First Fire had entered the Gorge from the southern end, incinerating every inch of the Low Quarter and most of the Down Quarter before it was finally put out at the steps of the Capitol. The lower quarters used the opportunity to rebuild their neighborhoods into a grid pattern of uniform buildings made of stone and brick so that a wildfire could never again steal the roofs from over their heads. The upper quarters had been saved from the flames by the S&R, so the streets still followed the circuitous walking paths of old, and the houses retained their mystical character with ornately carved timber frames.

As Zeno sat scanning the city, considering its complexity, he felt a biting-cold wind abruptly pick up from the northeast. He clasped the top button on his parka and looked over his left shoulder in the wind's direction. He couldn't believe his eyes—ink-dark storm clouds were accelerating along the ridgeline directly toward him.

How could I have missed a massive stormfront? Zeno slammed the mountainside with his gloved fist. *Ten minutes ago, the sky was clear in every direction!*

As distant thunder rumbled across the otherwise tranquil sky, Zeno's instincts kicked in. First, he tied one end of the rope to his harness in a double knot and looped the other end around a nearby rock. Then he secured himself to the slick mountain with his ice axe and crampons.

Within minutes, the storm was upon him. *How in the Gorge did I miss this? I've been reading the weather patterns all day.* Zeno was well aware that the extreme climate of the Cloudhorns was notoriously unpredictable, but the suddenness with which this storm arrived was so . . . unnatural.

With the storm's center directly overhead, Zeno found that its speed was not the only abnormal feature. When the charcoal clouds passed by, the sky lit up with streaks of pink and purple lightning, triggering thunder so loud that it felt like Mt. Southspur itself was shaking. The vibrations sent gravel and ice fragments tumbling down the precipice, pelting Zeno from above as he attempted to cover his head and face from the debris.

For almost thirty minutes he clung to the mountainside, his muscles convulsing in an effort to maintain his grip, but the vicious wind had more endurance, and it shook Zeno loose from his position. He began to slide down the Snake, bumping into scaly ridges and bouncing over cracks. He crashed into a boulder, which momentarily stopped his fall, and then the rope snapped taut against his harness. *Whew,* he thought. *My double knot held.*

But then that boulder began wobbling like a loose tooth. *If I don't move now, it's going to crush me.*

Zeno didn't have time to assess the path below him. He whipped out his pocketknife and sawed at the rope. When the safety line finally snapped, Zeno slid down the ice field feet first, carried by an avalanche of rocks, snow, and ice. Through the snow kicked up by the wind, he caught a glance at the runout ahead.

No, no, no, no! His momentum was carrying him straight toward the crevasse.

Flipping onto his stomach, Zeno held his ice axe diagonally across his torso. He pressed his chest and shoulders down, forcing the pick end of his axe into the glacier. He slid for twenty more yards, spraying ice particles like sparks, until the axe's teeth caught hold of the glacier and arrested his slide.

Zeno lay on his stomach, gasping for air. The flashes and rattle of the storm drifted away, vanishing as quickly as they came. He rolled over and sat upright, wiping the slush from his eyes. With his vision cleared, he saw how far the avalanche had carried him—about ten feet from the chasm.

Zeno took a deep breath and tried to remain totally still. The center of the storm had passed, but he wasn't out of trouble yet. His bottom half was covered in ice fragments, and he sensed that the snow around him was unstable. If he tried to stand up or shift his weight, the avalanche would sweep him into the crevasse.

Alright, I'll wait here until someone comes. Slowly, Zeno pulled his knees to his chest, trying to conserve heat. *Need to stay warm, need to stay still. Someone will come.*

One hour evaporated, and then another. Night settled into the Cloudhorns, the sky fading from sky blue to midnight blue to black. Zeno's entire body ached, and the warm droplets of blood that had leaked from the cuts on his face were frozen. At that point, Zeno acknowledged that his chances of being rescued by the S&R were slim. Not only was it too dark to climb safely; after the storm, the route would be covered with debris.

So, Zeno watched the gentle gleam of lamps gradually appear in the windows of homes all the way from the Up Quarter to the Low Quarter. He could no longer feel his frozen feet. Next, four lanes of light flickered on simultaneously, extending east to west across the river, as the bridgekeepers lit their candles. By then his hands were numb.

When the moon finally rose over Shoulder Ridge, the Capitol building's silver dome was illuminated in blue light as giant lanterns were lit at each corner of the roof. Zeno had been so focused on his training over the last few weeks that he had forgotten inauguration day was approaching. Tomorrow at moonrise, in the Capitol's council chamber, the new members of the Sterling City Council would be sworn in. To mark the occasion, everyone would celebrate late into the night with food, drink, and music.

Well, not everyone. Zeno was curled up, huddled under his coat, but his body was shivering uncontrollably. By then he had lost all feeling in his legs and, with that, all hope of rescue. *I should have turned around.*

Before his lips could freeze together too, Zeno reached into an inner pocket of his parka for a trillium seed. True climbers always carried a trill with them, for this was their original purpose. If a climber ended up stranded on the mountain with no chance of rescue, they would take a seed to ease the pain of freezing to death.

Here we go. Zeno planted the trill into his bottom lip. At first, he grimaced at the bitter taste, but the next instant a warm calm washed over his body. *This isn't as hard as I thought it would be,* he thought. *And at least I'll go out with a show.* Zeno remembered there was one more tradition to come on Inauguration Eve. Weeks ago, at the start of spring, the bridgekeepers planted trumpet bluebells in the gardens lining the bridges, in part to announce the upcoming ceremonies. But the hanging clusters of trumpet-shaped flowers served another important purpose: they attracted bluefire dragonflies.

These creatures are unique to the Gorge, so you probably haven't seen a bluefire dragonfly in your own garden. Although their anatomy is similar to that of a standard dragonfly, they're the size of a small bird, and the tips of their tails glow blue at night. As Zeno gazed out at the fragile city between the mountains, millions of tiny blue lights swarmed the bridges, shapeshifting in stunning waves across the sky. Zeno closed his eyes, holding on to the view as his last impression of his city.

Then he heard a distinct crunching sound in the snowpack behind him. *I must be hallucinating from the trill*, he thought. More footsteps crunched all around him, moving closer.

Zeno managed to pry open his eyelashes, which were lined with frost. A tall, slim figure glided down from the sky and landed in front of him. A bare hand with long fingers brushed against his cheek. He couldn't make out the person's face, which was masked in a shadow cast by a hood, but as the seed dissolved in his mouth, Zeno heard the figure speak.

"The boy is still breathing. If we hurry, he might make it. Quickly, grab his arms!"

Chapter II

Aris weaved through the packed streets of the Mid Quarter back to Mr. Marcel's shop, dodging the couriers delivering the traditional blue flowers and lanterns from house to house. He was returning from his last errand of the day, and twice he had almost been crushed by workmen unloading crates from their wagons, most likely full of food, ale, or wine. The moon had just risen, and the blue lanterns were lit, so the whole city, it seemed, had flocked to the bridges to watch the dragonflies arrive.

Mr. Marcel's shop was hard to find if you didn't know where to look. The surest way was to take Center Street along the riverfront until you reached Seventh Avenue. A few blocks to the north, if you paid close enough attention, you'd see a small sign, painted green, pointing down a narrow alley with ivy-covered walls. That's where the Odd Shop was located, at 135 Seventh Avenue.

Aris pushed open the heavy green door in the alleyway, jangling the bells on the doorknob.

"Hello, Mr. Marcel, I'm back!" Aris called out. "Mrs. Lewis was pleased with the silverware set, and sends her best wishes. I'll start closing up. Let me know if you need anything."

Aris set a stack of coins on the pay counter and began tidying up. Every night at closing, Aris tried to restore some semblance of order to the storeroom, yet it always seemed to be in disarray. He attributed the mess not only to the sheer volume of things but also to the fact that the many things had nothing in common—except, of course, that Mr. Marcel found them interesting in some way. The shelves were filled with many strange artifacts, ranging from rare books and antique furniture to old instruments and foreign clocks. Aris found the hand-woven rugs to be particularly interesting, as some of them depicted faraway places, like Imperial Bay, that he had only heard about in stories. On slow days at the shop, he passed the time trying on rusted sets of armor from back when the S&R carried weapons.

Many of the items had no apparent use at all, such as a jar half filled with snow-white sand and foreign coins that wouldn't be accepted at any market in Sterling. Perhaps the strangest item was a wooden cube the size of a cigar box that Mr. Marcel had affixed to a heavy bronze base. The chestnut-colored box was inlaid with an intricate maze of lighter woods on top. Although it felt solid and smooth, the box sounded hollow when Aris tapped the sides. He had spent countless hours trying to open it, to no avail. He had a mind to smash it open with a hammer if Mr. Marcel would let him.

Aris had finished sweeping when Mr. Marcel entered from the back room holding a platter with two teacups. He walked behind the counter and waved Aris over. As they sipped the hot, sweet drink—a combination of green tea and pomegranate juice—they could hear groups of people outside making their way to the Capitol, shouting and laughing in the street.

"It sounds like the celebrations are already starting, huh?" Aris asked.

Mr. Marcel nodded.

"Do you think the new council members will be better than the last?"

Mr. Marcel shrugged, his green suspenders with gold clips stretching over his round belly.

"Well, my mother is counting on it. She's been accepting more folks for dinner at our house, all of them addicted to those seeds. She says we need more help from the other quarters before the problem gets worse."

Mr. Marcel looked down, squinting. Wrinkles spread out from the corners of his eyes, and he stroked his long gray beard. Then he took another sip of tea.

"At least she's hopeful that our new council member, Numa, will look out for the Low Quarter. My mother writes letters to her every week, anyway."

Aris was used to these one-way conversations. For as long as Aris knew him, Mr. Marcel had never said a word. He communicated through his hands, body, and face, which were more than enough. In fact, Mr. Marcel was so expressive that Aris trusted him more than anyone. Without any words to hide behind, the man's thoughts were exposed with each subtle movement or reaction, his feelings flapping out in the air like clothes hung out to dry.

Many stories were told, in taverns and the like, that Mr. Marcel didn't speak because of an oath to protect a friend or lover, because his tongue had been taken by frostbite, or because his vocal cords had been severed by an enemy. The less imaginative surmised that the old man had simply run out of things to say. "Oh, those stories are nonsense," his neighbor, Ms. Simone, would say to anyone who asked. "Loneliness is enough to rust a voice; you'll see!"

Mr. Marcel had lived alone above his shop for as long as anyone could remember. He never married, never hosted family for the holidays, never traveled. His solitary lifestyle and his complete silence made many folks in the Mid Quarter uneasy (along with many customers, no doubt), but he always treated Aris kindly. He had given him the violin, the job at the shop, and usually extra food or coins each week to support his mother's shelter. So, Aris never asked why he didn't talk, and truthfully, never thought about it much.

"Well, enough about politics. Would you like to play some music? I brought my violin."

Mr. Marcel's bushy gray eyebrows lifted, and the wrinkles around his eyes smoothed slightly. He walked to the back of the storeroom and returned with his violin. After a quick tuning, he gestured with an open hand to Aris, his way of saying that the first song was Aris's choice.

"I was hoping you could teach me that old folk song about trumpet bluebells," Aris said as he adjusted his tuning pegs. "I know the chorus because my mother has been humming the tune for weeks, but she doesn't remember the verses."

As Mr. Marcel lifted his bow, Aris recalled the first time that he heard him play the violin. When he was around eleven, Aris had wandered away from the Low Quarter toward the shops in the Mid Quarter. As he neared Seventh Avenue, he heard a melody drifting over the ordinary street noise of carts and wheelbarrows. He followed the sound until he came upon Mr. Marcel—with the same gray beard hanging low between the same green suspenders—playing his violin outside the alleyway for passersby on Seventh.

Aris had never heard anything like it. The music was so graceful and clear that the songs felt instantly familiar. He returned to listen every day after school until one afternoon Mr. Marcel caught on to his young audience. He waved Aris into the shop and served him a cup of green tea. Aris spit out the first sip, but he liked it much better after Mr. Marcel added a splash of pomegranate juice for sweetness.

So, for nearly five years, Mr. Marcel had been teaching Aris how to play the violin, although, truth be told, the instructor was often learning more from his student. Aris had taken to the instrument quickly. Even early on, when he was still learning how to properly hold the bow, he had the uncanny ability to play a melody after only hearing it once. As a result, he never quite mastered how to read sheet music; he simply didn't need it. Mr. Marcel tried to teach him using old scores in the shop, but he abandoned that effort when he realized Aris's remarkable gift for improvisation.

Aris couldn't practice at home with the house full of his mother's guests, so he would head out to the clearing in the woods, sometimes with me, Kati, and Kevi tagging along. The Low Quarter was not known for its musicians (and admission to the concert hall was unaffordable for most). That left Aris with only the songs that Mr. Marcel taught him, which Aris would practice over and over again. When he tired of those, he would listen carefully to the birds and attempt to mimic their songs on his violin. At first he tried it in jest, to see if the birds would sing back, but with practice, it became more musical. Then he listened to the owls and tried to recreate the timbre of their calls, and then the wolves, to copy the crescendo of their howls.

What started as a game had become ingrained in his manner of performance. To every song Aris would add these stylistic elements that he borrowed from the forest. What made his violin playing so captivating was that it sounded both natural, and, well, *wild* would be one word to describe it. For instance, Aris would play a familiar folk melody, like "The Wind in the Pines," and people could feel a breeze on their cheeks during the high notes. Or he would perform the classic "Ballad of the Lost Sailors," but he could build the chorus to make it feel like the listener was adrift at sea.

On this particular Inauguration Eve, Aris and Mr. Marcel started with the song about trumpet bluebells and then moved on to their other favorite tunes—some named after soldiers and Philosophers, others after kings and queens. They played late into the night until the sound of the crowds outside began to fade.

"Well, I should probably head home," Aris said. "It seems the streets have emptied out, but it's a long walk back to the Low Quarter."

He took his time packing up. Although his violin was nearly spotless, he wiped it down completely, checking for any specks of dust on the top, neck, and fingerboard. Then he loosened the tension on the bow hair and placed it in the case. As he snapped the lid shut, Aris noticed the teacups and plates were still spread out on the countertop.

"Wait, do you need help cleaning this up?"

Mr. Marcel shook his head vigorously, pushing aside the platter before Aris could take it. From the drawer under the counter he took out a handful of coins and pressed them into Aris's palm.

"That's very generous, Mr. Marcel, but we can't accept this . . ."

Mr. Marcel squeezed his hands tighter around Aris's fist.

"Okay. Well, thank you. My mother will put it to good use, as always."

After locking the heavy green door behind him, Aris heard the bells on the doorknob echo softly down the ivy-covered alley. He made it out of the Mid Quarter and through the Down Quarter quickly now that the inauguration traffic had subsided. He walked briskly to avoid any encounters with drunken revelers who might find it curious that a boy from the Low Quarter was carrying a rare violin. Another reason to hurry was that Aris had also heard the recent gossip his mother mentioned about the ice thieves, mountain ghosts, and savages. The neighbors came up with many colorful names, but the creatures called themselves the Alpinees.

According to rumor, the S&R guards had spotted the Alpinees scrambling through the foothills, which was much closer than they usually came to the city. Aris was not interested in confirming any of those reports. While his father had always assured him that the Alpinees were harmless, that wasn't enough to make the nightmares go away. Aris had the same fear as all the other kids in Sterling—that the Alpinees would drop out of the night sky and carry him into the mountains. Without thinking about it, his pace turned from a brisk walk into a light run.

By the time he reached the Low Quarter, the streets were only dimly lit by a pale blue light from the few remaining dragonflies along the bridges. Aris turned down his street and heard feet shuffling in the dirt behind him. At any other time of day, it would be no cause for alarm—usually, that sound was me sneaking up on him. But at that hour, I was fast asleep.

To be safe, Aris ducked into an alley to listen. The lane was quiet and motionless except for the baskets of blue flowers swinging gently on a few porches. He looked to the left toward his house; no one was outside, not even the regular cigar smokers. Warm yellow light glowed through the front windows, which meant his mother had likely fallen asleep reading in her chair by the fireplace. *I asked her not to wait up for me.*

As Aris stepped out of the alley, someone grabbed him from behind. He tried to shout, but his mouth was quickly covered with a frayed, greasy cloth. It reeked of the bitter scent of trillium seeds. Another set of hands snatched his legs, and Aris was carried halfway down the dark passageway. He tried to twist out of the tight grip, but he was flipped around and pinned to the ground with a sharp knee. Then the punches began, to his back and his sides. At the same time, he felt hands reaching into his pockets, stealing the coins that Mr. Marcel had given him. The blows continued until Aris heard the clips of his violin case snap open. The thieves must have realized their good fortune, for they immediately took off down the street, kicking Aris once more in the ribs before they vanished with his instrument.

Aris lifted himself off the ground, sucking in the dusty air. He rolled up his sleeves and took a few shaky steps in the direction that his attackers had fled, but that was as far as he got. He tumbled face first into the dirt, knocking over a garbage can on the way down. *Get up!* he yelled at himself. *Go after them! If you don't get that violin back, you'll never leave the Low Quarter.*

But his legs wouldn't listen. The pain in his sides was pulsating. So, Aris crawled over to the nearest wall and collapsed. With his back against the bricks, he buried his head between his knees and sat there in silence in the pale blue light, crumpled up like all the papers and packages that had fallen out of the trash.

⬤

Zeno awoke to the loud snap of a low-burning fire that sent tiny embers floating into the cool air. The flames hissed as the damp branches caught fire. Zeno's eyes opened to the night sky. He knew by the position of the moon and the pale blue light emanating from the river that it was very late.

Based on the tall pine trees shape-shifting in the firelight, Zeno could tell he was lying in a forest, most likely in the foothills of the Cloudhorns. His head was resting on his rucksack, and he noticed his ice axe and crampons set evenly on the firm soil beside him. As Zeno rolled over on the floor of pine needles, he could feel his entire body, aching and bruised. He rubbed his face and felt scrapes and cuts. Zeno pulled the wool blanket more tightly around himself, thankful for its softness and warmth.

Wait, I forgot my blanket at home . . . and Erro was with me on the mountain.

"Erro!" Zeno bolted upright. "Erro, where are you?" His voice echoed off the trees before it was absorbed in the darkness. The massive trunks, covered in thick plates of reddish-brown bark, stood motionless, like soldiers-at-arms on guard. Zeno couldn't help but watch the shadows shifting between the pines, waiting for a human shape to emerge. *He must have gone to get firewood,* Zeno told himself, *or maybe to fill the canteens. He'll step out of those shadows any minute.*

Instead of his friend's voice, the shadows spoke. "Your friend is with the S&R; he's safe. They reached the outpost before the worst of it."

The worst of what? The fire popped again, and the few remaining logs, gleaming orange, collapsed into the white ashes. *Oh, those whipping winds . . . suffocating clouds . . .* The storm flashed by in bits and pieces, like a bad dream. *That thunder, lightning . . . violent, vicious.*

"How . . . how do you know?" Zeno asked the ring of trees, unable to discern the precise location of the voice.

33

"How do I know that he's safe?" the darkness responded. "Or how do I know he's your friend?"

Zeno hadn't considered the second question, but the mere thought of it made the hair rise on the nape of his neck.

The shadow speaker didn't give him time to clarify. "Regardless, the answer is nearly the same. For years, young Harper, my scouts have watched you and your friend explore the peaks along this range. Today was no exception—we had many sets of eyes on you. When the storm ripped through, we saw your friend take cover in the outpost shelter with two S&R guards. But one of my scouts spotted you near the summit. Stranded."

Finally, it all came back. Zeno remembered hacking through his rope and skidding violently down the Snake. *I stopped ten feet from that crevasse. Ten feet between me and the black abyss.* His toes curled in his boots at the thought.

"We came as quickly as we could," the voice explained. "But we had to ensure the storm was truly over. Otherwise, we would have been stranded as well."

"Who are you? Why did you come for me? What do you want?" The questions tumbled out of his mouth like dogs bolting through a gate that should've been locked, and Zeno wished he could've pulled them back. He didn't really want to hear the answers. He reached for his axe and squeezed its worn leather handle.

"One question at a time, young Harper." The speaker stepped into the firelight, and several others of the same stature and dress followed closely behind, flanking him on each side. He was twice as tall as any man Zeno had ever seen, and nearly twice as thin. He wore a pine-green jacket, fitted to his slender but muscular body, with a hood over his head. The jacket appeared spongy, like moss, but it also had a waxy outer shell made from pine needles, which were woven into the fabric. Diagonally across his chest was a broad leather strap to which various tools were affixed. In his left hand he held the head of a climbing axe that was easily taller than Zeno himself. He stopped a few yards from Zeno and stabbed the spike end of the axe into the soil.

"My name is Isolo Ranger. Standing beside me are my fellow Alpinees scouts."

The Alpinees. Like all other children in Sterling, from a young age Zeno had heard countless stories about these villains in the mountains, but had never seen them face to face. They lived in the highest peaks of the Cloudhorns and seldom ventured lower into the Gorge. Parents often warned their children (to keep them from straying too far into the backwoods) that the Alpinees could fly down from the mountains and snatch them from the sky. The Alpinees gained this notoriety for the featherlight material that lined their jackets, sewn between their underarms and sides. While it didn't enable them to fly, strictly speaking, they could spread their arms to glide effortlessly down the mountainside without touching the surface.

Not surprisingly, Zeno was less intrigued about the gliding and was more interested in their fabled climbing skills, for the Alpinees didn't use crampons or ropes. Their tall, light bodies and incredibly long wingspans enabled them to traverse almost any rockface. For the most difficult stretches they might use their ice axes, the ends of which could be removed and interchanged with the other tools on their leather straps.

In recent months, the S&R had reported sightings of the Alpinees roaming in the backwoods and foothills of the Cloudhorns. They were often the subject of heated debates in the council chamber, blamed for everything from stealing crops and livestock to robbing hunters and trappers. With this in mind, Zeno kept a tight hold on his axe as he studied the Alpinees scouts.

"As to your other questions," Isolo continued, "we came for you because we need your help."

Zeno stared back at the tall scout for a moment, taking in his words. Then he dropped his head and took a deep breath. *My help? For what?* Using his axe for leverage, Zeno stood up and brushed off the layer of leaves and pine needles sticking to his clothes. He stuffed his crampons into his rucksack and tightened the straps over his shoulders. It took him a second to regain his balance because his whole body was sore and stiff. After steadying himself, he was ready to speak.

"Thank you for rescuing me, but I have no way to repay you. I'm going home." Zeno began walking away toward the blue lights at the bottom of the valley.

"I realize I haven't yet given you a reason to trust me," Isolo said, "so let me offer one now: your father was willing to help us. And when Amos was killed, I carried his body down from the mountain myself."

Zeno stopped and turned around, his fists clenched around the shaft of his axe. "I don't know how you learned my father's name, but I won't fall for your lies. I've heard the story of my father's death a thousand times. His men carried him down from the Cloudhorns. They recovered his body after a freak storm."

"A freak storm? Did it resemble the one you just witnessed? Tell me, young Harper, have you ever seen storm clouds with such velocity? Have you ever seen lightning flash bright pink?"

All the strange features of the storm came flooding back; it really had come out of nowhere, without warning. Recalling those terrible flashes and booms made Zeno shiver.

"We know you're an expert climber, like your father," Isolo continued. "Amos spoke of you often. So please consider this, as one mountaineer to another: our people have lived for centuries at this altitude, and we have learned to read the character of many storms. Indeed, some say we have more words for weather than you have names inscribed into your bridges. And the storms of this peculiar variety—like the one that killed your father and the one that knocked you down the mountain—these storms are something else."

"I won't blame the weather for my own mistake." Zeno huffed, his nostrils flaring. "I should have turned around!"

"Ah, young Harper," Isolo said, "it's not for me to say what you should or shouldn't have done. But what I can tell you, with certainty, is that the cloud front this afternoon was impossible to see coming. These storms are manufactured, and your father knew it too. That's what brought us together."

Isolo pulled his hood back so that Zeno could see his face more clearly in the firelight. "One spring, Amos climbed alone to our village in the mountains. He came to ask us about strange storms that had recently appeared along the ridgeline. Somehow, the clouds only hovered at high altitude, sparing the City of Sterling of any wind or rain." The Alpinees scout paused, dragging his axe point in the topsoil. "Over several years your father and I became close friends. We chased these storms together, trying to discover their origin. Your father knew this effort was imperative for the well-being of our people, but he was also concerned about the city's safety. 'If a storm could be targeted here,' Amos said, 'why not elsewhere along the Silver River?'"

Zeno loosened his grip on his axe and lowered his gaze. He remembered that his father had been preoccupied with the weather for some time, but the details escaped him. Zeno had been so young then. Talk about strange mountain storms had seemed like a distant concern for a kid, especially compared to fishing, hiking, and swimming. While Zeno searched his memory for anything his father might have said, Isolo reached into the side pocket of his pine-needle jacket.

"I want you to have something." Sensing that Zeno was becoming less guarded, Isolo stepped forward—with his long legs, it only took a couple strides to reach him—and got down on one knee so they were at the same height. Zeno noticed that Isolo's skin was off-white and almost translucent, like a river pearl. His facial features from ear to ear were smoothed over, which Zeno imagined must help with the sharp mountain winds. His eyes, however, were most remarkable. The irises were as reflective as two tiny, circular mirrors. It must have been helpful at altitude, Zeno thought, for dealing with the harsh sunlight rebounding off the snowy ground.

Isolo handed him a round, ordinary rock.

"On one of our last climbs, your father gave me this stone. He said it came from the bed of the Silver River. I realize it may seem unremarkable to you, but I found it quite extraordinary. Up here, every rock is razor sharp."

Zeno rubbed his thumb and forefinger over the stone, which was so smooth from centuries of flowing water that it had a velvet-like texture. It was true that his father would take a small stone from the river bottom whenever he left for a climb, as a reminder of the river and of their stone house in the Low Quarter.

"Mr. Ranger, sir, if I hadn't seen the storm myself, I wouldn't believe you now despite the earnestness in your voice. But if what you say is true, how can I possibly help?"

"We need to meet with the Philosopher. Amos said that certain books in the Philosopher's collection mention a device that can control the weather. Based on the sketches he heard about, someone could conjure a storm simply by breathing."

Zeno shook his head. "Our Philosophers take credit for all kinds of inventions, but I have yet to see one. And if this contraption does exist, did my father mention that we're from the Low Quarter? It's impossible for someone like me to speak to the Philosopher."

"What if you had something to offer in return?"

Before Zeno could ask what that might be, Isolo took a bundle of flowers from his jacket's inner pocket.

"Young Harper, do you remember taking a trillium seed before we arrived to collect you on the mountain?"

The memory of the seed dissolving in his mouth came back, as did the feeling of warmth that had washed over his frozen limbs a second later. Zeno realized only now that he didn't feel any of the after-effects that usually tortured those who used the seeds—the unbearable headaches and nausea, the insufferable chills and cravings—symptoms that his mother attempted to treat at her shelter with all manner of medicines and herbs.

"The flower I'm holding is called snowrose. It grows near our village, and it's capable of counteracting the trillium seed's worst effects. You should notice it now. When we found you, we placed a few petals into your lower lip."

Zeno ran his tongue over his bottom gums and detected a slimy coating left over from the flower's petals.

"And we have many other remedies in the mountains. We will show your Philosopher how to make them."

Zeno paused for a moment, distracted by his own reflection in Isolo's mirror-like eyes. His face was illuminated by the small fire, but behind him the blackness of the forest extended endlessly in every direction. If the Alpinees had not arrived when they did, Zeno would have been frozen in that infinite night, just like his father. He clenched his fist around the river stone in his pocket. *If Dad trusted the Alpinees, then I must trust them too.*

"With the S&R on patrol, we'll never get you into the city," Zeno said. "But I'll ask the Philosopher about this weather device. I promise."

Isolo and the other Alpinees scouts lined up to thank him. Zeno shook each scout's hand, trying not to reveal how strange their long, ice-cold fingers felt when he squeezed them.

After the goodbyes were finished, Zeno threw on his backpack and took off down the path toward the valley. He could see the slate-rock roofs of the Low Quarter only a few miles in the distance, but it would take some time to get home, as the trail weaved back and forth many times through the woods. His cuts and bruises from the climb were nothing compared to his headache—without the sound of Erro's footsteps behind him, Zeno felt off balance and disoriented. If it weren't for the promise he made to the Alpinees, he wasn't sure he would have the strength to hike all the way back home.

When he finally made it to his street, the blue light from the dragonflies had mostly faded and the crowds had dispersed from the bridges. A mist drifted down from low clouds, and Zeno noticed the water droplets collecting on the surface of his parka. He thought back in wonder to the Alpinees' pine-green jackets, which looked so light and warm. Maybe one day they would invite him to climb with them. Maybe one day he would visit their village, up among those unreachable peaks, to see the world as his father had once seen it.

***

Aris was sitting in the alley with his back to the wall, half asleep, when a light rain began to fall. Even the threat of getting soaked could not compel him to stand up and walk the few hundred feet to his front door. The inertia stemmed not so much from his bruises, although those still ached. The real heaviness set in because he knew full well that he would never recover his violin. Chances were slim to none that the S&R could track down the thieves, who would surely sell the instrument at one of the Mid Quarter markets. He tried to swallow, but his mouth was painfully dry; he could feel the dust from the street at the back of his throat.

That's when he felt two hands grab him by the collar and pull him off the ground. *Not again*, he thought, lacking the willpower to fight back. *You already took everything from me.*

"Aris, what happened? Are you alright?"

He was relieved to find it was Zeno, dressed in his full climbing gear. "They stole my violin," Aris managed to spit out between coughs, trying to clear his throat.

"By the owl, I'm sorry, brother." Zeno wiped the dust and gravel from Aris's clothes. The rain drops left muddy streaks down Aris's face. Using his sleeve, Zeno cleaned his brother's forehead and freckled cheeks. "Let's get inside somewhere so we can talk. I need your advice, and I think we both need a drink."

With his arm around Aris's shoulder, Zeno led him several blocks northeast to Wasko's Tavern on the edge of the Down Quarter. It was well past midnight, but Wasko's still had a lively crowd, the tavern packed with carousers. The women were all wearing blue flowers in their braided hair, and half of the men were wearing matching blue vests. From the outfits, Zeno and Aris figured they must be attending the inauguration ceremonies the next day. They all kept Wasko busy behind the bar, pouring ale and rivershine from the barrels behind him.

Aris found a table in the back corner next to the fireplace. Like at home, a white owl was carved into the stone mantelpiece, but this one was holding a mug of ale in its curved talons (in keeping with Wasko's sense of humor). Zeno brought over two tin cups. When he set them down, a clear liquid sloshed over the sides. Before Zeno could remove his coat and sit down, Aris lifted his cup and took a deep draft, eager to clear his throat. The strong liquor, which tasted the same way that sticky pine sap smells, burned his throat all the way down to his stomach, making his eyes water.

"Go easy now," Zeno said. "Wasko's rivershine is strong stuff. So, tell me what happened by the alley."

Aris leaned in to be heard over the din of the barroom and provided his account of the night, from cleaning up the shop to playing songs with Mr. Marcel. When he described the attack in the alley, Zeno felt guilt wash over him. *I should have been here to look after him.*

"I'll find you another instrument, brother; I promise." He took a long swig of the rivershine. By then a handful of drunk men in blue vests had gathered at the bar, arms over each other's shoulders, belting out an old folk song. The lyrics were charming, something about spring rains in the Gorge. Unfortunately, due to the ale, each man was singing in a different key.

"By the damn owl, will Wasko shut them up already?" Zeno pounded his mug on the tabletop. Aris noticed his hand was shaking.

"Zeno, what's wrong? Where's Erro, by the way? Wasn't he with you?"

Zeno downed the rest of his drink. "Erro's fine. He decided to turn back with two S&R guards before we reached the summit."

"Wait, what did you do?"

"I kept climbing." Zeno recounted what had happened on the mountain, describing in detail the strange storm that overtook him. "It was impossible to see it coming. The clouds came out of nowhere, and the wind was unbearable. By the time the dragonflies came out I was half-frozen, assuming my time was up. I even swallowed a trill."

Aris shook his head solemnly. He needed another drink, but didn't have the strength to lift his arm.

"Anyway," Zeno continued, "they reached me just in time, before everything went black, and carried me down the mountain."

"Two guards were able to lift you on their own?" Aris asked.

"The S&R? No way. After the storm, they couldn't have reached me if they tried."

Aris's eyes grew wide when the only other answer sank in.

"The ice thieves. They saved my life." Zeno explained how the Alpinees rescued him and then reported his entire conversation with Isolo. He tried to capture every detail in case Aris saw an angle that he had missed. "I need to ask the Philosopher whether this weather device is real. Will you help me?"

Aris rolled the edge of his cup in a circular motion on the table. "I want to, Zeno, but I don't know what the Philosopher looks like. The Capitol is barely a mile from here, but it feels farther away than Imperial Bay."

Zeno nodded. "We'll find a way. By the owl, we might have to break into the Capitol and search the library ourselves. Can you imagine that?" Zeno raised his glass in a toast. "Here's to the Harper brothers, secret Philosophers!"

Aris allowed himself a quick laugh at the thought and then raised his cup. Before they could clink them together, a heavyset man dancing near the fireplace lost his balance and crashed onto their table, splitting it in half and spilling their rivershine all over the floor. His face was flushed, and his blue vest was sopping wet with brown ale. The singing by the bar stopped as several men from the group rushed over.

"I sincerely apologize for my friend here," said the first man to arrive, kneeling next to his unconscious companion. "I warned him that the ale is almost as strong as the rivershine. What are you drinking? Can I buy you another round?"

Now that Aris could see the men up close, he noticed their blue vests were embroidered with musical notes, woven into the garment with white thread.

"No, thank you," Zeno said. "We were about to head home."

"Very well, I'm sorry for the disruption. If you happen to be attending the inauguration tomorrow, we'll be performing. And I swear that our concert band plays better than we sing, although it looks like we've lost our lead violinist to a terrible hangover."

Zeno's ears perked up at the comment, as his promise to find another instrument for Aris came to mind. *Maybe he has an old violin I can buy . . . or borrow, at least, until I'm on an S&R salary.*

"Excuse me, sir; any chance you've got used instruments for sale?" Zeno asked. "My brother plays the violin, and he's in the market for a new—"

"*Used to* play," Aris mumbled, as if it had been years and not hours since he had been robbed.

"Is that so? In that case, maybe you should sit first chair for us tomorrow." His quip drew snickers from his bandmates, who had finally managed to sit the drunk upright. "We'll be playing 'The Eagle's Heavy Feathers.' Do you know it?"

"I've heard of it." Aris had never played the song, although the tune was well known. It was traditionally performed at the swearing-in ceremony for new council members.

"How about an audition, then? I'll grab my friend's violin for you. I think it's safe to say he won't complain."

Considering the day's events, Aris wasn't in the mood to play. What's more, besides Mr. Marcel, he had only performed for me, Kati, and Kevi, so this would be his largest audience by far.

Zeno, on the other hand, couldn't believe his luck. This man would bring a violin right to him. Now, he needed to convince the man to sell it on credit. "Go for it, brother," he whispered. "We can stay for one more drink."

"Alright, I'll give it a try," Aris said, figuring it was his last chance to play for a while anyway.

The man brought over the violin, which looked brand new. Its polished spruce top glistened in the dim light. While Aris tuned it, a few other patrons huddled around to hear the performance. Aris played several practice notes and tested different positions with the chin rest until he found one that felt comfortable. Then he turned out to face the center of the tavern, his back to the fireplace.

"You said the one about the eagle, right?"

"That's the one. We'll start it off, and you jump in when you're ready." The men who had gathered around Aris began singing the tune.

The eagle lets his feathers lift
His body to the sky.
"I am stronger than the morning!
And lighter than air!" he cries.

*But the world appears so vast up there
That his flight becomes unsteady;
He discovers just how small he is,
And his feathers, just how heavy.*

By the second verse, Aris had caught on to the melody. The onlooking crowd was making him more nervous than he expected, so he closed his eyes and rocked back and forth with the rhythm. It helped that the rivershine was setting in, calming his nerves. To focus he envisioned the flight paths of eagles that he had watched from the clearing in the woods, riding gusts of wind up into the clouds, only to come screeching back down into the forest moments later.

The band members were immediately impressed with the young man's skillful, albeit timid, performance. Their clapping and whistling caught the attention of several others at the bar, who made their way toward the music radiating from the fireplace. Aris failed to notice his growing audience, his eyes shut in concentration. The stranger's violin, which had felt so foreign at first (especially compared to his old instrument, of which he knew every quirk), was vibrating in his hands. Aris was quickly adapting to its unique strengths and weaknesses, much the same way that a mariner learns to navigate a familiar sea with new sails.

Halfway through the piece, his confidence returned. His finger placement became more secure, and each stroke of the bow was bolder than the last. Following the eagle's flight in his imagination, he took the song to its highest, brightest points, the sound swelling in the room like a rising tide. The double stops danced off his strings, sounding like a full orchestra, while the light from the fireplace reflected off the violin's smooth surface.

After sending the high, clear notes of the chorus ringing through the tavern, Aris gradually brought the song back down low to match the shallowness and darkness of the last verse. The decrescendo returned to the same melody, this time in a minor key, and Aris played it so softly that everyone in the tavern could practically hear the mist setting on the building's roof. The delicate sound brought to mind the silent night that was waiting for them beyond the tavern's walls. Folks who were there said that the silence outside felt so heavy by comparison that they feared the roof might collapse.

As the last lonely note rang out, the audience felt it resonate in their empty beer glasses.

When Aris opened his eyes, he discovered that every patron in the bar had congregated around him, staring in silent awe. One man sitting at the bar was so taken aback that his cigar had gone out in his hand, beer dripping down his beard. Zeno also couldn't believe that his little brother—with his wet hair matted over his muddy forehead—could play something so wildly beautiful. Even Wasko had come out from behind the bar to listen.

Considering the silence that hung in the room, for a second Aris thought that he had done something wrong. Then Wasko broke the tension with his booming voice.

"Tell us your name, lad."

"Aris Harper."

"And where are you from, Aris Harper?"

"The Low Quarter."

"Ladies and gentlemen!" Wasko shouted, turning to the crowd. "In all its years, this tavern has never heard such captivating music, and it may never again if you don't come back to play for us. You're always welcome here. Here's to Aris Harper of the Low Quarter! Cheers!"

The crowd buzzed around Aris, slapping him on the back and praising his rendition. Zeno stood next to his brother with an arm over his shoulders, trying to manage the throng. One woman plucked a blue flower from her blonde hair and tucked it into Aris's front pocket, sneaking a kiss on the cheek when Zeno wasn't looking. When the pack subsided somewhat, the man who had provided the violin approached them with two new cups of rivershine.

"Here you go, lads. This is to make up for my friend's clumsiness, and to make you an offer. I'm the conductor of this band, and we need a new violinist for tomorrow. From what I just heard, you are more than capable of filling in."

"That's very kind, sir, but I'll have to decline," Aris said without hesitation. "I've never heard a full concert band play before, let alone perform with one."

"Oh, that's nothing to worry about. You have the talent to blend in perfectly. Follow our percussionists' lead and you'll be fine."

"Even so, I don't have the proper attire." Aris patted down his gray tunic and brown trousers, both of which were still a little damp.

"That's no trouble either. We have an extra uniform in the wagon, and you can wear our friend's vest—after we wash the beer stains out. The vest will be quite large for you, but you'll be positioned in the back behind the trumpets, so no one will notice."

"I'm not sure—"

"It's up to you. But with talent like yours, I wouldn't skip this opportunity to play at the Capitol. This year we've been asked to perform during the swearing-in ceremony, so instead of our rowdy group, the council and the Philosopher will be your audience tomorrow."

Zeno grabbed Aris by the arm and pulled him close. "Aris, this is our chance. We'll be in the same room as the Philosopher!"

"But how will *you* get in?" Aris replied. "I'm not going without you."

Zeno winked at his little brother, banged their cups of rivershine together so that bubbles splashed out of the glasses, and then turned to the conductor.

"My brother will join your group, sir, as long as I can go with him."

"Very well. We'll need extra hands to carry the equipment. Meet us at the Mid Quarter Bridge at two o'clock tomorrow afternoon. I'll have your uniforms ready."

Aris and Zeno looked at each other, their faces showing equal parts excitement and uneasiness. They swallowed the rest of the rivershine without taking a breath. Both of them knew they would need it to fall asleep.

Chapter III

If you are ever so inclined to make the long journey to Sterling—and the journey is long, mind you, regardless of the roads you take—you must try to visit in the springtime. For in those mornings, from the eastern sky over Shoulder Ridge, the sun rises slowly and then all at once. What I mean is that the sleepy purple sky, dotted with pale stars, stretches its arms gradually over the valley. I like to wake up early on such mornings, brew a strong coffee, and find a spot on one of the Capitol's balconies to watch the transformation. Taking its time, the sky's transition to red is nearly imperceptible, but once it accelerates into orange, the yellow rays cascade over the rounded hills in a hurry. Daylight first strikes the bridge tops and then the silver dome of the Capitol building, giving time for the city to wake up in the layer of shadow below.

When I mentioned earlier that it was Aris who brought that dome crashing down, he was merely the one who pulled the trigger. In truth, Sera gave him the idea—she found our way out. So, let me tell you a little about her too.

When Ms. Sera Avery woke up on Inauguration Day, the ambitious yellow sun was beaming through the window of her bedroom on the third floor of the Capitol. She had forgotten to close the curtains the night before, caught up in the display put on by the dragonflies. The light show was Sera's favorite inauguration tradition. She pretended that the dragonflies could send her messages in their blue waves, so she spent all evening at her windowsill on the lookout for shapes and signs in the shifting dots of light.

Sera turned over to her other side to avoid the glaring sun a bit longer, tucked in snugly under her green quilt. Although she was not very tall to begin with, the massive bedframe made her look even smaller. With her head resting on the pillow, her toes only made it halfway down to the bedposts at the other end. Her shining blonde hair was fanned out over the white pillowcase, appearing practically golden in the morning sunshine.

As her dark brown eyes adjusted to the light, Sera admired how many angles the sun was capable of casting on the wall. Since she had begun her studies under the Philosopher—it was hard to believe that was nearly six years prior, when she was twelve years old—geometry had become her favorite subject. She spent countless evenings, after all her other research for the Philosopher was complete, combing industriously through the mathematics section of the Capitol library. Sera was drawn to the order and precision of geometry. Not only did she find the various proofs and theorems intellectually stimulating, she considered the shapes themselves beautiful in their utility: the elegance of a perfect circle, the simple grace of a straight line. Her interest was inspired one evening while she was searching the shelves on some assignment and stumbled upon the first major work of Aldo the Arithmetic, an early Philosopher who designed the Four Bridges. The leather cover was torn, the timeworn pages yellowing, but Sera could still make out his sketches penciled on the back pages. Poor Aldo passed away before his bridges were built, so Sera felt responsible to cherish his geometrical masterpieces by walking along the platforms every chance she could get—which, unfortunately, was not as often as she wished.

The life of a Philosopher's apprentice brought many exceptional opportunities, but it also came with significant limitations. Sera was seldom able to leave the Capitol building unless it was required as part of her studies. She spent most of her days in the library, researching and writing at the Philosopher's request. Sometimes she was granted leave to venture out for fieldwork, such as a visit to the bridges to inspect an inscription. On those rare occasions, Sera used the opportunity to explore the city's neighborhoods, although those brief walks required two S&R guards in tow, and she had to wear her violet scarf, discreetly concealing her face so as not to draw too much attention.

While it may sound quite stifling, Sera found the work very meaningful. Her fact-finding and analysis were used by the Philosopher to provide guidance to the council on all matters of public importance. Sera was passionate about her role serving the city and took every advantage of her ability to access the largest library on the continent—the tall shelves stretched across the entire basement floor of the Capitol. On more than one occasion, she stayed up reading by lantern light until the sun rose, carried away in books authored by Philosophers of old, such as Nina the Green (who specialized in botany), Haro the Handler (zoology), and many other subjects in between. She especially loved the library's peaceful solitude, as she could hear the Silver River running steadily below the library's floor.

As Sera watched the polygons of morning light gradually drift across her wall, she realized that she must have left the window open too, for she could smell the crisp spring air breezing through the curtains. She could also hear the river rushing slightly louder than the day before, which told her it must have rained during the night. The scent of spring was soon overcome by the aroma of strong coffee, a signal that Sera's maid, Roma, was coming down the hall with breakfast. A mischievous smile crossed Sera's face, revealing the dimples in her cheeks.

While Sera certainly had her serious, scholarly side, she also infused much-needed humor into the Capitol. She often played light-hearted tricks on Roma and her senior colleague, Ozar Wrinn, who held the official title of Junior

Philosopher. Ozar tolerated her jokes and Roma usually laughed along, but sometimes Sera's timing was inopportune, and it got her into trouble.

Roma rapped a few times on the door with her keys. "Time to wake up, sweet Sera. It's Inauguration Day." She opened the door and wheeled in a cart with an oval tray on top. Sera pretended to be sound asleep, complete with gentle snoring. Roma pushed the tray to Sera's bedside and leaned down to shake her. "Sweet Sera, it's time to wake up—"

"Swoosh!" Sera shouted, popping up from her bed. She threw the quilt over her shoulders like wings. "Look out from above! It's the Alpinees!"

Roma bumped into the tray, rattling the porcelain cups and platters. She gasped and quickly blushed as Sera hopped down from the bed and hugged her, wrapping the green quilt around them both.

"You little dandelion," Roma grumbled, squeezing Sera close to her. "On any given morning, I wonder whether I'll find a flower growing here or a prickly weed. But I'll love you 'until the Silver River runs dry,' as they used to say. If you keep up these antics, though, you'll be making your own breakfast."

"I don't know what I would do without you," Sera said, reaching for a slice of brown bread, covered in almond butter, honey, and cinnamon. She tore off a corner and popped it into her mouth. Roma, Ozar, and the Philosopher had truly become like family. Sera's schedule was demanding, which left little time for visits back to her childhood home in the Up Quarter. As she got older and plunged deeper into her studies, she sensed that separation growing. Indeed, Sera spent so much time reading that she felt closer to the ancient Philosophers than to her own parents.

As Sera chewed her toast, she noticed that her inauguration dress was hanging from the back of the cart. The traditional blue gown was modest but refined, the lone embellishment being the silver stripes at the bottom and down the long sleeves.

"Roma, why have you brought my formal dress so early? The swearing-in ceremony doesn't start until this evening."

"The Philosopher has asked that you and Ozar get dressed promptly and head straight to the library. An urgent request was received, and there will be no time to change before tonight's council meeting."

"What in the Gorge could be so important? It's only the first meeting. It's usually all formalities, with a little music in between." Sera reached for her coffee cup, took a sip, and then added more hot water from the kettle. She was still getting used to the strong brew, which was the Philosopher's favorite drink.

Ozar's butler, Palo, stopped in the doorway. "Ms. Sera, the Philosopher has asked that you hurry to the library," he said. "They are already at work."

Now Sera realized it must be important. She grabbed her dress from the hanger and changed quickly in the washroom. She put her blonde hair up in a neat ponytail and rushed down the hall to the staircase that led to the library, her shoes clicking on the intricate marble tiles.

As she descended the stairs, Sera pondered what could be so pressing, but no particular issue came to mind. The Sterling City Council was made up of four members—one representative elected from each quarter—so Sera considered each in turn.

I doubt that Veti had some urgent matter for the Philosopher, Sera thought. Veti was the veteran councilwoman from the Up Quarter and was well versed in council procedures. In fact, Veti was the longest-serving council member in Sterling's history, having held her position for nearly fifty years. Her main priority was preserving the Gorge's art and history, so she took a special interest in organizing cultural events at the Capitol and ensuring that the library was properly funded.

It's also unlikely that Taro made some last-minute request. Taro was the second-term councilman from the Mid Quarter. Before joining the council four years prior, he operated a jewelry business that was now run by his children. Taro was outspoken and steadfast in his opinions. He emphasized safety and security above all other concerns. As such, he took charge of foreign affairs and ensuring that the Search & Rescue was provided for. For many years, however, the City of Sterling had faced no outside threats and maintained peaceful relations with Imperial Bay. Indeed, the last time that any person of rank in the Royal Army had visited the Gorge was over a decade prior. So, Taro held quite a dull council post, in Sera's opinion.

The other two council members were new additions: Rolu from the Down Quarter and Numa from the Low Quarter. Sera had not yet met either of them, so her knowledge was limited to what was written in the papers. Rolu was a bridgekeeper who embodied the working-class values of the Down Quarter. Numa had won her seat by promising to bring more resources to the poverty-stricken Low Quarter. Sera guessed that one of these new council members, overeager to please their constituencies, must have made an inquiry of the Philosopher. *This question better be worth skipping breakfast,* Sera thought.

She made it to the bottom of the staircase and approached the library's northeast entrance. Two guards stood stoically in front of the wide double doors, wearing the typical S&R uniform: close-fitting gray jackets and tan canvas pants. The outfit was comfortable enough if stationed indoors but was better suited for patrols up in the mountains. Each guard held the standard-issue ice axe, the only weapon the S&R guards were authorized to carry.

"Good morning, gentlemen," Sera said. The guards bowed respectfully and then moved to the side. Sera took a deep breath, then leaned into the doors with all her weight to swing them open.

Vesu Doveney, the Philosopher, was seated at the end of a long mahogany table reading a tome laid open before her. With her head bowed over the pages, the lantern light glinted off the clips and pins, hundreds of them, that held up her hair in a tangled yet elegant tower of braids. That spiral of black and white locks, with what seemed like tiny stars strewn about it, reminded Sera of a miniature galaxy. And that image captured Vesu's spirit perfectly: always seeking answers for the unexplainable, searching for systems to improve the city.

While the Philosopher read carefully to herself, Sera saw that the rest of the table was covered with stacks of books, layers of parchment, and a half-dozen empty coffee cups. She wondered if Vesu had even slept the previous night. Her sleeves were rolled up, her gray undershirt rumpled.

Ozar sat across from Vesu in his formal attire, like Sera, and he looked stately by comparison. His black hair, flecked with gray on the sides, was neatly combed over to one side. Ozar was scribbling notes as Vesu read references out loud from behind the round, ivory-rimmed glasses that hung precariously on the tip of her nose.

"Good morning, madam," Sera said as she approached the table. "What are we working on?"

Vesu didn't look up. She stayed focused on the massive book in front of her, her wrinkled fingers sliding left to right across the text, reeling off citations as Ozar scrawled on. Although Vesu may have looked unkempt, her speech was exceedingly articulate, as usual, and her voice maintained its commanding tone. After another minute or so, she grabbed the page from under Ozar's pen and handed it to Sera.

"Sera, won't you go collect these books for us? Quickly, quickly now!"

Sera snatched the paper, irritated that neither Vesu nor Ozar had provided any information about the assignment. Technically, she was still an apprentice, but she was certainly no longer a beginner. Vesu usually gave her some background on the topic, and more recently had started asking for Sera's opinion on various matters before the council. Ozar didn't offer any details either, which annoyed Sera more. He had been appointed Junior Philosopher the year before, when he turned forty. Ozar, of all people, should have remembered what it felt like to be a Philosopher's apprentice. He was next in line to take over the position, and then Sera after him, if everything fell into place. *I will run things differently when I'm the Philosopher*, she thought, then stomped away down the aisle.

Sera scanned Vesu's list as she walked. She soon realized that all of the requested texts concerned the Gorge's North Gate. This was the enormous gateway of hardwood doors installed into the three-foot-thick rock wall at the north end of the valley. The North Gate provided the only passageway into the Gorge from that direction—unless, of course, one was foolish enough to try and climb over the mountain ranges on either side. Sera had recently read about the gate's pulley system (the design was based on a model first developed by Aldo the Arithmetic), but she could not recall anything else of historical significance. *Why is the council interested in this now?*

Fortunately, locating the books regarding the North Gate would be relatively simple. The library's collection, albeit vast, was meticulously organized. The catalog system passed down from Philosopher to Philosopher had been ingeniously designed by Inka the Librarian, who had founded the Capitol library centuries ago. Inka's system included symbols for the author, subject, and year on the spine of every book. If a bridge inscription had been made for a person or event, the appropriate notation was also included.

Although these classifications were very useful, one couldn't become a Philosopher's apprentice overnight. Inka was precise in her design, but she was by no means linear. Instead of straight rows of library shelves, Inka's aisles spiraled and curved in every direction, like tree roots spreading into deep soil. When Sera first began her training there, the maze seemed completely random, but over time the order revealed itself, and now Sera was starting to think like Inka, seeing similar connections between people and events.

Sera weaved between the floor-to-ceiling shelves, running her hands along the volumes until she found the right section. The shelf was ten rows high and Sera could barely reach the fourth row, so she rolled a ladder over and climbed up, cursing her long gown for getting in the way. She surveyed the spines and pulled the texts that the Philosopher had requested, most of them early reports of the North Gate's construction. One book on the list stood out, though, authored by Inka herself: *The Drowned King's War*. Uncertain of its relevance, Sera shrugged and put the book in her pile.

When she had gathered all the books that she could carry, she slid the ladder back over to the aisle's end. Along the way, it knocked a small book from the top shelf. Sera picked it up, and upon seeing the cover, laughed out loud. It was a study of the Nortleby Beetle, universally considered the ugliest insect in the Gorge. The beetle itself was blind (thank goodness, all scholars agreed), so it attracted mates using a clicking sound that was as harsh as its appearance. Sera thought the Philosopher could use a laugh that morning, so she placed that book on top.

When Sera returned to the table, she set the stack next to Vesu, who was scrutinizing another giant volume. The surface of the massive, dark-brown table was inlaid with a complex design of lighter-colored woods—golden oak, chestnut, cherry, maple—but Sera could barely see the pattern beneath the mounds of papers and books. She held back her smile so as not to ruin the surprise.

"Thank you, thank you, Sera," the Philosopher said. "We will need your ingenuity to handle what is coming our way."

Sera swallowed hard, for she sensed a worried tension in Vesu's voice that she hadn't heard before. Now that she was standing close to her, she could also see the disquiet in

Vesu's eyes, which were surrounded by dark rings from lack of sleep. Sera immediately regretted her joke and went to grab the book before Vesu could get to it, but she was too late. Vesu hastily opened to the middle of the text, which revealed nothing about the North Gate, only sketches of a hideous beetle.

The Philosopher slammed the book onto the table and stood up, her ashen cheeks flaring bright red. "By the damn owl, Sera!" Vesu shouted, her voice echoing through the library's tangled aisles. "We cannot afford such antics. Too much is at stake!"

"I'm sorry, madam, I was only trying to—"

"Sera, we must make use of every minute to prepare for the council meeting," Vesu said, calmer now. "I should have told you earlier. Taro has presented a motion."

"A motion? At the first meeting of the session?" Sera glanced at Ozar.

"Taro is demanding that the S&R lock the North Gate," he said, looking down at his papers. "He is requesting that nobody from outside the Gorge be granted admission until further notice."

Sera's eyes flashed at Vesu, who nodded in confirmation. Sera struggled to wrap her head around the concept. For as long as she could remember, the North Gate doors had always been open. Her parents had told her the same was true when they were growing up. Two S&R guards manned the gate at all times, but their purpose was less to protect the entryway than to offer guidance to visitors about where to go once inside. The North Gate was the longstanding symbol to the rest of the continent that any traveler, arriving in peace, was welcome there.

"But why?" Sera asked. "How could Taro possibly justify such a demand?"

"We won't know for sure until the meeting tonight," Vesu said, "and even then I wonder if all of his reasons will be revealed. I suspect it has something to do with keeping the Alpinees out of Sterling, but we need to consider every angle—and learn everything we can about the North Gate—in order to provide a recommendation to the council before the vote."

"Madam, has the gate ever been closed before?" Ozar asked. "It's the first question that came to my mind, so surely the council will ask."

"That's why we're here, to find out." Vesu reached into the stack of books that Sera had set down. She pulled out Inka's *The Drowned King's War* and held it in the air. "The only written account of the North Gate's closure—that I know of—is set forth in here, when King Avarin's Royal Army invaded Sterling three centuries ago. We closed and locked the gate back then for protection from the king's soldiers, who were charging the walls with cannons. *Many* cannons, I might add."

"I'm not the least bit surprised," Ozar said, scowling. He tapped the table with his pen in agitation. "Yet another reason why this continent shouldn't be ruled by a fickle family. Why did King Avarin invade the Gorge in the first place? I'm sure we didn't provoke that fight."

Oh no, Sera thought, *here we go again*. Ozar was a master of many subjects, but the topic he pontificated about most often was the politics of Imperial Bay. He detested that the throne was filled by arbitrary bloodlines. In his view the entire continent should be governed the same way as Sterling, where the Philosopher chose the most qualified successor. Fortunately, Vesu didn't let the conversation veer too far toward his politics.

"You are quite right, Ozar. Sterling dutifully paid its taxes, and we stayed far away from Imperial Bay, facts that have been confirmed by multiple historians. However, the young king was egomaniacal, to put it lightly, and he would not tolerate our quasi-independent city at the south end of his realm. In fact, King Avarin led the army here himself to join the assault. If loyalty would not be granted freely, you see, then he would take it forcibly. And that journey from

Imperial Bay to the Gorge can take six months or more, so he must have been determined to send a strong message."

"Why do historians call him that?" Sera asked. "The Drowned King?"

"Well, I suppose we were also determined to send a message." Vesu tapped a book on the table. "From what I've read, the Royal Army crushed the gate—no, splintered it into a million pieces would be more historically accurate—and took many lives in the process. But as evidenced by us sitting here today, the invasion ultimately failed. Despite being outnumbered, the S&R was able to fend off the onslaught with whitefire crossbows. The king was captured and tortured, and the council sentenced him to death by drowning. He was tied to one of his own cannons and submerged in the Silver River. The Royal Army's commander, however, was released by the S&R. He marched back to Imperial Bay and assumed the throne, passing the crown down to his heirs. In the three hundred years since that blood-soaked war, many kings and queens have come and gone, and most of them have left Sterling alone to largely govern itself."

Vesu was a natural storyteller, due in part to her eloquent manner of speaking, but her stories were also compelling because she had an astounding recollection of historical details. Her mention of the whitefire crossbows sparked the interest of both Sera and Ozar, as neither of them had ever seen the infamous weapons. Capable of killing hundreds at a time, the crossbows had been banned after the Disarming and remained locked away in the Capitol armory.

"Madam, in light of that history, what if Taro has information about a potential attack?" Ozar asked. "After all, he oversees foreign affairs and correspondence. Maybe he has discovered some credible threat."

"We certainly cannot rule that out, but I find it unlikely. We have not encountered any signs of hostility in this region for decades. And I know Ambassador Elerin well. He would warn us of any trouble."

"I agree it is unlikely, madam," Ozar replied, "but with all due respect, you said we should consider every angle, and the consequences of this possibility warrant some of our attention, at least."

"I suppose you have a point." Vesu tossed her glasses onto the table and rubbed her eyes. It was moments like these that reminded Sera why Vesu had chosen Ozar as her Junior Philosopher in the first place, even though they had such drastically different . . . well, there's no other way to say it: *different philosophies*. Vesu believed it was crucial to keep the counter-argument close at hand because it kept her intellectually honest. "Sera, why don't you look through the foreign correspondence we have on file? See if you can find any letters of interest from our old friend, Ambassador Elerin. Ozar and I will continue our search through these reports on the North Gate. And nothing about insects this time, understood?"

"Yes, of course, madam."

Sera headed back into the library's winding aisles. She knew exactly where to look, as she had been filing official letters from Imperial Bay for several years. Ambassador Elerin had a custom of sending a letter to Sterling each spring with general updates from Imperial Bay. Otherwise, letters only arrived if there was an urgent matter to report. Sera could only remember one or two letters of that nature, such as when the queen's son died in infancy or when the Royal Army successfully put down an insurrection on the Iceway Coast. Taro normally summarized foreign communications at the council meeting and then handed the letters to Sera for safekeeping in the library.

From a lower shelf, Sera pulled out a leather binder labeled "Elerin." By the weight of it, she guessed it contained over one hundred pages of royal parchment—a daunting amount to read carefully in a short timeframe. Like Vesu, she didn't expect to find anything noteworthy, let alone a declaration of war that they had somehow missed, yet she heard Vesu's voice in her head from her early research lessons: *Turn every page, Sera, every last page!* So, she started from the beginning.

In his early letters, Sera observed that Ambassador Elerin did not provide much detail in the way of government or politics. His descriptions of Imperial Bay itself, however, were nothing short of poetic. His writings painted a vivid picture of the royal grounds, from the castle with its stained-glass windows to the gardens with their gilded fountains. Sera was most intrigued by Elerin's description of the ocean itself: the way the waves curled into the white sand from the seemingly endless horizon. Never having seen the ocean, Sera imagined how immense it must feel, and for a moment the Silver River seemed most inadequate by comparison.

As Sera moved through the years of Elerin's letters, her admiration for the ambassador grew and grew. He cataloged the kingdom's everyday events as if they were special occasions, demonstrating how much he cared for and respected the royal family. Sera also marveled at his handwriting. The cursive script was strikingly beautiful, the letters running smoothly together despite the thick black ink on the rough parchment. Most of the letters showed wear and tear from the long delivery route, but Elerin's writing remained crisp on the page.

Then Sera turned to the last section of Elerin's correspondence, the period starting from about three years earlier. She read the opening lines, and immediately something seemed off—almost like Elerin was writing in a different voice. The language was so formal, stilted, bureaucratic. It lacked the romantic attention to detail of his early letters. Sera checked to see if the letter was actually signed by Elerin, and found the same swooping letters.

But the next letter in the stack was also different somehow. It was missing the passion that filled the other pages. *Maybe Elerin was tiring of his position,* she thought. *Maybe he asked others to compose these letters for him.*

Sera turned to the next letter and the one after that; something was definitely amiss. She flipped to the end of the pile to see if she had lost the true Elerin for good. As she did, the paper's edge sliced the skin on her finger, and a few drops of blood dripped onto the parchment. That's when it struck her. It was not only the writing style that had changed from Elerin's early letters; the paper was different too.

She picked up the last page and examined it in the light. The parchment fibers looked thinner, and yet the pages didn't show the same weathering from travel. The ink was not of equal quality, either. It had a bluish hue instead of the heavy black ink used in previous letters. Sera wasn't sure what it meant, but Vesu needed to know immediately. She stuffed the pages of parchment into the binder.

When she returned to the mahogany table, Vesu and Ozar were already standing up.

"Madam, I have something to show you," Sera said, the thick folder pressed firmly under her arm.

"What did we miss?" Vesu asked over her shoulder. "Any signs of aggression?" She and Ozar were already walking away from the table toward the library's southwest entrance, which was next to the Grand Fireplace. The doors opened directly into the council chamber. Sera glanced at the clock and saw it was almost six o'clock in the evening. She really had lost track of time.

"Well, no, not exactly."

"Can it wait until after the council meeting?" the Philosopher asked.

Hearing the impatience in Vesu's voice, Sera reconsidered the evidence. A change in writing style, parchment, and ink was nowhere near an imminent threat. *I can't embarrass myself twice in one day.*

"Never mind, it's probably nothing." Sera slammed the folder on the table next to the other stacks and raced after them through the aisles.

When they reached the room with the Grand Fireplace, Sera could hear the trumpets through the wall, meaning the council members were about to march into the chamber. Waiting behind Vesu and Ozar at the doorway, Sera looked over at the fireplace. The stonework was beautiful—a snowy owl was carved directly into the mantel—but Sera found the bird quite unnerving. Its glossy yellow eyes seemed to follow her as she moved around the room.

As Vesu opened the door halfway to check on the progress of the procession, she gave some last-minute instructions. "Sera, one more thing. Tomorrow, I need you to prepare the Grand Fireplace for a visit."

"Yes, madam, I'll be ready." Sera was not surprised by the request. In fact, she wondered why Vesu had not asked her to light the fireplace sooner. "Where are you going this time?"

Before answering, Vesu lifted the Philosopher's shawl from its hook next to the fireplace and wrapped it around her neck. She held it there until Ozar could fasten the clip in the back. The shawl was made from the speckled black-and-white feathers of a snowy owl, woven together like a scarf that draped over Vesu's shoulders. Sera always admired how humbly and reverently Vesu wore the shawl, even though it made her look so powerful.

"I'm not entirely sure yet, so take careful notes."

Vesu stepped into the council chamber precisely as the concert band's cymbals crashed together at the end of the opening song, the room erupting into applause as the Philosopher took her place at the podium.

○

Before the Silver River reaches the Gorge and absorbs the cold rushing water from the mountains, it meanders across the continent through many diverse lands. At some locations, you would barely recognize it. Near the mouth at Imperial Bay, its bed is comprised of white sand that leaks in from ocean beaches. When it flows south through the midland forests, the line breaks apart into countless sloughs and backwaters, roots creeping out of the banks and dipping into the lazy, leaf-covered water. Eventually, the trees thin out into meadows, and the terrain turns into miles and miles of grasslands. At this point the Silver River's veins reconnect, and the main channel passes through the Prairie Basin, where it takes on a rusty-red color from the earthen clay crumbling in at each side.

Sir Balton Orowin, colonel of the Royal Army's South Branch, crouched low in the reedy brush lining a stretch of the Silver River to wash his hands in the muddy stream. He removed his cap and splashed his face with the warm water, though it provided little relief. The sun had been up for not yet an hour, and his face was already burned. The water dripped down into the stubble that covered his square jaw, which had been a reddish-blonde beard in his younger years, but over time turned mostly to gray.

He untied the reins of his horse, Una, from the only tree remaining along this section of the riverbank. He wasn't sure the tree would survive much longer. The soil between its roots was eroding, and its gray bark had mostly peeled away, revealing an inner core that was as smooth and white as bone.

"Hang in there, Ms. Una," the colonel said, patting her tawny chest. "The hunt should be over soon, and I'll get you back to camp and into the shade." The heat was getting to Una too. Orowin felt a thin film of sweat forming on her body. "I'll grab you a pail of well water when we get back. This creek here is more clay than rain these days."

At moments like these, Orowin wondered if horses like Una had strong memories. *Does she remember anything from home? The constant sound of waves crashing or the salty air that sweeps in from the bay and settles on your skin? Or the smell of seafood dinners when we take the gravel road that passes along the piers?* Their home was so far from this unforgiving, wretched place that perhaps it was best if Una forgot it all.

Orowin held up his arm to shield his face from the sun as he looked out across the flat plains of cracked clay. His wrist was outlined in three bands of black ink, one tattoo for each two-year tour of duty in the Prairie Basin. Rather than consider them badges of honor, like the other soldiers did, Orowin joked that his tattoos stood for heat, hunger, and thirst. For him they represented six years of his life that he wouldn't get back.

When Orowin accepted this appointment, he told himself it was for the adventure, for the action, for the risk. At age fifty-five, he was the longest-serving standard officer in the Royal Army, and had always been stationed at Imperial Bay. Under this new assignment he would take command of the army's South Branch, a regiment of four hundred soldiers that kept watch over the vast territory that stretched from the midlands all the way to the Silver River Gorge.

Over the last six years spent guarding this wasteland, Orowin had come to learn why he had really accepted the post: it was the safest choice he could have made. He knew from the start that the appointment was largely symbolic; there had been no conflicts in the region for decades. Orowin's main task was to keep an eye on the Prairie Riders, an elusive tribe whose members roamed the red plains on their bison. In his military briefings, the Riders were described as quick, cutthroat warriors, capable of raiding two towns in one night if the South Branch wasn't vigilant. Like many of his predecessors' reports, though, Orowin found this threat to be inflated. So far, the Prairie Riders had proven to be quiet neighbors who avoided confrontation. Running into them was rare, for they had no permanent home. They simply roamed from pasture to pasture, seeking out taller grasses for their bison. When it came down to it, Orowin was more curious about the Riders than he was suspicious. In all those briefings, nothing was ever mentioned about their history, culture, or language. *Why do we know so little about them?* he wondered.

What's more, save for a few towns along the Silver River, the vast region was largely uninhabited. *Who am I out here to protect, anyway?* The most populated city was Sterling, and it was guarded on both sides by two armies much larger than Orowin's: the mountain ranges. In fact, he was under strict orders from the king not to go anywhere near the Gorge and to avoid all confrontation with the Silver River Search & Rescue.

So, Orowin knew full well that he had chosen the position as much as it had chosen him. He followed orders. He abided by every rule, always. That was how he had gotten noticed as a young officer in the Royal Army and why he had been promoted up the ranks—not because of his bravery but because he played it safe.

Of course, it also helped that his cousin, Ambassador Elerin, was a close confidant of the king. Elerin had recommended the assignment to Orowin in the first place, insisting that it was an opportunity he couldn't pass up. When he returned home, Orowin would finish his career residing in the main barracks as a general, dining on the same food and wine as the royal family. Moreover, while on this tour of duty, Elerin would be his conduit to the king. All correspondence to Orowin would come directly from Ambassador Elerin, who promised to keep him informed of every noteworthy event in Imperial Bay.

Well, cousin, I'm over sixty years old now, Orowin said to himself, *and this is how far obedience has taken me: halfway across the continent, hunting savanna rats in a desert.* And he still had to endure the sting of one more tattoo on his wrist before he could make the long journey home. Instead of wine and oysters, for the next two years he would be drinking warm rivershine that his soldiers bought in the small towns along the river (for twice the price the bottles were actually worth), and most meals would consist of roasted savanna rats—that is, if he could actually kill one or two this morning.

"Okay, hold there for a minute, Ms. Una." Orowin dropped the reins and reached over his shoulder for his quiver. He took out each arrow and examined the feather fletching, smoothing them out to ensure a straighter shot.

The feathers alternated red and white, like the broad vertical stripes on his uniform. Next, he examined the arrowheads, which were dull from years of use. Shipments of new equipment from Imperial Bay arrived once a year, if that, so they learned to make everything last.

"Alright now, Ms. Una," Orowin said, turning around, "let me see my bow." When he turned to grab his recurve bow from the saddle bag, he realized Una had wandered off toward the river to nibble on the reeds. Orowin's heartbeat accelerated immediately, and more sweat poured into his eyes. She was only forty yards away, give or take, but out there, well, that was the distance between the hunter and the hunted.

Forgive me that I have not yet fully described the peculiar species known as the savanna rat. If you've never heard of one, count yourself among the vast majority of folks, even the well traveled. These furry creatures somewhat resemble a fox, in their size and shape at least, but their skinny tails are hairless. They inhabit deep tunnels under the red clay of the Prairie Basin, moving together in packs. And they can always hear you before you can hear them. Savanna rats listen underground for the footsteps of prey on the surface, and when the timing is right, they shoot out from the red dust. Most unnerving, perhaps, is that the ravenous packs devour every centimeter of their prey, from hair to bone, leaving behind only their foamy drool on the clay. But that evidence also evaporates quickly under the hot sun.

These horrendous little beasts know their limits, however. They leave large creatures, like horses, alone. Many suspect they are able to sense the differences in gait over their hunting grounds. The Royal Army learned this defensive technique from watching the Prairie Riders over the years. The Riders never strayed more than a few feet from their bison.

So, now you understand why Orowin dropped his quiver and bolted toward Una. He tried to cover the distance as nimbly and quietly as possible, although his army boots struggled to find traction in the sandy clay. He stumbled over himself, kicking clouds of copper-colored dust as he crawled toward Una, who continued to chew casually at the riverbank.

Orowin noticed the landscape had gone strangely quiet. The silence seemed to amplify his efforts. Compared to the peaceful backdrop of the Silver River's soft flow, his scrambling in the sand seemed to echo for miles. With less than twenty yards to safety, Orowin heard a soft rumble that gave him the chills. He had heard the sound of stampedes through the basin before, but none so stealthy and ruthless as this one. The quiet hum seemed far off, but Orowin sensed the pack was nearly upon him. He turned around to face the rush of savanna rats that would soon overtake him, the wave of teeth that would tear him apart.

But to Orowin's surprise, instead of taking a straight line at him, the wave of animals veered to his left, and the pack erupted into high-pitched howls. Orowin glanced toward the right and saw what was driving the group in the other direction: two soldiers on horseback galloping across the plains at full speed, launching arrows into the ferocious pack. After every other shot, a savanna rat shrieked and skidded into the clay. The soldiers pursued the group until most of the rats had scattered back into their holes, seeking the safety of their tunnels, waiting and listening underground for the heavy thud of hooves to dissipate.

"If you won't let your colonel defend himself, at least allow an old man the dignity of retrieving his horse," Orowin muttered. He trudged over to Una. He couldn't see the two soldiers' faces through the dust, which hadn't yet settled, but he knew exactly who they were by the accuracy of their arrows. Carolin and Pearlin, his captains.

"We never doubted you had everything under control, sir!" Carolin shouted. Orowin could hear the grin on her face. "We just wanted in on the action." She rode up next to Una and grabbed the reins so Orowin could step into the stirrup.

"Yes, a very interesting hunting tactic, Colonel," Pearlin said. "Using yourself as bait is risky, but I suppose it worked out in the end. Looks like we have twelve pelts to carry home."

"Holy ocean . . . keep quiet, the both of you." Orowin clambered up his horse. "If you hadn't interrupted, I could have taken twenty with my bare hands." The two captains laughed, relieved that their colonel was safe and his sense of humor intact.

Orowin straightened himself up in the saddle and sighed. His military career had not lent itself to marriage or children (or maybe it was another risk he was unwilling to take), so Orowin didn't know what it felt like to have daughters. But the affection that he felt for Carolin and Pearlin, and his constant worry for their well-being, had to be somewhere close.

He thought back to the gray morning when the army set out from Imperial Bay. Carolin and Pearlin rode beside him at the front of the regiment. In a quiet voice, he offered them a chance to turn around, to stay home, no questions asked. They just laughed and kept on marching. Their laugh was so similar and their physical appearance so alike, most people assumed they were sisters. "Maybe you should turn back, Colonel," Carolin joked. "We can lead the army from here."

Back then they laughed a lot more. Back then their uniforms truly did look royal, the bright red-and-white coats pressed into tight creases. Now Orowin's uniform was faded and wrinkled, while Carolin and Pearlin still managed to look like captains somehow. They had cut off their uniforms' sleeves at the shoulder, showing their smooth olive skin and toned arms. Their windblown black hair, long and wavy, contrasted sharply with their turquoise eyes, making them appear both fierce and alluring.

"In all candor, though, I owe it to both of you for keeping me alive. Not just today but over these last six years. I wish I could say I'll repay you one day for all it has meant to me, but I'm not sure the imperial treasury presses enough coins." Orowin nodded at each soldier. "I made a grave mistake this morning, and the desert took every advantage."

"In fairness, sir, it's not entirely your fault." Carolin pointed at the vegetation along the riverbank. "Remember when we arrived here years ago? Those shrubs grew out thirty more yards from the river than they do now, and these plains were spotted with tall green grass that would blow in the wind instead of all this dust. Oh, and remember the trees that used to line the river all the way back to camp? Those were great places to rest in the shade and maybe find some fruit. Come to think of it, we never called this place a desert until the last few years."

"She's right, Colonel," Pearlin added. "The sun has always been brutal here, but now it's an order of magnitude worse. It's not only the plants—you can see it in the way the savanna rats move. They're more aggressive than they used to be. And can you blame them? They're as desperate for food as we are."

Orowin knew his captains weren't exaggerating. Each year had been hotter than the last, and each year his troops became hungrier and thirstier while out on patrol.

"Morale is extremely low, sir," Pearlin said. "The soldiers want something to eat besides savanna rats, and something cooler to drink than well water. Could we move the troops upstream to gain the cover of the forests? The Silver River runs clearer up there."

"Pearlin, you know I've already asked for permission to move northward. You helped me draft that letter to the ambassador. But the king has commanded that we hold our position for the time being."

"That was two years ago, Colonel," Carolin said. "Is it time to march south, then, toward the Gorge? We're charged with protecting the citizens of Sterling too, are we not? On hot days like this, I dream of the cool breeze coming off those mountains, drinking a frosted glass of brown ale."

"Captain, I proposed that relocation to Ambassador Elerin months ago, and I expect to receive a response any day now. We will do as we are ordered."

"I understand, Colonel. Pardon my impatience."

"Sir, we should really start heading back to the fort," Pearlin said. "The reason we came to get you is that a tribe of Prairie Riders is congregating a few hundred yards from our camp."

"And what are they doing?"

"Well, it appears they're simply grazing their bison," Carolin explained, "which in itself is no cause for alarm. But four bison broke off from the herd and are standing near the fort's main doors."

"Why should a few stray bison concern me? It sounds like a situation you two soldiers are fully capable of handling on your own." Orowin kicked Una to set her trotting back toward the camp.

"Pearlin thinks they're waiting for you, sir!" Carolin called after him. Orowin sensed the hesitancy in her voice. He pulled back the reins and swung Una around.

"The Prairie Riders, you mean? Now that is strange, for in all my years here I've never met one, and I'd be interested to learn—"

"No, sir," Pearlin piped up. "Not the Prairie Riders. The bison."

Chapter IV

"Welcome, fellow countrymen and friends, to the two hundred and twenty-seventh inauguration of the Sterling City Council." Vesu's voice rebounded off the high ceilings of the council chamber, making Sera shiver. The echo added more gravitas to Vesu's already distinguished voice. "We gather here today, as we do every fourth year, to witness our elected council members take their oath of office and assume the safekeeping of our common home. Undeniably, we have many reasons to celebrate—the Silver River flows strong, and our bridges stand tall as landmarks of history and ingenuity. But we also face tall obstacles—the river's current does not carry all of us quickly, nor does it nourish all of us equally. So, as we begin our legislative session this evening, I challenge our council members to ensure that our Four Bridges also stand for mercy."

Sera watched in amazement as the entire audience rose from their seats and burst into applause. For Sera, moments like these justified all those long hours in the library, for she had the best seat in the chamber. Vesu's podium was set in the center of the circular room, and Sera was seated directly to her right, Ozar to her left.

While the clapping carried on for a minute or two, Sera glanced around the room to admire the architecture. Next to the bridges, she considered the council chamber Aldo's second-greatest achievement. The stadium-like seating rose up in concentric circles around the stage, like a staircase leading to the sky, where members of the public could observe the proceedings. Perfectly vertical columns held up the domed ceiling, which was silver on the outside but on the inside was decorated with stained glass in every imaginable shade of blue. The mural did not depict any particular scene, and Sera preferred it that way. She let her eyes roam across the abstract artwork, each pass finding new geometrical forms among the million tiny glass pieces. Instead of light coming in from the outside, the glass bits were lit up by chandeliers hanging below. Sera couldn't credit Aldo for the chandeliers because another Philosopher had designed them, although they suited the elegant chamber well. The fixtures resembled giant raindrops made of silver, crystal, and glass, and they were cleverly designed such that fifty candles alone could light up the entire room.

Vesu administered the oath of office for each council member at center stage under the chandeliers and then the concert band performed a song to mark the transition into the legislative session.

Sera would be the first to admit she could keep neither rhythm nor tune, but even she could tell the band was terrible. The percussionists could not maintain the tempo, and the horns sounded off-pitch on the high notes. Fortunately, the audience knew the words and sang along, which made the performance, on the whole, tolerable. The band was easy to pick out in the crowd, lined up along a middle-tier balcony in their matching blue vests. Sera couldn't sing either, so instead she scanned the line of musicians as they played, starting with the percussionists on the left, followed by the brass toward the middle. When she got to the string section on the far right, she nearly burst into laughter—a violinist near the end was wearing a uniform five times too big for his frame. *Ha! He looks a bit like melting ice*, Sera thought.

After the song ended, Vesu introduced Numa and invited her to take the podium. The council rules established that the Low Quarter had the first opportunity to address the assembly, followed by the higher quarters in order. As

Numa stepped up to the stage, the light from the chandeliers bounced off her curly blonde hair. Sera was sitting close enough to be drawn in by Numa's lively green eyes, which struck her as eager and compassionate.

"Ladies and gentlemen, I am humbled to join this esteemed body. As the Philosopher so wisely stated in her opening remarks, the Silver River does not provide for us all equally, and, indeed, it reaches the Low Quarter last. Our community faces unprecedented levels of pollution from both the water and the air. When we draw water from the river to drink, it is often full of dyes and sawdust from the textile manufacturers and woodworking shops upstream. Not to mention—"

"With all due respect, councilwoman, those shops provide for the livelihood of our communities," said Taro, the councilman from the Mid Quarter. "Have you considered, perhaps, that—"

"Taro, let the councilwoman finish her comments," Vesu said. "You'll have your turn to address the assembly soon enough. Please continue, Numa."

"As I was saying, our community also suffers from air that is unsafe to breathe. Our children walk to school through smoke that drifts in from the Down Quarter's blacksmith shops—"

"For the record, I'd like to reiterate that those blacksmiths employ many residents of the Low Quarter," Taro interrupted again, this time standing up behind his desk at the side of the stage. "As a unified council, we must consider the best interests of Sterling holistically. If I were councilman Rolu, who represents those smiths of the Down Quarter, I would be insulted that—"

"Taro, that's enough," Vesu said firmly. "You will have your opportunity to respond when it is your turn to speak. If you interrupt again, I will have you removed from the chamber."

Taro sat down in his high-back leather chair, and Numa finished her opening statement without further disruption.

She used the opportunity to emphasize the severity of the addiction problem in the Low Quarter, describing how the trillium seeds hooked more residents each day. She implored the upper quarters for assistance. "This seed will not obey our neighborhood boundaries. Soon the crime and homelessness that we are fighting will cross over our bridge into other communities. This problem demands a *holistic* solution, as I'm sure the councilman from the Mid Quarter will agree."

After Numa, Rolu tramped up on stage, taking hold of the podium with both hands. It was the first time Sera laid eyes on him, and at first she was concerned he might break the wooden podium into pieces. Not because Rolu was gripping it that tightly, but because his hands were so huge. The sleeves of his work shirt were rolled up, so Sera could see his forearm muscles flex under the thick black hair. His baritone voice hovered between powerful and protective.

"Brothers and sisters of Sterling, the councilwoman's prediction has already come true. As a bridgekeeper I see almost everything that comes in and out of the Down Quarter, and these seeds are already bought and sold in our streets. To that end, I look forward to working together this session to prevent this epidemic from spreading further."

Rolu paused and took a deep breath, his round torso expanding and contracting like a fireplace bellows. "I do fear, however, that we face a more imminent threat than the seeds. We have all heard the rumblings that the Alpinees have been sighted on the outskirts of our city. We do not yet know why they linger in our forests, but the council should assume the worst and take precautionary measures. This is not one of those ghost stories that our parents told us when we were children. This afternoon I was informed by the S&R that a young mountain climber has gone missing."

The audience released a wave of whispers that fluttered up the rows like leaves in the wind. Sera glanced over at Vesu and Ozar, who appeared equally surprised at the news.

"I'm told that the young man was climbing in the Cloudhorns, training to join the S&R. By all accounts he was an experienced climber, and yet the guards cannot find him in the area where he was last seen. The investigation is ongoing, so we cannot be certain, but the S&R have reason to believe that the Alpinees were involved in his disappearance."

The audience began to buzz again, this time escalating beyond whispers into shouting and questioning. Vesu stood up and rang the bell next to her seat to signal the public to quiet their voices, but the sound went unheard. She was about to ring it a second time in an attempt to regain order in the chamber when a drumbeat pounded through the commotion.

Sera immediately looked up to the percussion section on the balcony. The steady booms were coming from a young man who was banging wildly on the timpani drums. When he had gained the chamber's full attention, he shouted to the crowd. "That's not true! The Alpinees need our help. Please listen to me—"

That's all that Sera heard him say. The young man's voice was drowned out by yelling and boos. The crowd was quick to realize that he was merely a musician's assistant, dressed in a simpler version of the concert band attire. Sera was curious to hear what the young man had to say, but the audience had no patience for such an interruption. The cursing and shouting made that clear.

"Madam Philosopher, remove that boy from this chamber immediately," Taro demanded. "We must address this serious matter in an orderly fashion."

Vesu signaled to the S&R guards to take care of it. Sera watched as the young man was dragged along the upper-level aisles to the chamber's back doors, shouting the entire way.

When the chatter finally subsided, Rolu cleared his throat and continued. "Now, I will readily acknowledge that we know little about our neighbors in the Cloudhorns, although recent signs have not been signs of friendship. Crops have been stolen from fields at night, prized livestock gone missing. With this disappearance, are our children in danger? I recommend that the council take appropriate safety measures."

Half the room gave a standing ovation while others argued fervently amongst themselves in their seats. Sensing another upheaval, Vesu rang the bell and stepped up to the podium to introduce Taro. After his multiple interruptions thus far, she was not inclined to allow another long-winded address, so she tried to head off his remarks.

"Councilman Taro, you may step up to address the council. I understand that you would like to make a motion this evening, is that correct?"

"Yes, Madam Philosopher, I do intend to make a motion. And my remarks will be brief, as councilman Rolu has already made my argument for me, by and large."

Unlike the first two speakers, who were new to the council, Sera had observed Taro for a full term already. She was very familiar with his rhetorical style, which she considered as slick as his attire. He was sharply dressed in a charcoal-colored coat, a spotless white shirt, narrow gray pants, and shiny black shoes. His shoes were so polished, in fact, that Sera could see the multiple chandeliers reflecting off their surface. He moved his arms and hands excitedly as he argued, and the bright gemstones in the rings that he wore were very distracting. Taro also had a habit of combing his hair before taking the podium, which Sera found peculiar because it was already neatly in place.

"Fellow council members, Rolu is right to raise the alarm about the Alpinees. As your liaison to the S&R, I have kept a watchful eye on this potential threat, and I am here to report that the Alpinees are not only unpredictable; they are also armed. The S&R guards who patrol the Cloudhorns inform me that each Alpinees scout carries a climbing axe with a blade so sharp, even Rolu here could be sliced in half." Taro smacked the podium with his hands, startling the audience members sitting in the first few rows. "And I think that leaves little room for doubt that the council must take proactive safety measures, as Rolu suggests."

Sera was taking careful notes of Taro's talking points, but she shot a glance at Vesu to gauge her reaction. The Philosopher seemed completely taken aback, rubbing her temples nervously with her forefingers. Ozar stared blankly into the crowd. Never in Sera's six years as a Philosopher's apprentice had they been so unprepared for a council session. Never had she seen Vesu so on edge.

"Councilman," Vesu interjected, "we appreciate your detailed reporting, but you stated at the outset that your remarks would be brief, and you have not yet disclosed the subject matter of your motion."

"Madam Philosopher, I thought the purpose of my motion would be evident to all by now. I move that we close and lock the North Gate until further notice. That is, until the threat posed by the Alpinees has been properly assessed by the council."

As expected, the chamber erupted again into raucous debate. More than a fair share of the audience cheered the proposal while others turned to their neighbors in disbelief, asking if they had heard the councilman correctly. Vesu rang the bell several times, although it was barely noticeable above the clamor. She had no choice but to wait until the uproar settled down.

"Ladies and gentlemen, your attention, please!" Vesu rang the bell one last time to recapture the attention of the room. "Before we vote on the motion, we have one more council member left to speak. I invite Veti from the Up Quarter to the podium."

Veti rose slowly from her seat, assisted by an S&R guard. Veti was somewhere in her seventies, Sera guessed, so she needed a hand ascending the lofty steps to the stage. Other than that, though, Veti could readily hold her own during council debates. This would be her eighth term on the council, and Sera had watched her in action for the last two.

Sera did not always agree with Veti's arguments, but she respected their logic. Veti's mind was sharp and her memory clear. She could recall council decisions from decades ago, bringing them to bear on current subjects.

"Oh, dear. I intended to share my plans for the Up Quarter's annual art fair and my proposal for a summer recital, but it seems a more pressing matter has absorbed the council's attention." Veti's introduction drew some lighthearted laughter from the audience. She adjusted the lace scarf draped around her neck, which was decorated with a floral pattern. The white scarf matched a band of flowered trim that started at the bottom of her blue gown and spiraled up, wrapping around her slender body like a spring. Not only could Veti influence the politics of her fellow council members, she was also quite the trendsetter.

"As for the Councilman's motion, I have never taken the city's defense lightly. Our generation has had the fortune of living through peaceful times, but it was not always so. My parents lived through the Disarming and other battles before that. Those conflicts seem distant to us now, although only a century stands in between. And a century is merely a fleeting moment in the Silver River's long history.

"Nevertheless, the additional protection provided by the North Gate's closure must be measured against the consequences. And in this regard, I have reservations. What message will this send to the rest of the continent? That outsiders are no longer welcome here? We keep our doors wide open because we have much to share with the world and much to learn from it."

Several audience members applauded and whistled, although Sera recognized the response fell short of the public support that Taro had garnered during his speech. She scanned the other council members, looking for any signs that Veti's comments were persuasive enough. For a motion to pass the council, it required a majority vote, which meant three out of four needed to vote in favor of the measure. In the event of a tie, the Philosopher had the authority to cast the tie-breaking vote.

Taro rapped his rings on his desk, signaling to Vesu that he wanted to speak. Sera cringed whenever Taro sought attention that way, but at least it was less rude than blatantly interrupting other council members.

"Any final arguments, Councilman?" Vesu asked. Taro slipped his thin ivory comb back into his coat pocket, which did not go unnoticed by Sera. She had caught him discreetly combing his hair again while Veti made her remarks. Taro addressed the council and the public from behind his desk.

"I hear the concerns of my colleague, and I acknowledge that this decision has significant consequences. But before we cast our votes, there is another variable we must consider. Forgive me for not raising it sooner, Madam Philosopher, but it is a sensitive subject and I was not sure whether the timing was appropriate."

This is unbelievable! Sera thought. *What could it be now?* Again, she looked over at Vesu and Ozar in disbelief. She could tell by the way Vesu was sitting—arms crossed, hunched over in her chair—that the knot in her stomach was just as tight. Ozar was also leaning forward, his elbows on his knees, cracking the knuckles in one clenched fist, then the other.

"As the councilman assigned to foreign affairs, I have been handling correspondence with the king's diplomat, Ambassador Elerin. The council should be advised that I have not received a letter from the ambassador for many months now. He usually sends a message each spring with news from Imperial Bay. This year, however, no such letter arrived. Although I care little about the everyday occurrences up north, I find this recent silence disturbing. It leaves us completely in the dark about the location, and the intentions, of the Royal Army's South Branch."

"Taro, are you suggesting that the king might be considering military action against us?" Vesu asked.

"I'm not suggesting anything of the sort, Madam Philosopher. I'm merely pointing out, for the council's consideration, that we have absolutely no clue regarding the whereabouts of the largest military force in our region."

"Well, Councilman, that changes my calculus considerably," Veti said, having remained at the podium for the entire exchange. "I can't recall a single year in recent memory where Ambassador Elerin failed to send his annual report. His letters usually bring good tidings from the king and updates on the military movements in our area. Has that goodwill shifted in the wind? It's impossible to say, but I will lose sleep over this news."

After Veti sat back down, Taro wrapped up his argument. "Madam Philosopher, let each council member consult their own conscience. Take the roll call at your discretion."

Sera watched as Vesu's face went pale, and for good reason. This was the most unpredictable session Sera had ever sat through. Under normal circumstances, Vesu, Ozar, and Sera would spend weeks preparing for the monthly council meeting, anticipating likely questions and concerns. The Philosopher's role was to guide and inform the debate, remaining impartial unless called upon to vote. This last-minute motion caught them all by surprise, and now Vesu had lost control over the proceedings entirely. She removed her glasses and rubbed her eyes. Her hands looked especially frail under the bright chandeliers. The prolonged silence made everyone in the chamber uneasy.

"Since we do not normally consider such significant decisions during the first meeting, let's give the new council members a few minutes to consider their vote," Vesu suggested. "I'd like the concert band to play a song to allow us time for reflection. Mr. Conductor, could you perform 'The Anthem of the Swans?'"

The conductor was startled by the sudden request, as he too had been closely following the debate. However, he spun around and raised his baton, the musicians racing to adjust their instruments and tune up before the first downbeat.

She's trying to buy time, Sera thought.

The band played the opening notes of the song, which was a well-known piece composed shortly after the Disarming. The melody drifted along, cheerful and calm. The song had been written to signify the peace that settled into the Gorge after the civil war ended, and the whitefire crossbows were locked away. Despite the song's simplicity, the concert band sounded worse this time around. The woodwinds were out of tune, the trumpets screeched through the chorus, and the bass notes from the tubas could not keep up with the percussion section. By the time they reached the second verse, Vesu's face was bright red. The racket was simply unbearable.

By the owl, Sera thought, *is the whole world falling apart?*

"Please, Mr. Conductor!" Vesu yelled from center stage. "That's enough for now. That will do." She made no effort to conceal her disgust at the poor performance. The conductor lowered his baton, and the musicians dropped out, one by one. Vesu returned to the podium to take the roll call vote.

Before announcing the motion, however, she paused for a moment. The band had stopped playing, but the music hadn't completely faded away. Somehow the melody was still swirling around the council chamber. Sera assumed it was an echo at first, although the notes were too cheerful, calm, clear. She scanned the room and discovered that the sound was emanating from the balcony on the far right. A violinist continued to play, rocking back and forth with his eyes closed. *It's that funny little man! And he doesn't see that the conductor has stopped the music. Oh my, how embarrassing . . .*

Instead of directing the man to stop or ordering the S&R to take him away, Vesu just stood there, listening intently. The little soloist kept on playing, the notes rising along the columns and reverberating around the rotunda. Sera and Ozar (and the rest of the audience, for that matter) now realized what had caught Vesu's attention: the music was breathtaking.

The little soloist carried on with the piece, unaware that his colleagues had stopped performing. With the help of the chamber's perfect acoustics, he was capable of filling the room with sound all by himself. The melody echoed off the ceiling and drifted back down to dance with itself, twirling around the room. Sera couldn't help but look up, expecting to see a hidden orchestra in the walls, but all she saw were the chandeliers spinning slightly on their chains from the vibrations.

Sera glanced over at Vesu and saw that the worry had washed out of her eyes. Sera couldn't help but smile. She surveyed the audience, and they were also incredibly moved. Many people were holding their neighbor's hand, as if they were in church and not at the Capitol building. Whereas ten minutes ago the tension in the room was so deep that one could drown in it, when the last note of "The Anthem of the Swans" rang out, the final bit of fear left the room, like the last drop out of a sponge.

The little soloist was clearly shocked when the applause started. He blushed and tried to hide behind a fellow bandmate, but Vesu wouldn't let him escape that easily.

"Very impressive, young man," she said, loud enough to be heard above the applause. "I invite you to come down after our session adjourns. I'm interested to know how you learned to play so wonderfully, and I'm certain that Councilwoman Veti, our director of cultural affairs, would like to speak with you as well. Veti, we have been searching for a Capitol musician for some time, haven't we?"

"Yes, we have, Madam Philosopher. And we're still interviewing for the position."

"Very well then." Vesu seized the podium with both hands. She rolled her shoulders back and planted her feet firmly on the stage. Sera studied the faces of the council members. Apparently, the soloist's anthem had inspired them too. The look in their eyes was more confident, maybe even hopeful.

Everyone except for Taro, that is. He was sliding his rings on and off each finger, trying to figure out what happened to the momentum behind his motion. Sera couldn't tell if Vesu had also noticed this change in the council's demeanor, or if she was simply ready to deal with the motion's consequences, whatever they might be. Regardless, she pressed forward.

"We will now take a roll call vote on the motion to close the North Gate, presented by—"

"Madam Philosopher," Taro interrupted, "I would like to defer the motion until the next council meeting. Such an important measure warrants further study, I believe."

"Is that so, Councilman? Well, it is your right to do so under the council rules. Are there any other questions? Hearing none, I will see you all again in one month. Our session is adjourned."

◉

Before I became a Philosopher, I was fortunate enough to have explored the farthest reaches of this broad continent, from top to bottom and end to end. Many places I dream of visiting one last time, to hike in certain hills once more, to paddle familiar streams, and to camp on forest floors that might remember my shape. But my time is limited, and so I must be deliberate with my list. For this reason I'm doubtful I'll ever return to the Prairie Basin unless I'm only passing through. I remember that landscape as severe, hostile, and empty. Save for a few crossroads along the Silver River, it lacks the kind company of Sterling and the lively culture of Imperial Bay.

Many creatures call the Prairie Basin home, though, and find a way to survive. Take the volt of vultures, for instance, that was quick to congregate for an easy lunch around the savanna rats Carolin and Pearlin took out with their arrows. The captains retrieved every dart that was still intact, but the vultures were content to eat around the broken shafts that they left behind. A few vultures that circled in late, coasting down on their sooty black wings, saw the colonel and his captains from above, riding off toward the barracks as three streaks of smoke, their horses kicking up sand.

Colonel Orowin had to squint hard to prevent the dusty gravel from stinging his eyes, but soon enough an outline of the army campgrounds emerged on the horizon. He could see it from afar because the garrison was situated on an outcropping of bedrock. The elevated granite formation was mostly flat, which made it easier to construct the fort when they first arrived while also providing long-term protection against tunneling savanna rats. Toward the front stood the main barracks where the colonel resided. Behind that were several rows of cabins for the captains and other officers. The rest of the rank and file slept in tents, three or four under each tarpaulin roof. The settlement was sufficient at first, when they expected their stay to be short, but those days had accumulated into years of sleeping on the rocky ground.

Columns of light-gray smoke rose up between the tents where the soldiers were cooking lunch. It was a day of rest from their regular drills and training sessions, so the South Branch soldiers passed the time drinking rivershine and betting their wages on card games and dice. The colonel considered the gambling harmless enough; the money mostly made its way back and forth between the soldiers over time. The drinking, on the other hand, was becoming a serious distraction.

Since the day he set out from Imperial Bay, Orowin could think of a thousand reasons to complain about this assignment, although the caliber of his troops was never one of them. The king had supplied his regiment with tough, spirited soldiers who lived by the motto "ride far and shoot fast." But now those fighters were stuck in the Basin without a clear cause to fight for and no outlet for all their energy. So, his men had no place to turn for excitement except bootleg bottles of rivershine. They wound up picking fights amongst themselves just to feel some sort of intensity.

Within a few hundred yards, the bison that Carolin and Pearlin reported came into view: four brown-black boulders standing in an even line facing the main barracks, separated from the mass of Prairie Riders farther out in the field. A few soldiers paced around the bison on foot, holding their bows at chest level with arrows nocked.

"What do you think they taste like?" one soldier asked.

"Better than savanna rat, I'm sure," another replied.

"How many arrows do you think we'll need to take one down and find out?" a third soldier asked, aiming his arrow at the middle bison's chest.

"I need only one arrow to take you down, Private!" Carolin said as she rode up to the group with Orowin and Pearlin behind her. "Didn't I instruct you to leave these animals alone?"

"Yes, Captain!" The soldier dropped his bow, startled by the officers' arrival. "I was . . . was . . . not going to ha-harm them, Captain, I was only . . ." Orowin could tell by his stammering that he was half drunk already, and it was not even noon.

"Go make yourself useful," Pearlin said, tossing him a canvas sack full of savanna rats, which almost knocked him over when he caught it. "Take these back to camp and get a fire going. It should help you sober up."

Orowin ignored the soldier stumbling back to the fort. He had already turned his attention to the row of four bison. He lifted his reins to direct Una in a slow walk around them, inspecting the massive animals from all sides. The hump over their shoulders rose taller than Una, and their hulking bodies were twice as wide. Orowin was baffled that their skinny legs could hold up such a bulky core. Their shaggy fur was light brown on the sides, matted down with clumps of dirt, and darkened to a brownish-black mane around their low-set head and neck. Short gray horns curved to a sharp point above their ears.

Holy ocean! Every aspect of these creatures is intimidating, Orowin thought. *In fact, if not for that strange sadness in their eyes, I'd guess they were indestructible.*

The bison had their heavy heads tilted downward. Their round, glossy eyes were the same dark brown as the fur in their beards. Something in their stares didn't fit with the rest of their powerful presence. Instead of strength, Orowin sensed helplessness. When they exhaled into the heat from their wide nostrils, he saw their breath steam out in swirls of dust.

"I'm Colonel Orowin of the Royal Army's South Branch," he said, halting Una in front of the line, facing the bison. "What brings you to our barracks?"

The animals stood there indifferently, not making a sound. Orowin looked over at Carolin, lifting his eyebrows and shrugging. She returned the gesture.

"Tell us, why are you here?" Orowin let the silence hang in the air for several seconds. The bison remained quiet and still. He gave it another try. "How can we help you?"

No response. The bison stayed rooted in place, the mangy tufts of hair at the end of their tails swishing back and forth.

"Sir, I don't think you're asking the right questions," Pearlin said, hopping off her horse. She stepped up to the bison, her wavy bangs draped over her eyes. Orowin's stomach turned at the sight of Pearlin standing only a few feet away from those eight sharp horns. Before speaking, she casually tucked her hair behind her ears with both hands.

"Do you understand me?" Pearlin asked, slowly and calmly. The bison in the middle responded with a short, low-pitched grunt.

"Alright, let's give this a shot. Are you hungry?" This time, the middle bison scraped his hoof a couple of times in the dirt.

"No. Okay, are you thirsty?" Pearlin's question elicited another low groan from the bison's throat. "So, you're thirsty. Now we're getting somewhere. Private, go fetch a few buckets of water from the well," she ordered of a soldier standing by.

"Captain, is this some kind of joke?" Orowin scoffed. "You can stay here and play these games all day if you'd like, I'm riding over to the Prairie Riders to speak with someone in a position of authority."

Orowin kicked Una in her sides with his heels, and she started to trot through the line of bison, aiming toward the group of about one hundred Prairie Riders huddled together out in the field. As Una was about to pass between the two on the left, the bison stepped together, bumping into Una's chest and blocking her path. Una snorted anxiously, a bit rattled from being knocked around. Orowin backed her up and tried passing on the right, but they were intercepted again as the four animals moved together to form a tighter wall. Una neighed loudly in frustration, and Orowin was forced to pull back on the reins, retreating with Una to a safe distance behind Pearlin. Together all four bison stomped their hooves into the ground, smashing the clay's red crust.

"Pearlin speaks bison better than I do," Carolin said, grinning widely, "but I think that means they're in charge, sir."

"Alright, you have my attention." Orowin patted Una's neck to calm her down.

Pearlin stepped in closer and stretched out her arm to rub the flat forehead of the middle bison. Her hand looked so tiny compared to the animal's massive skull and so smooth compared to its scraggly fur.

"Listen, we're not going to hurt you, we're trying to figure out what's wrong. I've been stuck here in the Basin long enough to know you've never come this close to our camp. Are you in danger?"

The bison let out a longer grunt, more strained than before.

"What kind of danger?" Pearlin asked, with genuine concern in her voice. "Our scouts haven't seen anyone out here in any direction for many miles. Please, tell us, what are you running from?"

After this last question, all four bison swung their heavy heads from side to side, grunting in unison and shuffling their feet. Pearlin jumped back nervously, trying to avoid getting crushed between the mammoth bodies. She soon realized, though, that the bison were simply turning around to face the Prairie Riders standing in the open plain. She walked between them to get a better view, her hand gliding along the middle bison's scruffy hair. Orowin and Carolin followed suit, leading their horses forward to stand in line beside the bison to see whatever it was they were looking at out in the field.

For the first time, Orowin, Carolin, and Pearlin saw the Prairie Basin as the bison must have seen it. The intense sun baked the barren landscape laid out before them, the air shimmering in wavy lines along the horizon. Only a few patches of wilted grass remained in what was once a full field. No more daisies, coneflowers, or primrose. No more birds or butterflies. The trees no longer had leaves to shade themselves, let alone other creatures seeking cover from the sun's glare.

The Prairie Riders staggered toward them across the desert ground like ghosts. Orowin's eyes grew wide; it struck him that he had never actually seen a Rider up close. For years he had watched them charge across the fields by the hundreds, but only from a distance. Only from a *safe* distance, where he was confident that Una could race him out of harm's way if the Riders turned in his direction. From that distance, all Orowin could ever make out was the outline of their wiry bodies as they straddled their massive mounts, gripping them tightly. Come to think of it, Orowin couldn't have said if the Riders had skin, scales, or fur. Until now.

The Prairie Riders walked slowly through the hazy heat. Orowin's instinct was to shield his eyes, but at the same time he couldn't look away. The Riders were certainly shaped like warriors, but that was about the only thing that looked familiar. Their arms, legs, fingers, and toes were made of dense vines that twisted and turned like veins. Those spindly limbs connected to a torso that was itself a thicket of stringy plants, tangled up to form their shoulders, chest, and back. Instead of a rib cage protecting heart and lungs, the Riders were built like a skeleton of leaves, roots, and stems wrapped endlessly around each other.

Orowin had never seen anything—or anyone—quite like this. He couldn't help but imagine the Prairie Riders as gardens grown inside empty suits of armor, except when all the silver plating was removed, the gardens walked around with a life of their own.

Orowin was stunned by their elegant features, but he sensed immediately that the Riders were not healthy. The leaves in their spiraling ivy hair were starting to shrivel up. The clovers that shaped the outline of their lips were withering away. And most of the tiny flower petals that formed their eyelashes had fallen out. Orowin had to look away, at last, although that might have been worse. The harsh sun pierced the Riders' hollow bodies, casting eerily empty shadows on the red earth. Orowin was enraged. *When was the last time it rained?*

"Set those buckets down now!" Orowin yelled at the soldiers who had just returned with the well water for the bison. Several others tagged along, curious to see what had caused the commotion in front of the barracks. As each soldier approached, they couldn't help but wince as Orowin did. The Riders stood silently, their scorched nervous system of brambles, brittle and cracked, was enough to convey their thirst.

"Go get more water, as much as you can carry!" At Orowin's command, a group of soldiers scrambled off toward camp.

The middle bison leaned his head down to drink. Pearlin patted his mane and gently rubbed the fur behind his ears. As Orowin watched her comfort the enormous animal, he suddenly realized what Pearlin had already figured out: it wasn't the Prairie Riders who had tamed the bison; it was the other way around. All at once the mystery of the Riders made more sense. Out there in the Basin's open fields, a bison herd would be tempting prey for hunters. If they had been grazing alone all this time, the South Branch surely would have stalked the beasts to extinction. But no hunter wanted to fight a battle for every dinner, so the bison struck a clever bargain: these prairie creatures could hitch a ride wherever they wanted to go, as long as they looked like soldiers.

Is this their natural shape? Orowin wondered. *Or do they take the form of warriors out of necessity?* As much as he wanted to ask, Pearlin had more pressing concerns.

"Drink up," she said, "we'll bring more water for your Riders." Pearlin rubbed the tattoos on her wrist. "Colonel, we need to do something. Our well isn't deep enough to fill so many mouths for long."

"Let's bring the Riders back to Imperial Bay," Carolin suggested. "We'll find better rangelands closer to the ocean."

"In this condition, I doubt they'll make it that far," Pearlin said. "Colonel, we need to lead the Riders to the Gorge. The weather will be cooler between the mountains, and we can ask the City of Sterling for help."

By then a large number of soldiers had assembled around the colonel and the bison, drawn to this unusual confrontation. Many of them nodded in agreement at Pearlin's suggestion, but they dared not speak until they heard from the colonel.

"We will do whatever we can to help the Riders here, but we are under strict orders to remain at our position. The king has given us specific instructions."

"We don't actually know what the king commands anymore, do we?" Carolin asked. "We haven't received a message in months."

"Colonel! Colonel Orowin!" squeaked a short soldier as he pushed through the circle of troops gathered around the Prairie Riders. Orowin couldn't see the little man's body squeezing through the rows of soldiers, only his fist held high in the air, bobbing above the uniforms. In his hand he clutched a roll of parchment, tattered at each end. "Colonel, we received a letter from the messenger this morning while you were out hunting."

"Why didn't you inform me sooner? Hand it over immediately!" Orowin's face was flushed with anger. The soldier had to stand up on his toes to reach the colonel, turning his head to the side to avoid making eye contact. Orowin snatched the parchment, which was worn and torn from the long journey, but still rolled up and tied with the king's ribbon. Carolin, Pearlin, and the rest of the regiment watched in suspense. Nearly every soldier had wandered over from the campgrounds to observe the rare encounter with the Prairie Riders.

Orowin didn't even take the time to dismount from Una. He ripped the seal with his teeth, unfurled the paper, and read silently to himself.

Dearest Orowin, I hope this letter finds you in good spirits. Imperial Bay is as exquisite as you remember . . .

Orowin skimmed through the flowery introduction. Ambassador Elerin had a habit of beginning his letters with detailed descriptions of the royal grounds and special events, and this letter was no different. At times his letters inspired some nostalgia in Orowin, but today he had no patience for such minor details. He skipped the summary of the royal family's social calendar and turned his attention to the last few paragraphs.

> *... but as it relates to military matters, the king commands that you remain at your current location in the Prairie Basin. The king is a student of history, and he would like to maintain amicable relations with the City of Sterling. Therefore, hold your position. We do not want to make any movements that might send the wrong message to the Search & Rescue. We trust you will understand. Continue to monitor and protect those royal lands northeast of the Gorge where the Prairie Riders roam.*

Orowin looked up from the letter and found the entire South Branch staring back at him. He lifted his reins to spin Una in a circle, scanning his troops. They looked exhausted; not as weakened as the Prairie Riders, but at this rate it was only a matter of time until they too succumbed to the heat, hunger, and thirst.

He swiveled Una around again to face the barracks. Without any wind to lift them, the two Royal Army flags on each tower hung at rest in the dry heat. The harsh sunlight had faded their red and white stripes long ago. More than anything in the world, he simply wanted to go home. He could spend the rest of his mornings fishing from the seashore, maybe go for a swim in the afternoon. He could finish each long day drinking those royal red wines—the ones with notes of cherry, blackberry, and plum—until a deep sleep set in for the night.

He turned back toward his troops and met the gaze of Pearlin and Carolin, their vibrant blue-green eyes staring at him through the strands of black hair masking their faces. In all this excitement, their eyes regained a hint of the ambition they used to have when they set out from Imperial Bay. *My goodness, that color reminds me of the sea,* Orowin thought. *And not only of the water's surface but all the life that swims beneath.*

Carolin and Pearlin aren't ready to go home. They need an adventure. They want to serve.

Orowin ripped the weathered parchment down the middle, then in half again and again until the fragments tumbled away into the dust.

"Captains, order your divisions to disassemble their campsites and pack up their belongings." Whispers raced amongst the soldiers, from those in the front row to those in the back, who were craning their necks to hear the conversation.

"Sir, where are we going?" Carolin asked. She hastily swiped the hair away from her eyes as Orowin continued his instructions.

"Ensure that each division packs enough food and water for several weeks of travel." Many of the troops started to whistle and holler, grabbing at each other's uniforms.

"Are we going home, sir?" Pearlin asked, a trace of nervousness in her voice. She was rubbing the middle bison's mane as he gulped water from the bucket.

"No, no, we're not going home yet." Orowin announced it loud enough for the entire regiment to hear. "The king has directed us to visit the City of Sterling to ensure its protection. We leave tomorrow at daybreak. And as part of our assignment, we will assist any Prairie Riders who may need it along the way." The troops exploded into cheers, which soon escalated into a rhythm of vigorous chants. One side of the ring yelled "Ride far!", the other side, "Shoot fast!"

"Pearlin, can you take us there?" Orowin asked.

"I appreciate your confidence in my wayfinding abilities, Colonel, but this is a rather easy route. If we follow the Silver River south, we'll run into the Gorge eventually."

"Very well then. Lead the way."

Chapter V

Zeno sat on the floor with his back against the brick wall, drifting in and out of a light sleep. He couldn't tell what time it was because the tiny room on the lower level of the Capitol had no windows. The only natural light that made its way in had to sneak past the guards whenever they opened the door at the far end of the hall. Otherwise, the jail was lit with a few dim lanterns. The underground air was cool and damp, forming condensation on the walls and ceiling. The intermittent dripping sounds and the perpetual darkness combined to create a dreadful sense of timelessness.

Zeno rubbed his shoulders and neck, which were sore from sleeping on the floor. He could have slept in the bed that was pushed up against the other side of the cell, but he refused, purely out of principle. He didn't use the thin pillow or blanket that the S&R guards had provided either, just to make a point. Zeno's head was throbbing, and his thoughts were a little groggy, so at first he didn't hear the raspy voice calling to him from across the hall. But the pestering was so persistent, eventually he realized someone was trying to get his attention.

"Hey, kid! Hey! Are you awake? Wake up already."

Zeno rubbed his eyes and blinked several times until his vision cleared. In the cell across from him, behind another set of iron bars, a scrawny man was pacing back and forth.

"Alright, now he's awake. You missed breakfast, but you didn't miss much. Lunch around here is better, and it should be coming soon. Any minute now, any minute."

Zeno was not in the mood for conversation, friendly or otherwise. He stood up to stretch his legs, hoping that if he stayed quiet long enough the man would leave him alone. Zeno was still wearing the bottoms of the concert band uniform from the previous night. The matching blue vest was folded on the bed.

"Nice outfit, kid. Do you play in a band? I always wanted to play in a band. Never had the chance though. Couldn't afford the lessons."

Zeno simply ignored him. He couldn't wait to get home, change out of his damp clothes, and sleep a full night in his own bed. *The S&R have to let me go soon, right? All I did was speak up at the council meeting.*

"What are those boots you got on? If you ask me, those look like climbing boots. So, are you a musician or a mountain climber?"

Zeno was indeed wearing his father's climbing boots because they were the only shoes he owned that seemed to go with the band uniform. He admitted that the worn leather looked rather awkward with the blue pants, but he decided there was no one at the Capitol he was aiming to impress.

"Well, if you're a climber, do you carry any of those trills?" The man stopped pacing for a moment and gripped the bars with both hands. Zeno had gotten used to the constant shuffling back and forth, so when the man stopped so abruptly, it startled him. Zeno shot a sideways glance at the other cell. The man stood there with his mouth open, gritting his teeth, a line of drool sliding down his chin. When the lamplight flickered across his face, Zeno saw that the man's bottom teeth and gums were light green.

Despite the fact that the endless chatter was making his headache worse, Zeno couldn't help but feel sorry for the poor fellow. After the incident in the Cloudhorns, Zeno knew from experience what the high from those seeds felt like. When he thought about how the Alpinees could help this man, along with so many others in the Low Quarter, it made him angry that the S&R had dragged him out of the council chamber before he could speak with the Philosopher. So, Zeno felt that he owed the man some kind of response.

"No, I'm all out. Sorry."

"It's alright, kid. I had to ask. I'm starting to feel those jitters all over. When I saw your climbing boots, I thought I was in luck, but I never seem to have any luck these days, no luck at all."

"Hey! Leave the kid alone, will you?" An S&R guard walked up between the cells, balancing a tray of food in each hand. "You've been so busy causing trouble, Gobu, you're making it hard for luck to find you these days."

"Yes, sir, yes, I'm sorry." Gobu seized the tray as the guard slid it through an opening in the bars. He sat on the floor, tore off a hunk of bread, and dipped it into the steaming soup.

"Are you ready to eat something?" the guard asked, turning to Zeno.

Zeno didn't respond. He was resentful that the S&R had locked him up without listening to his full account of his encounter with the Alpinees. In fact, when Zeno tried to tell his story to the guards on duty the night before, they mocked him. "If your Alpinees friends were willing to rescue you in the mountains, surely they'll bail you out of jail." If the S&R wasn't going to listen, Zeno wasn't going to speak.

"It's almost noon, you've got to be starving." The guard crouched to place the tray on the floor next to Zeno's cell. The handle of the ice axe hanging from his belt clinked on the floor.

"He's still not eating, huh?" another guard asked. "Well, if you're not going to eat, talk to us at least. Where do you live, kid?"

Zeno stared at the brick wall in silence. Besides the runnels of water dribbling into the rusty drain in the corner, the only other sound was Gobu slurping across the hall.

"Whoa, check out his boots." One guard slapped his partner's arm and pointed at Zeno's feet. "That's an old pair of S&R boots. They don't even make those anymore. Where'd you find them, kid?"

Zeno ignored the question and turned away to face the opposite wall. Under normal circumstances, if given a chance to talk to S&R climbers, he would have asked a million questions about their training, equipment, assignments, everything. But after the way they had treated him the night before, he couldn't stand to look at them. *These men are nothing like my father*, Zeno thought. *What's the point of being an S&R climber if you're stuck inside? When I make the S&R, I'm not leaving the mountains.*

"Alright, have it your way. We're just trying to make conversation. But the chief will be expecting answers, so you better be ready to talk when he gets here." He stole the slice of bread from Zeno's tray. "If you're not going to eat it, I'll help myself."

The two guards walked away down the hall, leaving a trail of crumbs behind them. Except for the metal key rings swinging and clicking on their belts, the jail was quiet. The other cells lining the hallway seemed empty, so Zeno could hear their exchange quite clearly from his cell.

"So, how long are we going to keep him?"

"Until the chief gets here. He heard the kid was babbling about the Alpinees, so he wants to ask a few questions, make sure the story checks out."

"Do you think they're really that dangerous?" The guard was talking a little softer now, so Zeno moved closer to the iron bars to hear them better. He sat down cross-legged next to his food tray, pretending to eat.

"If that kid really saw the ice thieves, we'd still be searching for his body in the mountains." He bit off a chunk of the bread.

99

"Alright, but what about the crossbows? Do you think the chief is right about the armory?"

The other guard didn't wait to swallow. He spit out his answer while chomping, spilling crumbs all over his uniform. "Councilman Taro wasn't exaggerating at the meeting last night. The Alpinees scouts carry axes that are sharp enough to slice through a tree branch, according to a guy in Unit Four. Would you feel safe out on patrol if those savages could swoop down without warning and cut you in half?"

The other guard stopped mid-stride. "How do the crossbows work, anyway? Have you ever fired one?"

"No, sir. No one has. They've been locked up in the armory for over a hundred years. But the Philosopher says that when you pull the trigger, a ring of whitefire is launched from the barrel. The circle expands as it gets farther away—you know, like the first ripple when you throw a stone into a pond—but this ring burns everything in its path until the heat fizzles out."

"Incredible," the other guard whispered. His eyes shot back and forth, like he was trying to visualize a battle with these weapons in action. "They'll teach us how to shoot them, right?"

"There isn't much to learn. With one blast, you could take out a swarm of Alpinees scouts or a quarter of the Royal Army, if you had to."

"So, why have they been locked up all this time?"

The guard who answered lowered his voice, so Zeno couldn't hear his response. But Zeno remembered enough from his father's lectures to fill in the gaps. During the civil war that led to the Disarming, the factions within the city burned down nearly every building. And there wasn't an enemy involved: they were shooting at each other. One side wanted to bring the whitefire north and use it to take over the throne at Imperial Bay; the other side wanted to toss the crossbows into the river, so the embers would die out forever. According to the Philosophers, the Gorge lost

100

more lives in that conflict than in all the previous wars combined. As Amos explained it, the suffering was so senseless that the council voted to lock the crossbows in the armory indefinitely. "And that's where they should stay," he always said.

One of the guards down the hall began coughing. It sounded like the mealy ball of bread had gone down the wrong pipe. His partner slapped him on the back a few times.

"Are you alright? What were you saying?"

"I was saying that I agree with you. The Philosopher is out of touch. At the end of the day, the council still controls the S&R's movements. If you ask me, Chief Gaffney makes a strong case that we need those crossbows back."

"How do you unlock the armory?"

"Well, I heard that—"

"Hey, kid! Hey! You going to finish your soup?" Gobu asked from across the hall.

"Shhh, be quiet. Here, you can have all of it if you stop talking for a minute." Zeno pushed his tray of food across the floor to Gobu's cell. Instead of gliding smoothly, however, the tray hit a crack in the floor, and the bowl tipped over, spilling vegetables and broth all over the hallway. The clanging of the tin bowl on the floor immediately caught the guards' attention.

"Hey, what's going on over there? What'd you do that for, Gobu?"

"It wasn't me, sir." Gobu crawled over to the corner of his cell. "It wasn't me. I finished my lunch, and it was most delicious, sir. Thank you."

"Alright, kid," the guard said, stepping up to Zeno's cell. "Do you want to spend another night locked up in here? I'll grab a mop because you're going to clean this mess before the chief gets here."

"For the stunt he pulled last night, we should make him clean the entire floor," the other guard proposed.

"Settle down there, gentlemen. Take it easy on him," a gruff but good-natured voice said from down the hall. Zeno couldn't yet see the speaker, although he cast an imposing shadow. His body blocked nearly all of the light that normally flashed in when the door swung open.

"Good morning, Chief," the guards responded in unison, stepping aside so Chief Gaffney could walk between them. The chief was thickset and tall—his cap nearly brushed against the jail's low ceiling—so he easily stepped over the puddle of soup in one stride.

"Let's hear the young man's side of the story first, and then we'll decide how many floors he has to mop." The chief set his hands on his hips and smiled. In fact, it was almost like he smiled twice: the yellowish-gray mustache under his round nose and ruddy cheeks also lifted, following the upward curve of his lips. "I'm Chief Gaffney. What's your name, young man? And where do you live?"

While he waited for Zeno to answer, the chief grabbed the keys from the guard next to him and unlocked the cell door, swinging the iron gate open. His wide stance filled the entire doorway. He stood so straight, with his chest out and his shoulders back, that Zeno's first impression was that the chief had one of the iron bars for a spine.

Zeno took a breath, finally ready to speak. The way the chief carried himself, the way he projected security and authority so naturally, Zeno's instinct was to tell him the whole story from start to finish—the strange storm, the crevasse, the rescue, the Alpinees, the weather, and the snowrose. For the first time, he actually felt like he had found someone who could help him.

As he was about to introduce himself, however, Zeno was distracted by the chief's uniform. He knew the standard S&R attire well, and something seemed out of place. The heavy boots, tapered pants, and leather belt all appeared normal, fit for climbing. The jacket itself was also unremarkable, stitched in the same style as all the other S&R climbers: gray fabric, blue buttons, and long sleeves. Then a few flickers of polished metal caught Zeno's eye. Four silver medallions hung from white ribbons on the chief's chest pocket. *That's what seems so strange.* He recalled that his father had similar badges—two, in fact—that were intended to designate his rank as a staff sergeant. But his father refused to wear the medallions while on duty. He said they were too flashy and too heavy. "When I'm out climbing, they'll get in the way," he complained. At the inscription ceremony Zeno asked if they could keep his father's medallions, one for him and one for Aris, but tradition dictated that Amos Harper was to be buried in uniform, so his father's badges were buried with him. *He really would have hated that.*

"He's been like this all morning," one of the guards said, feeling the need to fill in the awkward silence. "The kid won't say anything, won't eat anything."

"And look at those old S&R boots, Chief. He won't tell us where he got them either. I'm guessing he has sticky fingers like Gobu over here."

"Hold on now, wait a second." The boots seemed to spark something in the chief's memory because his eyes grew wide as he said it. "By the owl, are you Amos Harper's kid? At your height, you must be the older one. Zeno, am I right? My goodness, the last time I saw you was at your father's funeral, and you were only about this big!" The chief hit his hip with the side of his hand. "Your father was respected by many, always spoke his mind. And he was a fearless climber, let me tell you. Ah, but you already know that. Anyhow, I considered your father a friend, and it's a shame what happened." The chief shook his head. "How is your mother doing these days?"

Leaning back against the bars, the chief stuck his hands into his pockets and waited for an answer. Zeno could tell the chief was strong, but not in the way that S&R climbers were usually built. Gaffney was heftier. His belly sagged slightly over his belt line, and his climbing jacket fit a bit too snugly over his upper body. *He might be able to wrestle me to the ground,* Zeno thought, *but there's no way he could keep up in the Cloudhorns.*

The chief was either growing impatient or simply bored because he pulled a cigar out of his pocket and lit a match. He took a few heavy puffs to get the cigar going and then continued with his questions.

"I'm sorry the guys locked you up in here last night; they were just following procedures. The report says you came across a group of Alpinees in the Cloudhorns. Is that true?" Zeno kept quiet while the cigar smoke circulated around the cell with nowhere to go. "Come on, Zeno, I think we can help each other out here. If that was really you on Mt. Southspur, how'd you get down? Did the Alpinees help? If they threatened you, don't worry; we won't let them hurt you. The sooner you tell me your story, the sooner I can let you out of here."

As Chief Gaffney probed him about the Alpinees, Zeno thought about the conversation between the guards. *Did the chief really plan to arm the S&R with crossbows? Would he actually use them against the Alpinees?* The chief didn't come across as overly aggressive or impulsive, but Zeno wasn't ready to trust him yet. He knew his father had been opposed to the idea of equipping the S&R with any weapons. He would complain about the proposal to Zita over dinner sometimes, and she immediately added it to the list of concerns in her letters to the council. Zeno couldn't remember the details because he had been much younger then, but he was willing to trust his father's instincts. He decided it was better to proceed cautiously.

"Let me speak to the Philosopher first," Zeno said.

"Alright, kid, let's see if we can compromise here." Gaffney was having difficulty hiding the irritation in his voice. "I can't let you see the Philosopher. It's simply not going to happen. Tell me where you saw the Alpinees, and you can walk right out the door." He gestured with the hand that was holding the cigar, a wisp of smoke twisting up and slithering out between the bars.

"Please, you don't understand. I need to speak with the Philosopher." Zeno tried to say it as politely as possible, although it did not have the intended effect. In fact, it only made the chief more upset. He took another long puff of his cigar, so deep that the layers of rolled leaves crackled, glowing orange. Then he stubbed out the cigar on the brick wall, where it sizzled on contact. Gaffney walked over to Zeno and blew the smoke directly in his face.

"You're as stubborn as your father, do you know that?" He was standing so close that Zeno could smell the stale tobacco on his breath. "But he had the opposite problem. Amos never knew when to keep his mouth shut."

"What's that supposed to mean?" Zeno reached out with both hands and grabbed a fold of the chief's jacket in each fist. He tried to pull him forward, but the chief was so solid that he didn't budge. The guards darted over and seized Zeno under each arm, tackling him to the floor. After several attempts to squirm out, Zeno realized he could not overpower two guards at once, and he gave up trying. When his body relaxed, one of the guards reached for the handcuffs on his belt.

"Oh, leave him be. He's harmless," Gaffney said. He walked backward and plopped down on the bed. The guards gave each other a surprised look, then released their grip.

"I'm sorry, young man. I let my temper get the best of me. I didn't mean to be disrespectful. I truly considered your father a friend." With one hand Gaffney unclipped the ice axe from his belt and with the other he stroked his mustache, deep in thought. "However, I'll admit that Amos and I didn't always see eye to eye. We both cared immensely about Sterling's safety, but we had different views about what that entailed." He ran his fingers along the pointed end of his ice axe as he spoke. "Remember how your father led those long expeditions in the Cloudhorns, up near the Alpinees' settlements? I ordered him to end those excursions on numerous occasions because he was putting himself and others in danger. Do you think he ever listened to me? No, of course not. He was intent on proving his absurd theories about the weather." Gaffney shook his head. "And he simply would not let them go."

"What theories?" Zeno asked. "What did he say?"

"Now you're asking me questions when you haven't answered any of mine?" Gaffney stood up and reattached his ice axe. "Learn how to compromise, kid. I give up something, you give up something. That's how the world works. Where did you see the Alpinees? What did they tell you? I'm trying to help you out here."

"I need to speak with the Philosopher."

"Alright, have it your way. Let's try another night in here and see how you feel about all this tomorrow."

As the chief pivoted to exit the cell, the jail's door creaked open, and a full column of light flashed in, followed by a woman's voice.

"Hello? Hello? Chief Gaffney, are you in here?" The chief's mustache twitched, and he held up his finger for the guards to hold still. Then he shuffled out of the cell to greet the unexpected visitor. Zeno was relieved to see several shadows hustling down the hall.

"Councilwoman Veti! What a surprise. It's a pleasure to see you." Gaffney offered his greetings with a slight bow as Veti strolled up to Zeno's cell in her high heels. She was wearing a puffy purple dress that looked completely out of place in the dingy basement. "And good morning to you, Ms. Sera," the chief added. "I'm sorry, I didn't see you there at first. What can I do for you this morning?"

From behind the councilwoman, Zeno watched a young lady step forward. Her long blonde hair was pulled back into a ponytail. Somehow it managed to shine like honey in the poorly lit hallway. He was struck by her playful cinnamon-brown eyes, which appeared lively and mischievous, like they were holding back a secret. He had no idea who she was, but when their eyes met he felt instantly underdressed. Zeno rushed over to the bed to throw on the vest.

"We don't need a thing, Chief Gaffney," Veti said. "We've come to introduce you to the Capitol's new musician. Sera and I are giving him an official tour of the building."

"Ah, yes, I heard about his inspiring performance last night. I wish I could have been there. What's your name, young man?"

Zeno realized the chief was addressing another person in the hallway, so he pushed his face between the iron bars to get a better view.

"I would like you to meet Aris Harper." Veti moved to the side so Aris could shake Gaffney's hand. "And it appears you have already become acquainted with his brother, Zeno."

"Aris?" Zeno asked in disbelief.

Aris walked up to the jail cell and tossed his brother a change of clothes.

"You didn't think I would leave you in here for another night, did you?"

"Chief Gaffney, we'll be taking Zeno with us on the tour," Veti said. "Hurry up and change, young man. We have much to see around the Capitol."

"Councilwoman, I could use more time with Mr. Harper. We aren't quite finished with our questioning."

"You'll have plenty of time for that later. I expect you will be seeing Zeno around here more often anyway. The Philosopher has offered Aris a bedroom in the third-floor living quarters."

"As you wish, councilwoman. Mr. Harper, I will try to catch you at a better time so we can finish our discussion." The two guards watched, perplexed, as Zeno exited the cell and followed Veti, Sera, and Aris down the hall.

"So, what do you want to see first?" Sera asked the two brothers. "The concert hall? The living quarters? The library?" Zeno noticed she was practically skipping down the hallway, her ponytail bouncing.

"Be patient, Sera. We'll show them everything in due time."

"How about the kitchen?" Zeno suggested. "I'm *starving*." He projected that last part loud enough so his voice could be heard down the hall.

"Yes, an excellent idea," Veti responded. "It is lunchtime, isn't it? In all this excitement, I nearly forgot!"

⬤

On days when the sun sleeps in and low clouds move over the valley, covering the Four Bridges in a thick fog, I pass the time strolling through the halls of the Capitol admiring Sterling's other works of fine art. I must concede that I have always been clumsy with a paintbrush and clueless with a drawing pencil (except to dash off a few lines of poetry now and again). Despite lacking any artistic ability of my own, I have developed a profound appreciation for the creativity on display in the Capitol. With so many stunning paintings and sculptures, each with its own significance and secrets, it's impossible not to be taken in by their stories. I spend more hours lost in the library than I care to admit, trying to learn about the lives behind the artists and the sources of their inspiration. So, if you've been waiting for one more reason to visit the Silver River Gorge, look no further. I promise to give you a tour of the Capitol building when you arrive, and I'll show you all the pieces that captivate me most.

I cannot claim to be the most knowledgeable guide to ever walk these halls, however. Sera surely deserves that distinction.

After a brief but satisfying lunch in the kitchen (the boys devoured Roma's toasted sandwiches with tomatoes and melted cheese), they dropped off Aris's few belongings in his living quarters on the third floor, only a couple doors down from Sera's. With the practical stops out of the way, Councilwoman Veti asked Sera to lead the rest of the tour in her place. She claimed to have an appointment in the Up

Quarter, although in truth she saw how eager Sera was to spend time with people her own age.

Sera brought Aris and Zeno around to her favorite places in the Capitol, starting with the concert hall (where Aris would supposedly be spending most of his time) and then to the council chamber. Along the way, Sera made sure to point out each architectural feature of significance, and she often stopped to give the history behind noteworthy frescos and busts of famous Philosophers. Despite her efforts and enthusiasm, Sera grew frustrated at her guests' apparent lack of interest. She couldn't understand why they weren't as fascinated as she was by all the architecture and history.

In actuality, Aris and Zeno were awed by the Capitol building, and they were equally impressed by Sera's knowledge. In her excitement, though, Sera had missed the signs. She mistook their quiet, polite nodding as a sign of boredom, when in reality they were overwhelmed. For two boys from the Low Quarter, the place was a lot to take in (in fairness, so was Sera). They were not bored by any means. They were simply curious about other things.

" . . . and that's how Cian the Colorful developed the brushstroke technique that you see here, about four hundred years ago." Sera finished one of her mini-lectures, standing in front of an enormous oil painting of Imperial Bay. In the foreground, white sandy beaches lined the coast while several giant ships fought to stay upright among turbulent waves in the middle of the canvas. At the top of the painting, the greenish-blue ocean blended seamlessly with the sky, making it difficult to tell the difference between the water and the clouds.

"Have you ever seen the ocean?" Zeno asked out of the blue. To Sera it sounded like a challenge, but his tone was sincere. "I mean, is that really what it looks like?"

"I've never been to Imperial Bay myself. It's quite a journey, as you know. But I have read many books about it, and I would love to visit if I ever get the chance. Vesu traveled to Imperial Bay once many years ago, when she was a teenager. She ran along the beaches in her bare feet while the sun was setting, holding hands with . . . oh, you should ask her to tell you the story herself sometime. She tells it so wonderfully! And yet she still claims that Cian captured the 'boundless spirit' of the ocean better in this painting."

"Vesu is the Philosopher, right?" Zeno asked. "Can I meet her?"

Aris was embarrassed that Zeno's question was so cavalier, but Sera didn't seem to mind.

"Of course," she said, as if this was a common occurrence. (And I suppose for her, it was.) "If we run into her today, I'll introduce you. Oh, and that reminds me: you should ask Vesu about the time she sailed on a Royal Navy ship with the ambassador. She said those boats are more amazing in real life."

Sera twirled around to face the painting. "As you can see here, Cian was not only a pioneer of color theory. He was also a master of perspective. He meticulously studied the proportions of every object in his paintings, including these ships. Check out the fine details in the sails, for example, and the ropes dangling from the masts. If you look carefully, each shadow is . . ."

When Sera turned back around, instead of an attentive audience, she found that her guests had wandered off down the hall, gazing at other pieces of art. She huffed in frustration and hurried after Zeno, who was already moving his hands along a large mural that spanned an entire section of the wall.

"Be careful! You shouldn't touch that!" Sera shouted, running to catch up.

Zeno was so engrossed in the scene that he didn't hear her warning. The mural was so different from all the others that he couldn't look away. Instead of the typical watercolor on plaster, the panorama was carved directly into the stone panel, which was relatively soft and grainy to the touch. And rather than the peaceful scenery that usually adorned the

Capitol's walls (flora, fauna, landscapes, and the like), the mural depicted a gruesome, chaotic battle: S&R guards fought each other fiercely with ice axes, fists, and crossbows. He couldn't tell who was on which side, let alone which side was winning or losing. Every fighter was frozen in the same grayish-tan rock, either attacking or being attacked.

On the panel's far right, the sculptor had chiseled a line of S&R guards firing crossbows into the fray. Their stone silhouettes were lifelike, nearly true to size, so Zeno stood before them eye to eye. Their ferocious, greedy glares were haunting. Zeno traced a ring of whitefire with his fingers until it ran into the buildings in the background. Up close the structures appeared wavy, abstract, distorted, so he couldn't quite tell what the artist was illustrating. But when he took several steps back to observe the entire display from a distance, the imagery became clear: behind the violent combat of the S&R guards, every building was burning.

"This is the armory," Zeno said.

Sera wasn't sure if it was a question or a statement. While she was normally a quick study when it came to reading people, Zeno still puzzled her. At lunch he mostly talked about his adventures in the mountains, so she assumed he was another self-absorbed climber (and a bit of a show-off). But as they walked together through the Capitol, Zeno was proving to be cleverer than she expected.

"Yes, this is the armory. Well, technically it's the *entrance to* the armory. How did you know?"

"I overheard the guards talking about it in the jail earlier." Zeno glanced down the hall toward the library and noticed two other S&R guards keeping watch at the double doors. There was little chance they could hear him at that distance, but he leaned in closer to Sera anyway, cupping his hand around his mouth.

"They said that Chief Gaffney wants to rearm the S&R with crossbows," he whispered.

Zeno was standing so close to her now that Sera noticed his eyes glowed like that intense glacier-blue you can sometimes see in the mountains on a clear day. She had never been climbing, although she would go in a heartbeat if she had the right guide. *Maybe I can tag along with Zeno sometime, if Vesu will let me.*

"Oh, I wouldn't worry too much about the crossbows, those are rumors," Sera said in her normal voice, disregarding the common courtesy of responding to a whisper with a whisper.

Zeno wasn't reassured that easily, so he continued to lean in, speaking softly. "How do you know? The guards seemed pretty sure about it."

"Zeno, take a closer look at that wall. Do you see any hinges or handles? Any doorknobs, dials, or keyholes? The Philosophers who constructed the armory made it impossible to break into. And we know because people have tried. Fortunately, the old Philosophers were cautious, and they considered that risk when they built it. They lined the entire chamber with a strange mineral that's unbreakable, uncrushable, un . . . you get the picture. To be honest, no one really knows what the armory is made of, let alone how to get inside."

"But if the Philosophers didn't want the S&R to ever use the crossbows again, why not destroy them?"

Maybe he isn't just a clueless climber after all, Sera thought.

"Okay, so they didn't lock us out completely. The old Philosophers figured the weapons might be needed at some point. If the council votes unanimously to access the crossbows, including the Philosopher's vote, the key to the armory is supposed to . . . uh . . . reveal itself, I guess."

Zeno stared at her skeptically.

"Now that I say it out loud, I realize how strange it sounds. But those are the only instructions that the old Philosophers passed down to us. According to their journals, after a unanimous vote the Philosopher will find the key in the Silver River."

"In the river?" Zeno asked. "The Philosopher will need to search for quite some time. The river stretches for hundreds of miles."

"I can't explain how it works, although Philosophers have built stranger inventions than the armory, believe me. Really, you shouldn't worry about it. From the day Vesu was sworn in as the Philosopher, she promised never to open the armory. How could she when she has seen all that horror firsthand?"

"Firsthand? What do you mean?" Zeno looked up at the ceiling, and Sera could tell he was trying to do the math. "The Disarming was over a century ago."

Suddenly, Zeno's cleverness, which Sera had found so charming minutes earlier, was making her nervous. She had definitely overshared. This was more information than a Philosopher's apprentice should have disclosed.

"Wait a second, where did your brother go? I can't lose him on the first day!" Sera spotted Aris standing by the two guards at the double doors to the library. Before Zeno could ask anything else, she took off after him. "Do you want to see the library? If we don't go now, we might miss our chance."

The distraction worked perfectly. Eager to see whether the library would live up to his expectations, Zeno let the mystery go for the moment and followed her down the hall.

Sera knew it would be difficult to get her guests into the library without Vesu's permission, but she was still desperately trying to impress them. Without the necessary paperwork in hand, it took ten minutes to persuade the S&R guards to allow the boys inside. When the guards learned that Aris was the new Capitol musician, they finally relented.

"You've got twenty minutes," one of them grumbled, and then pushed open the doors.

When I mentioned that Aris and Zeno were overwhelmed by their tour of the Capitol, that was nothing compared to their reaction when they stepped into the library. The seemingly endless aisles of curving bookshelves, stacked to the ceiling in neat multicolored rows, were absolutely mystifying. Both brothers took a deep breath, mainly to compose themselves but also to take in the uniquely sweet scent of leather-bound books and ancient parchment. Before Sera could offer a basic overview of the library's layout, Aris and Zeno took off in different directions to explore on their own.

"Where do they keep all the books about the weather?" Zeno asked, bolting away between the stacks to the left.

"The weather? What makes you so interested in the weather all of a sudden?" *Where does he come up with these questions?* "Anyway, you won't find them over there. Those are mostly biographies."

"This table is magnificent," Aris said. He had wandered off in the opposite direction toward the mahogany table in the center of the room. The fact that the boys split up put Sera more on edge than she already was. It was easy to get lost inside of Inka's literary labyrinth, and they didn't have much time to look around before the guards would get suspicious. But she decided to stay with Aris for now, to make sure he didn't disturb any papers by mistake.

"If only Mr. Marcel could see this piece," Aris said. "I've seen similar antiques at his shop but nothing of this quality. By the owl, it must have taken years to finish this woodwork."

As Sera watched Aris glide his fingers over the table's gold, chestnut, and cherry-colored inlays, she realized that Palo must have tidied up that morning because she could actually see the tabletop for once instead of all the usual clutter.

"This is where we do most of our research and writing to prepare for council meetings," Sera said. "The Philosopher sits here, at the head of the table." She plunked down in Vesu's tall leather chair and leaned back, kicking her feet up on the mahogany. Then with one hand she twisted her ponytail up on her head to make it look like

Vesu's winding braids. With her other hand she pretended to ring the bell in the council chamber. "Ding, ding, ding! Have all voted who wish? Have all voted who wish?" Sera announced this dramatically, as if she were presiding over a council meeting. Aris burst out laughing at the imitation, which was just the reaction Sera was hoping for. She was relieved that this new addition to the Capitol had a good sense of humor, even if he did come across as a bit timid most of the time.

"When will you become the Philosopher, Sera?" Aris asked.

The question caught her off guard. Almost everyone she encountered in the Capitol knew exactly who she was and the importance of her role. Aris's question subtly reminded her that residents of the Low Quarter had many other matters to worry about besides the esoteric rules governing the succession of Philosophers.

"Oh, that won't be for quite some time, Aris. Ozar was recently appointed Junior Philosopher, so he's next in line after Vesu. And then I'm supposed to take over after him, if all goes according to plan. Well, technically speaking, none of that's guaranteed. Under the council rules, the Philosopher selects her own replacement, and it can be anyone she feels is best suited for the position. But Ozar is older and more experienced than I am, and Vesu trusts him, so it's highly unlikely she would choose someone other than him to take her place. And that's how it should be. Many years from now, when Ozar is ready to step down, I hope he'll have the same confidence in me."

"I'm sure he will," Aris said. "I would never be able to handle all that pressure, but you'll make an excellent Philosopher."

It was a simple compliment, but Aris said it so genuinely that Sera blushed all over. On the surface Aris seemed shy and reserved, although she found him much easier to read than his brother. He had a tendency to lay everything out in the open, his thoughts and emotions included. In fact, when

Aris shared what was on his mind, Sera felt like he was reading the room (and the people in it) like a sheet of music. True to form, he saw that his compliment surprised Sera, and he took it upon himself to tactfully change the topic.

"Tell me about this Grand Fireplace that people are always talking about."

"How about I show you? Swear you won't tell a soul, or Vesu and Ozar really will pass me over as Philosopher."

Sera grabbed Aris by the wrist, and they ran together through the bookstacks to the southeast corner of the library. Of course, Aris couldn't tell which direction they were headed, with the narrow passageways so tangled and disordered. More than once he was sure they had doubled back toward the main room, only to enter a new section of the library he hadn't yet seen. All of the twists and turns made him completely disoriented, which compelled Aris to switch his grip; he took hold of Sera's hand instead, squeezing it tightly. He was afraid that if she let go, even for a second, he would never find his way out of that maze on his own.

To Aris's relief, the aisles eventually opened up into another expansive room, and he immediately spotted the Grand Fireplace at the center of the back wall. The opening was as wide as a wagon and tall enough to walk through standing up. Instead of logs, a row of candles lined the hearth, unlit, and the firebox behind the candles was pitch black, making it appear more like a tunnel than an enclosure. The darkness contrasted sharply with the snowy owl that was carved into the mantel and painted so flawlessly that it appeared lifelike. Its sharp yellow eyes were cut cleanly into the pure white feathers on its face and chest while black feathers speckled its wings and legs all the way down to its curved talons.

"So, what do you think?" Sera asked.
"They're terrifying."
"What's terrifying?"

"The eyes of that owl. Doesn't it feel like they're following you?"

"Oh yes, very much so. It's quite uncomfortable. You never really get used to that."

"What's hanging from the hook over there?"

"That's the Philosopher's shawl. Vesu was wearing it during the council meeting, remember? When the Philosopher makes her decision about who will replace her, she will pass it down to her successor."

Sera reached up, removed the feathered shawl from its hook, and stretched out her arms, offering it to Aris.

"Would you like to try it on?"

"Oh, no, no . . ." Aris stammered, backing away. "Thank you, but I don't think I should."

"Alright, alright, I won't make you wear it now. But let me know if you change your mind. You know, it doesn't actually mean anything unless the Philosopher hands it over herself. And it has to be done freely, intentionally. The appointment of a Philosopher isn't legitimate if it's made under duress." Sera draped the shawl over her shoulders and turned to Aris. "Could you fasten the clasp for me?" Aris clipped one end to the other and then Sera spun around, the feathers swishing from the movement.

"How do I look?" she asked, continuing her imitation of Vesu from earlier. "Have all voted who wish? Have all voted who wish?"

Instead of laughing along this time, Aris gazed past her with his eyes wide open, and Sera noticed his complexion had gone pale. He was trying to say something, but he couldn't spit out the words. "Come on, Aris, do I really look that bad?"

"Good . . . good . . . afternoon, Madam Philosopher," Aris was finally able to squeak out.

"Aris, you don't have to be so formal, I was only playing around—"

"There you are!" Vesu stormed into the library from the council chamber, Ozar trailing close behind. "Sera, where in the Gorge have you been all day? And why are you wearing my shawl?"

"More importantly, what is *he* doing here?" Ozar pointed at Aris, who was frozen in place.

"Sera, did I give you permission to bring anyone to the library?" Vesu glared at her.

"No, madam, but the guards said—"

"The guards are not responsible for the safekeeping of the library, I am! You must be more cautious about our work, especially during times like these. We bought ourselves a few extra weeks with Councilman Taro's motion but not due to any of our efforts. We can thank our young musician here for that extra time."

"I'm very sorry. I'll show Aris back to his quarters right away."

If it had been any other visitor, Vesu would have escorted them out herself. But this soft-spoken boy could fill an auditorium with music compelling enough to move minds, and she wanted to learn the extent of his abilities. Moreover, while Vesu had no intention of stepping down as Philosopher any time soon, she couldn't hold the post forever. *Maybe it's time to bring on another apprentice*, she thought.

"Oh, by the owl, at this point he might as well stay," Vesu said. "From the looks of it, it seems you've told him everything there is to know about our little library."

"Are you sure that's a good idea, Madam?" Ozar asked uneasily, off to the side.

"I am quite certain, yes. We will need his talents again, and sooner rather than later, if I had to guess. Mr. Aris Harper, do you swear to protect the Silver River Gorge and every citizen inside?" Vesu rattled off this last sentence so quickly that Aris wasn't sure he caught everything.

"Me? Oh! Yes, Madam Philosopher, I'm at your service."

"That's good enough for me. Welcome aboard. Ms. Sera, will this be the end of your surprises for today?"

"Yes, madam."

"Thank goodness. Now, let's get moving. Aris, help Sera light the fireplace while I get a few other things ready."

Aris followed Sera to the giant fireplace. She stepped over the candles into the dark opening, then crouched and lifted a heavy iron gate until it crashed in place against the back of the hearth, revealing a rectangular cavity in the floor. The firebox was still dark, so Aris couldn't see what was in the hole, but when he leaned in closer, he heard the trickling, swishing sound of flowing water.

"That's the Silver River," Sera said, catching Aris's puzzled look. She dipped her fingers into the stream and flicked them at Aris so that a few drops splashed onto his cheeks. "The library's in the basement, remember?"

Next Sera snatched a tinder box from the mantel shelf and lit one candle at each end of the row. Instead of the warm yellow light that Aris was expecting, the wick ignited into a tall silver flame. "You start lighting the candles at that end, and I'll start over on this side. Go slowly, and be careful."

When they met in the middle, Sera and Aris stepped back to watch the fire grow. The flame of every candle rose taller and taller until the tips almost reached the mantel. Then each flame began to flicker and expand, blending together with the flame next to it until the fire formed a smooth wall of wavering, simmering, silver heat.

"Pretty neat, huh?" Sera said. "Don't get too close though; it's unbelievably hot."

When the silver fire was fully lit, Vesu returned wearing the Philosopher's shawl over her shoulders. On a nearby desk, Ozar had dumped out a box of papers, each rolled up with a ribbon, like miniature scrolls. As he opened them one by one to read the small script, Aris saw that the lettering was crudely scratched in charcoal.

"Vesu, where are you going today?" Sera asked.

"That is precisely what we are here to decide." Vesu smoothed the feathers on each shoulder with her long, wrinkled fingers. "Tell me, Sera, what did you learn at the council meeting last night?"

"Well, Taro seems to believe the North Gate was built solely for defense. In the books we pulled, however, the Philosophers had more in mind. The wide gates also symbolize acceptance; they signify this city can be a sanctuary. To find out for sure, I think you should visit Aldo—he was a key architect of the North Gate."

"Not a bad idea, I hadn't thought of that. Ozar, what do you think?"

"Madam, I think your time could be better spent. If the Alpinees were our only threat, I might agree with Ms. Avery. But Councilman Taro is right to be worried about the Royal Army—the lack of reporting from Ambassador Elerin is especially a cause for concern."

Ozar always assumes the worst, Sera thought. *He's paranoid the Royal Army will just show up one day, unannounced.*

"You should go back to the Drowned King's War," Ozar suggested. "You could observe the military movements from that battle in real time, and explore the potential weaknesses of the North Gate. That will give us concrete information to share with the council in case we have to defend the city."

"Ah, yes," Vesu said, pacing a short path back and forth in front of the fire. "Taro rattled every spine in that chamber when he mentioned the Royal Army, didn't he? My own included. I share your fears, Ozar, believe me. I'm also worried about why we haven't heard from the ambassador. But I've known Elerin for many years, and his silence alone does not convince me that the king intends to attack the Gorge. Not yet, at least. For some reason my instinct tells me our trouble is closer to home."

Vesu sat in a chair next to the fireplace and closed her eyes, massaging her temples in contemplation. The feathers resting on her shoulders moved gently up and down with each meditative breath as the fire hissed quietly in the background. The extended silence was making Sera restless, and apparently Ozar felt the same way. He was watching Vesu and cracking his knuckles one at a time while he waited for her to make a decision. At last she broke from her concentration, her comment taking everyone in the room by surprise.

"I think we could use another opinion. Aris, you were at the council meeting last night. Where do you propose that I go?"

"Oh! What do *I* think? Well, where to go . . . hmm, let's see . . ." Aris stared into the fireplace searching for an answer. Sera felt so nervous for him that she had to look away. *I'm so sorry I got you into this*, she thought, wishing Aris could somehow hear her apology. Only a handful of seconds passed by, but with the owl's sharp yellow eyes fixed on her, each second felt heavy and slow. *Would you leave me alone already?*

"Madam Philosopher, forgive me if I don't exactly understand your question," Aris said, "but with all these problems we're facing, I don't think you should go anywhere. We need you here."

His honest, innocent response drew a chuckle from the group. Even Ozar took a momentary break from his constant brooding to smile.

"Oh my, I'm sorry, Aris," Vesu said, shaking her head. "I assumed Sera had explained all of this already. Let me tell you what I can in the short time that we have. And I won't swear you to secrecy because I doubt anyone outside these walls will believe you anyway."

Vesu stood up and started pacing, her hands folded together behind her back. "As you know, the Four Bridges of the Gorge are held in high regard, and for good reason. By connecting our neighborhoods, the bridges tie us together as one community. And by standing tall as monuments of ingenuity, artistry, and craftsmanship, they remind us every day of what is possible, what we can build together.

"However, for Philosophers in particular, the Four Bridges serve another essential purpose: they connect us directly to our past. When we carve the name of someone we've lost into those structures, it enables us to return to them, to observe them, to see what they saw. When I walk through the Grand Fireplace and peer into the river, I'm able to follow our ancestors from above, close enough to catch their thoughts. Though they can't see me or hear me, sometimes they feel that I'm there, watching, learning. The same is true for the important events depicted on the bridges. We can revisit those times and learn from old mistakes. I find it helpful to think of it like this: in the normal course of events, the centuries flow through us like a river, and we only get one chance to drink the water as it rushes by. But the Four Bridges enable the Philosopher to hold that river in our hands a little longer, before it slips away, in order to make the most of it. To master many subjects, develop new inventions, and offer guidance to the council for the benefit of the Gorge.

"So that's why we're here. We have exactly one month before the next council meeting when Taro will reintroduce his motion to lock the North Gate, and I want to hear any ideas you have for how our history might help us advise the council."

In the otherwise quiet library, the Grand Fireplace crackled and splashed.

"I have an idea, Madam Philosopher," Zeno announced, stepping out from his hiding place behind the bookshelves.

"By the owl, who are you?" Ozar asked.

Zeno? I completely forgot! Sera screamed at herself. *How long has he been hiding back there?*

"Palo, call the guards!" Ozar shouted.

"Wait a minute," Zeno begged. "I need to speak with you. I think I can help."

"Sera, is he with you?" Vesu asked. "You better have a good explanation for this."

"Not exactly. Well, kind of . . ."

"It was my idea to come here," Zeno interjected, saving Sera the trouble of making up another story (and she was completely out of excuses anyway). "I'm Zeno Harper, Aris's older brother. A few days ago, the Alpinees saved my life in the Cloudhorns, and I promised to deliver a message." His straightforward report was quite effective at grabbing Vesu's attention.

"I thought you looked familiar, Mr. Harper." Vesu crossed her arms over her chest. "Was it you who interrupted my meeting last night?"

"Yes, madam, but only because the message is so important. Councilman Taro is wrong about the Alpinees. Please give me two minutes to explain, and then you can send me back to jail or drop me in backwoods, whatever you wish."

"We don't have time for this," Ozar protested.

"Mr. Harper, I'll give you one minute. If you waste a second of it, I *will* leave you for the bears in the backwoods."

Zeno got the message. He divulged everything as quickly as he could without glossing over the key details: the sudden storm with its pink and purple lightning; Isolo and the other Alpinees scouts with their translucent skin and reflective eyes; the taste of the snowrose, and the slimy film it left on his gums. His account had gone well over a minute by the time the S&R guards arrived, but Vesu shooed them away. Only someone who had actually seen the Alpinees up close could have described their features in such detail. And this possible cure for the trillium seeds sounded promising if it turned out to be true. She let Zeno continue.

"As I was saying, my father and Isolo were friends. They tracked these storms together for years, trying to find the source so that life could return to normal. The last thing the Alpinees want is to harm us. They desperately need our help. Madam Philosopher, if that fireplace can do what you say, you have to visit my father. Once you see the storms for yourself, you'll know the Alpinees aren't a threat."

"My goodness, you have been through quite a lot these last few days, haven't you?" Vesu's voice was warmer now, a touch of empathy between her words. "I can see how much your father meant to you. Indeed, your candor reminds me of his own. I did not know Amos well, but I recall that he addressed the council on several occasions."

"What did he say?" Zeno asked eagerly. "He asked you about a weather device, right?"

"Show some patience, Mr. Harper, and I'll share what I remember. Several sessions ago, your father spoke to the council about unpredictable weather patterns he had observed in the Cloudhorns. At first the council dismissed his reports as nothing more than the chaotic mountain climate, considering that only the Alpinees were affected by storms at such altitude. However, when your father returned the following year with reports that the weather was worsening, we all started to take notice. The council realized that our S&R guards who patrol the mountains might be at risk. I advised the council that we would search the library for any information that the old Philosophers left us about the weather.

"What I did not tell the council, so as not to build up false hope, is that certain literary works make passing reference to a device capable of controlling the weather. The authors called it a 'weatherbox.' Now, these are works of fiction, and I highly doubted that any such device was ever built outside of a Philosopher's imagination. But your father spoke so earnestly that I decided it was worth exploring. I asked Mr. Wrinn here to search everywhere—to follow every lead, turn every page. Ozar, tell us what you found."

"Well, I found much less than we had hoped for, I'm afraid. I started with those tales that Vesu mentioned and then pored over the writings of every Philosopher from that time period who showed an interest in meteorology. Although I came across some interesting theoretical contraptions—rough sketches and blueprints, even—the designs were all dead ends. Over the many months I spent searching, I found no evidence that a 'weatherbox' is scientifically possible. The old Philosophers invented many useful gadgets to read temperatures, pressures, and so on, but controlling the clouds was apparently beyond their reach."

"We must find some other way to help them, then," Zeno pleaded. "Madam Philosopher, let me take you to meet Isolo. You need to hear from the Alpinees directly."

"I would appreciate the introduction. I need to learn more about that snowrose you described; it might be the key to curing this city of its addiction to those horrible seeds. However, we can only tackle one problem at a time, and right now our focus must be on the North Gate."

With Vesu's position on the matter made clear, Zeno accepted that any further arguments on his part would be futile. Sera watched the fierce blue color of his eyes melt away to gray. Now that she had heard all he had been through, she couldn't fathom the pain that he carried. And she couldn't decide which was heaviest: the legacy of a lost father, or the unpaid debt to those who saved his life.

Sera's thoughts were interrupted by Vesu, who had dashed over to the pile of scrolls and was rummaging through them so hastily that several papers tumbled off the desk. "Sera, where is the parchment for the Disarming? Have you seen it?"

"The Disarming again?" Ozar groaned. "Madam Philosopher, what good will that do? You have seen that horrible war too many times already. What's left to learn there?"

In this regard, Sera agreed with Ozar. Whenever Vesu went back to visit the Disarming, which she had done a handful of times over the past few years, she always returned dispirited and drained. That was the one place Sera told herself she would never go as the Philosopher. The suffering would be too unbearable to witness. Though the past could often help make sense of the present, she wondered whether some lessons were worth the cost. *Maybe some things ought to be forgotten*, she thought, glaring at the owl over the fireplace. *Have you ever considered that, you strange old bird?*

"Ozar, this is my decision." Vesu continued to unfurl the scrolls in search of the right one. "And to be honest, I don't know what I'm looking for this time around. But lately it seems as though most of our troubles can be traced back to that conflict, doesn't it? It's like the earthquake that reset the ground on which we stand. Whenever I find a fault line, I can usually follow it back to . . . oh, here it is!"

Vesu held up the parchment with "The Disarming" scribbled on it in black lettering. She hurried over to the fireplace and straightened the feathers over her shoulders. Sera watched Aris and Zeno grow tense, wanting to look away but unable to turn their heads. She couldn't blame them. It was one thing to hear about walking through fire and another thing to see it. Vesu tossed the paper into the flames, where it sparked and snapped like fireworks, sending smoke up and around her in a slow-motion swirl. Then the Philosopher bowed her head and walked through the fire as smoothly as if it were a waterfall.

▥

I wish I could adequately describe for you what it's like to pass through the Grand Fireplace, to feel the smoke squeeze you, to see history appear in the ripples on the river's surface, to swim against the current of time, to fly over your ancestors like a bird, to inhale and exhale ancient air, but such an experience is impossible to communicate. Even if I could put it into words, it's like Vesu said: no one would believe me anyway.

▥

When Vesu stumbled out of the fire a few minutes later, she nearly collapsed. Ozar and Sera were quick to catch her, each taking an arm to guide her to the closest chair. Beads of sweat lined her forehead, and a few stray curls of white hair were stuck in the wetness. Sera saw that Vesu was completely worn out. Her skin was so pale, thin, and wrinkled that it reminded Sera of the pages in an old book that had been read too many times. Vesu was trying to tell them what she saw, but her voice was too weak; she was still trying to catch her breath.

"I never noticed it before . . . the North Gate . . ."

"Shhh . . . you can tell us later," Sera said, holding Vesu's hand. "You need to rest."

"The S&R . . . the North Gate. They closed it . . . locked it . . ."

"But that doesn't make any sense," Ozar said. "Were they expecting a siege from the outside?"

Vesu managed to shake her head slowly from side to side.

"Then why would the S&R close the gate?" Sera asked, equally confused. "The Disarming was a conflict between factions *within* the Gorge. According to every historical record we have, all the fighting took place inside the city walls."

Vesu was too exhausted to say anything more. She leaned her head back and closed her eyes. The fire had gone out by that point, leaving the library nearly silent, save for Vesu's breathing. So, when Aris cleared his throat to speak, it startled the others. He had been standing so quietly off to the side that Sera had almost forgotten he was there.

"Perhaps Councilman Taro is not trying to keep the Alpinees or the Royal Army *out* of the Gorge," he said warily, taking a deep breath. "Maybe he's trying to keep everyone else *in*."

Chapter VI

On days when I need to escape the Capitol—when the balcony views don't feel high enough, the hallway paintings not interesting enough, or the library aisles not long enough—when I simply need a break from my work, I head out for a walk in the hills of Shoulder Ridge to fill my lungs with fresh air. And, more importantly, to rest my eyes.

Before I became the Philosopher, I preferred the steep trails of the Cloudhorns, both for the physical challenge and for the striking views at the end of every climb. Believe me, when you're standing at certain outlooks up there, you have to remind yourself to breathe. You can see the entire city, from the North Gate to the Low Quarter, cradled between the arms of the mountains with homes and buildings filling in the space like a honeycomb. If you're anything like me, the sight will make you wonder how the views might look to the Alpinees, who spend a lifetime observing the world from even higher. At those heights they can watch over the roads and trails that crisscross the valley, and with their mirror-like eyes, they can see far beyond the North Gate, many miles into the Prairie Basin (and farther on the clearest days, if you believe the stories.)

And yet the Alpinees taught me that you can't find the truth with your eyes alone. You need to listen hard for it. So these days I spend more of my time in the hills of Shoulder Ridge, walking and listening. When I reach the end of a trail, I close my eyes and listen for messages in the air. If you get the chance to walk in these mountains one day, I recommend you do the same. Then slow your breathing, calm your heart, and quiet your mind, and you should be able to hear the Alpinees calling to each other through the wind.

Isolo, do you see them?

Yes, I see them.

Why are they moving in this direction?

I don't know.

How many do you think there are?

It's hard to say. I count almost five hundred bodies, but they're not all wearing red and white uniforms. Prairie Riders must be marching with them.

How long before the army reaches the Gorge?

At this rate, seven or eight days. They still have a long stretch of the Basin to cover.

It's been three weeks since we asked the boy for help. How much longer can we wait for him?

He will come. We must be patient. Let's give him a few more days.

Isolo, we can't wait that long! If another ice storm blows in, come morning, we'll be frozen in our homes.

Tomorrow, then. We will give him until tomorrow. If young Harper does not come with the Philosopher, we will move down into the Gorge and find the shelter we need.

We will take *the shelter we need.*

Yes, if we must. But tonight we wait, and we rest, and we hope that the sky remains clear.

⬛

With their new insights into Councilman Taro's motion to lock the North Gate, Vesu, Ozar, and Sera spent the next few weeks in serious preparation for the upcoming council meeting. Vesu was confident that the Royal Army advance was nothing more than a distraction, so she moved on to the next pressing question: a distraction from what? From prior experience, she knew Taro was capable of tying the council into complicated knots, but with enough focus she could unravel them. She set Ozar and Sera loose in the library to compile all the journals and manuscripts that made even a passing reference to the Alpinees. They needed to convince the council that Taro's proposal would be a grave mistake. And this time around, they had extra help.

Vesu asked Zeno to serve as her personal aide, running errands all across Sterling. He picked up packages that Vesu ordered, delivered letters to council members on her behalf, and often ran out to one of the bridges at a moment's notice whenever Vesu decided to take the Grand Fireplace to a new destination.

For his part, when Aris wasn't busy rehearsing (as the Capitol musician, he performed at all official events), he helped Sera and Ozar with their research. Every night during that first week, after a full day of running in circles through the library, Aris would lie in his bed in the Capitol with his arms spread out, gripping the sheets tightly. It was the only thing that helped. He had a constant waking dream of treading water at sea, sucked in by the force of a massive whirlpool.

But his nervousness didn't last long. The thrill of each new discovery and the excitement of being at the center of city government was invigorating. Once he settled in, Aris slept so soundly in his plush, springy bed that he wondered how he ever got a full night's sleep on his straw mattress at home. He was becoming more familiar with the library too. After a few weeks of following Sera through the stacks, he was beginning to understand Inka's chaotic (but admittedly brilliant) design. He was also starting to see why Sera loved swimming in that swirling ocean so much.

With seven days remaining before the council meeting, Vesu emerged from the fireplace and immediately collapsed on the armchair. She had paid a brief visit to Aldo, as Sera had recommended earlier, to see what else there was to learn about the North Gate. But the previous three weeks had left Vesu exhausted. Even a short trip through the silver fire made her feel dizzy. When the room finally stopped spinning, Vesu could see that the rest of the group was equally tired. Fortunately, she had enough sense remaining to do something about it.

"Listen, everyone. I am very grateful for your tireless efforts these last few weeks. I finally feel we're in a position to provide the council members with the information they need to vote on Taro's motion. Now it's up to them to make the right decision. Let's take the day off. Go for a walk or go get some rest; it's up to you. I'll see you back here tomorrow morning."

Sera was thrilled to receive the news. She had made plans with Aris to explore the city together when they found some free time. The two had become close friends, and Sera was dying to meet Aris's friends (including me); his mother, Zita; and the mysterious Mr. Marcel, all of whom she had heard so much about. Zeno had to finish a delivery for Vesu in the Down Quarter, but after that he agreed to meet them for dinner at their house in the Low Quarter.

Before leaving the library, Sera turned around to check on Ozar. He was also drained by the last few weeks and had become increasingly distraught as the days wore on. The work wasn't easy. Ozar took on the toughest research assignments, though he continued to voice his concern—fervently but respectfully—that they were underestimating the Royal Army. Sera watched as he hung the Philosopher's shawl on its hook (Vesu was too shaky to reach it) and then disappeared behind the book stacks. She wasn't surprised. Ozar was never one to take breaks, especially when important matters were pending. She still felt sorry for him, though. Ozar didn't have any close friends or family, which was not uncommon for Philosophers, although neither was loneliness. That much Sera knew from her own experience; she would be the first to admit that the isolation could be painful.

So, for a brief second, Sera considered inviting Ozar to dinner at the Harpers'. She got ready to call out his name, but then thought better of it. *Why make him come up with an excuse?* She knew with certainty that he would decline. *Ozar*

131

rarely leaves the Capitol grounds. And if he needs anything, Palo will be here to get it for him.

Leaving Ozar with his work, Sera rushed to her room to change her clothes (she had to wear something more discreet for venturing out into the city) and then met Aris by the northeast entrance.

"Now it's your turn to be the tour guide," Sera said, draping her violet scarf around her head to partially cover her face. "And don't mind them," she added, waving at the two S&R guards behind her. "Chief Gaffney makes us bring security whenever we go out. But they'll stay out of our way—eventually you'll forget they're even there." With that, the two set off toward their first stop: Mr. Marcel's shop.

Sera and Aris followed the same route I would have taken to the Mid Quarter from the Capitol, Center Street to Seventh Avenue. It was a gorgeous afternoon for a walk. Spring had almost transformed into summer, and it was evident that the whole neighborhood had been waiting for a warmer sun to arrive. Taking advantage of the fine weather, waves of people strolled along the riverfront, talking and laughing, while others settled down on the grass for lunch or tea.

By the time Sera and Aris reached the shops on Seventh, the sidewalks were overflowing. Ladies had lined up around the corner outside Simone's Clothiers to try on the new arrivals. Pearlmann's Fine Paper Products had its own steady stream of customers, coming and going. The Mid Quarter Grocer was quite busy too, although it took only a minute for Sera and Aris to buy a box of chocolate scones to share with Mr. Marcel.

When Sera turned down the ivy-covered alley, she smiled when she saw the little green sign for the Odd Shop. The sign was exactly as Aris had described it, and when he opened the heavy green door, the bells on the doorknob jingled just as Aris said they would. Now she hoped that the mysterious Mr. Marcel would also live up to her expectations. The S&R guards stayed on watch in the alley while Sera followed Aris into the store.

"Hello, Mr. Marcel! It's Aris, I'd like you to meet someone."

Sera heard dishes clanking in the back, followed by hurried footsteps creaking along the old floorboards. Mr. Marcel bounded out from the back room, his beard bouncing expectantly as he maneuvered around the assorted items strewn about the storeroom floor (or stacked precariously high on the shelves). It was no easy task, the shop having become even more cluttered without Aris around to manage things.

To Sera's delight, Mr. Marcel was as charming as she had imagined. Of course, he didn't say a word as he came to greet them, but he didn't have to. Sera could tell how excited he was to see Aris simply by the way his cheeks squished up from smiling.

"Mr. Marcel, I'd like you to meet Ms. Sera Avery. She's the Philosopher I was telling you about."

"Philosopher in training," Sera corrected him, reaching out to shake Mr. Marcel's hand. "It's a pleasure to meet you. You're quickly gaining a reputation as the best music teacher in Sterling, you know."

Mr. Marcel playfully pulled on his green suspenders and let them snap back into place, then proceeded to squeeze Aris firmly on the shoulder, all as if to humbly say, "Why thank you, but I had little to do with it. Aris, here, always had the talent." He gracefully took Sera's outstretched hand and kissed it.

"Oh, and we picked up some chocolate scones for you," Aris said, placing the box on the counter. Mr. Marcel flicked his finger in the air as if he had remembered something vitally important. The kettle whistled in the back room, and he scurried after it.

"That must be the famous green tea," Sera whispered. "I can't wait to try it."

While Mr. Marcel prepared the tea, Sera and Aris poked around the storeroom shelves. After a first pass down the nearest aisle, Sera didn't see anything that stood out. The shelves were stocked with everything you'd expect to find in an antique shop—lamps and luggage, furniture and rugs—each with its fair share of rust or dust lining the edges.

But as Sera followed Aris to the last aisle, she sensed something different. It was like walking down a long city street and suddenly realizing she was in a new neighborhood. At that end of the shop, every artifact was something she had never seen before—a candle in the shape of a sea creature, a birdhouse made of ivory and jade. Each object she examined was more peculiar than the last. *Wait, this clock has too many numbers around the face, and this one doesn't have any at all.* Most of the items Sera couldn't name, let alone figure out how they worked. *Okay, this looks like a mirror, but I can't find my reflection. What in the Gorge is this thing? Where am I?*

For a second, Sera really did wonder whether she was still inside the little shop on Seventh Avenue or if she had stumbled into a strange museum at the other end of the continent. And "stumbled" is an apt description, for Sera was feeling both lost and unsteady. She was used to living like a Philosopher, where she expected to have all the answers all the time (or at least know where to find them). But in the last aisle of Mr. Marcel's shop, nothing felt familiar. The coins had faces and figures on them that Sera didn't recognize, and the books were written in languages that she couldn't read. The few maps she dared to open depicted cities that she had never heard of (and islands she was pretty sure didn't exist).

Then a particular item on the top shelf caught Sera's eye. In fact, it stood out precisely because it seemed so ordinary compared to everything else. Sera knew exactly what it was because she had been dreaming about it for some time.

"Aris, come over here. You've got to see this."

Sera climbed onto a short step stool and carefully slid a clear jar off the top ledge. It was heavier than it looked. The jar was nearly three-quarters full of sand, and the tiny crystalline grains were perfectly smooth and white.

"You know what this is, don't you?"

"It looks like regular sand to me."

Sera unscrewed the silver lid and let it fall to the floor. With the jar cradled in both hands, she lifted it to her nose, closed her eyes, and took a deep breath.

"Do you smell that?"

She held the jar toward Aris, her arms fully extended. "That's the scent of the ocean," she said. "This sand came all the way from Imperial Bay."

"That's a long way to carry a heavy jar of sand. Why's it so special?"

"Are you kidding me? I would give anything to see the ocean. And so far, this is the closest I've come. Vesu got to see the ocean when she was my age—that's where she fell in love, you know—and all I have here in the Gorge is the Silver River. It gets old after a while, don't you think?"

Aris grimaced.

"Okay, okay, 'old' is not the word I was looking for. It's just that the river is so predictable, knowable. The ocean, on the other hand, it's practically endless. It's like someone placed a copy of the sky right here on earth. It's as close to infinite as you can get."

"I never thought of it like that," Aris said. "But I prefer the Silver River anyway. A river is more relatable. It's more . . . I don't know, *human*."

"So, if I decide to visit the ocean one day, you won't come with me?"

"Well, someone has to look after things in the Gorge until you return. And can you imagine what this shop would look like if I was gone for two years?" Aris wiped a thick layer of gray dust off a suitcase on the floor. "Don't worry, though; I'm sure you won't be traveling alone. We both know someone who would follow you to the ocean in a heartbeat."

"What? Who?"

"Come on, Sera. You've seen the way my brother looks at you. Before he met you, all Zeno talked about was climbing, and now he spends most of his time hanging around the Capitol with Philosophers. Why do you think he agreed to run those errands for Vesu?"

"Wait, what? I mean . . . well, how would I know?" Sera pretended to examine the jar, turning it upside down so the sand swished around inside. But she didn't have any witty response this time. Or, to put it more accurately, she didn't want to share what she was thinking in case it didn't come true.

"Because he gets to be around you," Aris said, answering for her. "You didn't think Zeno was showing up at the Capitol every day simply to admire all the old statues, did you?" At this suggestion, they both burst out laughing.

"Alright, alright, are you ready to try those scones?" Sera put the jar back on the highest shelf and followed Aris toward the front counter.

On the way there, about halfway down the center aisle, Aris stopped so abruptly that Sera bumped into him. "By the owl, I almost forgot. I want to show you something." Aris pushed aside some rusty tools and perfume bottles and pulled out a wooden box from a middle shelf. "I've been trying to figure out what this thing is for over a year, and I still haven't got a clue. Any ideas?"

Sera examined it. "Hmm . . . Based on the shape, it's probably some kind of jewelry box. Or maybe an old cigar box."

"I thought so too, but feel how heavy it is." Aris handed her the chestnut-colored cube, which was fastened to a heavy bronze base. As she examined it, Aris rapped the top with his knuckles. "It's hollow on the inside, although I can't find any way to open it."

"That's strange. And check out the pattern on the top. The lines look familiar, don't they?"

Aris traced his finger along the intricate design on the surface, which was made of tiny wooden pieces in various shades of brown. "Not really, doesn't ring any bells." He shrugged. "Oh well, I thought it was worth asking in case you had seen something like this before."

"No, nothing like this. Then again, everything in this shop is . . ." Sera stopped mid-sentence, distracted by the sound of porcelain cups sliding around dangerously on a tray. While he wasn't in view yet, Mr. Marcel was clearly struggling to keep the tea tray balanced as he navigated around all the junk on the storeroom floor.

"Aris, you better give him a hand—"

Crash. Mr. Marcel tripped over an old lamp and the whole tea set went flying. The platter knocked over a stack of books, which toppled into a shelf of ceramics. The teapot caused damage of its own, smashing into a stained-glass window on the counter. The sound of it all was so startling that Sera instinctively covered her ears, letting the wooden box fall to the floor.

Aris rushed over to check on Mr. Marcel. Fortunately, only his pride was injured, and he was already bent over, picking up pieces of stained glass from the floor. Aris could tell by his annoyed huffing and puffing that he was more embarrassed than anything else.

"Be careful, those pieces are sharp," Aris said. "Hold on, let me grab the broom."

"Aris, wait!" Sera yelled. "The box! I figured it out."

Sera approached the counter, brushed away some glass and ceramic bits, and set down the wooden cube. However, it wasn't just a cube anymore. Two rows of little structures were sticking out of its surface, like miniature buildings lined up along a city street.

"Are you serious? How did you manage to open it?" Aris swung around the counter to get a closer look.

"I wish I could take credit, but it was mostly by accident. When I heard the sudden noise, I dropped it. After the bronze base hit the ground, the whole thing tipped over. I thought for sure it was broken, but when I picked it up I noticed the wood pieces on top had slid out. That's when it hit me—it doesn't open like a normal box with a lid; you have to turn it upside down, and then the pattern on the surface drops out."

Aris placed his elbows on the counter and leaned in, inspecting the box. Sera was right. A tiny three-dimensional streetscape was poking out of the cube. To test her theory, he pushed down on the buildings and they slid back into place. Then Sera flipped the box upside down again, and the scene reappeared.

"Now I know why the pattern looked familiar," she said. "Do you recognize where this is?"

"The buildings remind me of the Mid Quarter."

"Exactly! This is Seventh Avenue. There's the grocer, there's Pearlmann's, and there's Simone's on the corner. And there's the Odd Shop in the alley."

"Do you think it's a game of some sort? A puzzle, maybe?"

"No, it looks too valuable to be a toy. Maybe it's some kind of map, or a model, or . . . maybe Mr. Marcel knows?"

Sera and Aris lifted their eyes toward Mr. Marcel, who had stopped cleaning up some time ago and was standing at the counter. Instead of his usual cheery demeanor, he had his arms crossed over his chest and a concerned look on his face.

"Mr. Marcel, do you know what this is?" Aris asked. "Could you show us how it works?"

Mr. Marcel clenched his teeth and shook his head, his beard following the movements of his chin like the wake of a boat. *I really shouldn't say,* he communicated clearly. *It would be better if you didn't know.*

"Okay, fine," Aris said, disappointed. "Maybe some other time. Let's get this place cleaned up."

138

But Mr. Marcel didn't move. He leaned on the counter with one hand, and with the other he combed his long gray beard, from his chin all the way down to his belly. Sera could tell that he hadn't made up his mind just yet.

"Please, Mr. Marcel? I've never seen anything like this."

Mr. Marcel squeezed his suspenders with both hands, looked up at the ceiling, and drew a deep breath. Sera couldn't help but smile. The build-up reminded her of a swimmer deciding whether to jump into water that he knew was freezing cold.

Mr. Marcel scanned the room to make sure it was empty, then hopped over the toppled books and locked the front door. He also closed the white curtains on the two front windows so nobody could see in, although the bright afternoon sun shone through the thin fabric. The two S&R guards were still keeping watch outside, but they didn't notice. Sera and Aris could see their silhouettes pacing back and forth in the alley.

When Mr. Marcel returned to the counter, he hovered over the little replica of Seventh Avenue and held his finger up to his lips.

Sera and Aris got the message: *You better not tell anyone I showed you this.*

Mr. Marcel pulled out a piece of stationery from the drawer and held it over one end of the box so it cast a shadow on the miniature buildings below. Then he moved the paper above the street until the shadow covered the tiny neighborhood, including the narrow alley leading to the Odd Shop. At that instant, the bright light streaming through the storefront windows dimmed, as if clouds had covered the sky outside. The shop went almost completely dark. After a brief pause, Mr. Marcel pulled the paper away, and sunlight flooded back into the shop.

"Wait a second," Sera said. "How in the Gorge . . ."

Mr. Marcel placed his finger over his lips. Apparently, the demonstration wasn't over. He took out a matchbox from the drawer, struck a match, and lit the paper on fire.

He held it over one end of the tiny street until a fair amount of smoke formed, and then blew the smoke across the little model of Seventh Avenue until it filled every street, sidewalk, and alley.

Barely two seconds later, the bells on the shop's doorknob jingled outside in the breeze. Aris and Sera glanced at the door, not ready to believe what they had heard, and yet everything they saw confirmed it was real. Through the front windows they watched an S&R guard's hat fly off in the wind. As his partner ran after it, a layer of fog moved in through the alley, seemingly out of nowhere, and then dissipated as quickly as it had arrived.

Mr. Marcel fanned out the flame and waved his arms around to clear the air. He was expecting to find the delighted smiles of Sera and Aris once the smoke cleared, especially after he managed to blow the hat right off that guard's head. But Sera and Aris didn't seem pleased at all. In fact, they both appeared worried and afraid. Mr. Marcel raised his eyebrows innocently and turned up the palms of his hands, silently asking them, *What did I do wrong?*

Sera had so many questions, but she wasn't able to speak. Remembering the storms that Zeno had described, her throat went dry. She glanced at Aris, who was still in shock, trying to make sense of everything. With one look, they each knew what the other was thinking. Sera nodded for Aris to go ahead and ask the question that was on both of their minds.

"Mr. Marcel, would it be possible to make a box like this the size of a mountain range? Or maybe the size of the entire Gorge?"

Mr. Marcel shrugged as if to say, "I don't know," but at the same time suggesting, "I don't see why not."

"What's this thing called?" Sera asked.

Mr. Marcel tore off another page of stationery, scribbled down a word with his green pen, and then turned it around so Sera and Aris could read it:

Weatherbox.

"We need to tell Zeno about this," Aris said. "It's exactly what my father and the Alpinees were afraid of."

"I have to inform Vesu right away. Ozar won't believe that he missed this . . ." Sera didn't finish her thought, distracted by something else on the counter. She snatched the page that Mr. Marcel had scribbled on and held it up to the sunlight, which was streaming in again through the windows.

"Aris, where does Mr. Marcel buy his stationery?" Sera asked.

"We buy our supplies from Pearlmann's, down the street."

"I've seen this kind of paper before." Sera bent the page back and forth, apparently testing its thickness.

"Of course you have. Pearlmann delivers his products to most businesses in the Mid Quarter."

"I've seen letters from Ambassador Elerin written on the same stationery. Does Pearlmann deliver to Imperial Bay too?"

Mr. Marcel and Aris stared back at her, baffled. They had no idea what she was talking about, but they both shook their heads in unison. "No, that would be impossible," Aris said.

"I thought so. Mr. Marcel, thank you for everything. Your shop is lovely. I'll be back again soon to try the green tea. Aris, we need to find Zeno. Can you take us to your house right away?"

"Will you tell me what's going on?"

"I'll explain along the way. We need to go now."

⬛

Aris and Sera bolted out of the Odd Shop and sped down the ivy-covered alley so fast that the two S&R guards had to sprint to catch up.

"Ms. Avery! Don't get too far ahead!" one of the guards called out as they ran after her, his axe swinging back and forth on his belt.

"We have a dinner appointment in the Low Quarter," Sera responded, without looking back. "And we're in a hurry, so try your best to keep up."

Aris led the way through the Mid Quarter, following the most direct route he knew, taking side streets to save time. The sun had dipped behind the Cloudhorns, spreading an orange glow across the sky so that the darker mountains in front appeared purple by comparison. As twilight set in, the air felt cooler than it had in the afternoon.

The letters. The lovely handwriting, the vivid descriptions. Sera told Aris everything she could remember about the early correspondence from Ambassador Elerin, and then how it all abruptly changed. Not only the writing style, but the paper and ink too. To prove it, she showed Aris the little scar where the parchment had sliced her finger. The recent letters were too well preserved to have come all the way from Imperial Bay. Sera had suspected that much all along. But when she discovered the same stationery at Mr. Marcel's shop, that was better proof than a paper cut.

"I'm certain those recent letters weren't written by Ambassador Elerin. Who could have sent them?"

Aris knew she was on to something, but his attention had drifted elsewhere. The atmosphere outside had changed drastically since the afternoon. The evening air was colder, sure, but that wasn't what was bothering him. The parks along the river walk were empty. The paths and the greenways were nearly deserted too. A few hours earlier, Aris and Sera wouldn't have been able to find a place to sit down, and now the only people along the riverfront were S&R guards. And they were apparently on patrol, instructing the few families who remained to go home.

Aris was only half listening to Sera as he tried to figure out what was going on. As he watched the people passing by on the boulevard, he sensed a mixture of confusion and panic. Couples whispered to each other as they walked. Parents squeezed their children's hands, keeping them close.

Families rushed into their houses, locking the doors behind them.

"Aris," Sera whispered, also sensing the fear in the air. "What's going on?"

Aris didn't know, and it wouldn't have done any good to guess. He took Sera's hand and led her across the bridge into the Down Quarter, hoping to make it home before dusk. He was sure that his mother and Zeno would have heard some news about what had caused such a stir around town.

When they reached the other side of the river, Aris expected to hear the familiar sounds of the Down Quarter, the steady buzz of people at work: sawing, chopping, hammering, and chiseling. That night, though, the whole neighborhood was silent. Apparently, the blacksmiths, carpenters, and bricklayers had all gone home. Only a few buildings still had their lights on, and the only sign of activity was a stableman locking up his yard at the end of the block. As he wrapped the metal chains around the iron gate, the clinking sound seemed excessively loud compared to the quiet, empty street. Aris couldn't wait any longer. He had to find out why everyone was acting so strangely.

"Excuse me, sir? Could you tell us what's going on? It seems like the Down Quarter shops closed early tonight."

"Haven't you heard?" The stableman's voice echoed off the brick buildings, and the sound caused the horses to snort and shuffle around in their stalls. He lowered his voice. "The Alpinees kidnapped a boy from the Low Quarter two hours ago. Then they set fire to the S&R outposts up in the mountains." He paused for a moment, noticing the two S&R guards standing behind Sera. "I'm surprised your friends haven't told you this already. Anyway, the S&R came by and instructed everyone to go home early, to be safe. You kids better move along." He pulled hard on the chains twice to make sure the gate was locked.

"He can't be serious," Sera said. Her comment was intended for Aris, but the streets were so quiet that the stableman overheard.

"If you don't believe me, see for yourself." He pointed up at the mountain range behind them. The fires were impossible to miss. Against the dark purple-brown backdrop of the Cloudhorns, little points of light flickered yellow-orange at seven or eight places along the ridge. Aris could make out light-gray lines of smoke twisting above them.

"What in the Gorge . . ."

Aris was also having trouble making any sense of it. *Why would the Alpinees attack the outposts?* Everything they had learned over the last few weeks indicated that the Alpinees were the least of their worries. Something was not adding up. *Are the storms getting worse? Are the Alpinees that desperate?*

"Thank you, sir, we'll head home straight away," Aris said, as calmly as he could. Sera, on the other hand, directed her shock and anger toward the guards.

"Why didn't you tell us about this?" she asked. "If I find out that you knew—" Aris grabbed her hand and pulled her away toward the Low Quarter. The guards didn't have any information; they had been following him and Sera around all day.

"Sera, let it go. We need to keep moving. We're almost there."

⬛

They arrived at the Low Quarter Bridge by nightfall. The bridgekeeper had set out the candles along the railings, so the platform was fairly well lit. Sera could read most of the family names flickering in the candlelight as they rushed by: Dillon, McCarthy, Downey, Ferrick . . . Thousands of Low Quarter family names were etched for eternity into the ancient oak: Begley, Langan, Harper . . .

Sera stopped abruptly near the end of the bridge, before Aris and the guards cleared the platform. "Aris, come back for a second. I need a hand." She took a candle out of the handrail and held it close to the wood panel, tracing the cursive script with her fingers. Simply by where she was standing, Aris knew the name that Sera was looking for. He didn't want to walk back there. Too many memories and mixed emotions. But Aris turned around anyway because he didn't want Sera to linger any longer than necessary. He wanted to get home.

"Hold this for me," Sera said, handing the candle to Aris. With one hand she unrolled a piece of parchment and pressed it down on the oak floorboard. With the other she ran a charcoal pencil back and forth across the paper. Aris forced himself to watch over her shoulder as the outline of each letter appeared, one at a time: AMOS HARPER.

"I'm sorry. I know it hurts to be here." Sera rolled up the parchment and put it back in her pocket. "But after what we found in Mr. Marcel's shop, Vesu needs to visit your father through the fireplace. He may have information that we need."

Aris nodded. He knew she was right. His father was somehow at the center of all this. But Aris also had a feeling that his father's curiosity about the weather device was the reason he ended up frozen in the Cloudhorns.

"I'm alright, let's go. I need to get home."

Sera followed Aris as closely as she could, afraid she might lose him in the shadows if they got separated. Without any streetlamps, the Low Quarter's dirt streets were pitch black at night. The guards weren't used to such darkness either. Both unclipped their axes and carried them against their chests, ready to swing. With the recent warning about the Alpinees on their minds, they nervously scanned the tree line of the backwoods, searching for figures to drop out of the sky.

Aris stopped at the corner of the last row of stone houses and listened. *The sounds are different here too.* Usually at that time of night in the Low Quarter, he could only hear the forest sounds of the backwoods, the call of crickets, critters, and owls. But now he heard voices, many of them, drifting down the street.

Dozens of people were gathered outside Aris's house talking to each other in hushed, hurried voices. He couldn't see their faces, but Aris knew something was wrong. It wasn't the regular group of his mother's houseguests outside having a smoke. Half the neighborhood, it seemed, had assembled around his front yard, the crowd spilling out from the porch onto the sidewalk and the street.

In the darkness and dust of the roadway, Aris and Sera approached unnoticed. The fireplace in the living room was going full blast, so Aris could make out a few faces in the arc of yellow light. Zeno was arguing with S&R guards by the sidewalk. His mother was comforting several neighbors near the flower bed, holding their hands. Kati and Kevi were sitting together on the front porch, wiping tears from their eyes. *What happened?* Aris wondered. *Are they hurt?*

"Aris! They took him!" Kati leapt off the stairs. She was the first to see Aris as he walked into the front yard. Kevi jumped up a second later, and together they tackled Aris with hugs, nearly knocking him over.

"Do you think . . . do you think they'll hurt him?" Kevi asked between breaths.

"Are you two okay? What happened?"

Aris's arrival grabbed everyone's attention. Many of the neighbors had stuck around, hoping he might bring news from the Capitol. But it was clear that Aris knew even less than everybody else. The crowd moved in closer on the lawn to hear Kati and Kevi tell their story one more time.

"We hiked together to the clearing, where we always go," Kati said. "And we were jumping between boulders when I lost sight of Bimo behind the rocks. I assumed he was hiding from us, like he always does, but this time he had wandered over by the trees at the north end of the field."

"Then the Alpinees grabbed him," Kevi said. "They carried Bimo off into the woods. I should have helped him, but I just stood there."

"And all I could do was scream," Kati confessed.

I didn't *want* to see this moment, by the way. It was devastating to watch my closest friends believe I might be dead. If only I could have whispered, across all those decades, that I was safe. But Kati and Kevi couldn't have heard me if I screamed. The Grand Fireplace doesn't have that power. Instead, I watched the scene helplessly while Aris squeezed his arms tighter around his friends.

"Hold on a second!" Zeno shouted from across the lawn. He had abandoned his argument with the S&R guards and pushed his way through to the center of the crowd. "Did you get a good look at the people who grabbed him?"

"Not really," Kevi replied. "It all happened so fast."

"Try to slow everything down. Were they short? Tall? Were they carrying anything?"

"I'm sorry, I'm not sure. It was getting dark, and Bimo was halfway across the field."

"Could you tell if they had green jackets on? With hoods, maybe?"

"It's possible, I guess. They sort of blended in with the trees."

Those answers didn't give Zeno much to work with. With his hands in his pockets, he rocked back and forth in his climbing boots, biting the inside of his cheek. Aris knew his brother well enough to know exactly what he was thinking. Zeno didn't believe the Alpinees had kidnapped me. Or maybe he *couldn't* believe it because he had promised to help them. Regardless, Aris wasn't so sure anymore. For the first time since meeting the Philosopher, he had to ask himself: *Has Vesu got something wrong? Maybe we're missing something.*

Zita weaved her way through the crowd until she reached the center of the lawn. She wrapped her arms around the three kids and kissed the top of Aris's head. Then she began to hum, very quietly, the song that Aris liked. The one about the trumpet bluebells. The one she didn't know all the words to. Aris never understood where she got that power, but whenever she sang softly like that, his doubts and fears seemed more distant. More manageable, somehow. He was still terribly worried, of course, and he blamed himself for not being there to protect me, but the simple melody gave him hope that I might be safe somewhere. And that was enough for the moment.

After his questioning went nowhere, Zeno returned his attention to the S&R guards. Most of the neighbors were heading home, so the guards had assembled their horses and carriages in the street. They were preparing to return to the Capitol building, but Zeno wasn't through with them yet. He was furious.

The S&R had informed everyone that the guards would not begin their search for me until the morning; that they had no choice but to wait. "The Alpinees are armed and dangerous," the staff sergeant said, "and they have an advantage in the mountains at night." He reminded the neighbors that the S&R's outposts had been destroyed, along with the supplies stored inside them. "We simply don't have the resources for an extended search at this hour."

"You really won't go after him?" Zeno asked the guards as they lined up in the street. He didn't agree with the sergeant's decision, and he wouldn't let it go. "Isn't that your job? *Search and rescue*? The longer we wait, the harder it will be to find Bimo's tracks. And if it rains tonight, we'll have no chance at all."

The guards ignored him as they hitched up their harnesses and tightened their saddles. Well, they tried to ignore him. Earlier in the evening the guards had been more understanding. They knew that emotions were running high, so they let Zeno blow off some steam. At that hour, though, the guards were tired and annoyed.

"Why don't you go find him yourself?" one of them snapped.

"Good luck catching the Alpinees in those old boots," another quipped.

"If you're going to stand around, then I will go after him," Zeno said. "I can find Bimo on my own."

The guards snorted and shook their heads. The kid couldn't possibly be serious. They called for the next two horses in line and finished tacking up. If they had watched Zeno run off, however, they would have seen him head straight to the front porch where his climbing gear had been laid out to dry. He stuffed his equipment into his backpack, laced up his boots, and tightened the straps of his gloves. He shouldered his bag and headed down the porch stairs. The first step creaked under his weight. It was going to be a long hike to the clearing in the dark, but at least he knew where to start looking.

"Zeno, wait!" Sera called out. She had been standing off to the side, listening and watching everything going on around her. (Maybe she was more prepared to be a Philosopher than she gave herself credit for.) Although she had never met me before, she was heartbroken. And like Aris, she knew exactly what Zeno was thinking: *The Alpinees have nothing to do with this.* To be fair, that morning she would have agreed with him. That's what all the history seemed to support, anyway.

Except now there were fires burning in the mountains, and Sera couldn't come up with another explanation. The outposts had been attacked by *somebody*. She stopped Zeno before he reached the bottom of the porch stairs.

"Zeno, listen to me." She shifted her violet scarf away from her eyes. "I realize you want to find Bimo, and I know you're brave enough to try. But it won't do any good to go searching for him alone." She took his hand and pulled him closer. They were standing on the same step, but Sera was much shorter than him, and she wasn't sure where to look. So, she simply rested her head on Zeno's shoulder and closed her eyes.

"Come back with us to the Capitol," she said quietly. "Vesu will know how to find Bimo. Then we can try to rescue him together, okay?" She lifted herself up on her toes and kissed him on the cheek.

For most people a kiss like that will send their heart rate through the clouds like a weather balloon. For Zeno it had the opposite effect, although it was equally powerful. His thoughts settled down, his breathing slowed, and his pulse tapped lighter than leaves falling from a tree.

Zeno let go of his backpack. It bounced on the bottom step and rolled onto the ground.

"You'll really come with me?" Sera asked as she took her scarf off completely. She needed to see him better, and her scarf was only getting in the way.

Zeno shoved his hands into his pockets and bit his lip. What he wanted to say was that he would follow her anywhere—all the way to the ocean, if she asked. But he kept that to himself for the moment.

Sera pulled his hands out of his pockets and untied the leather straps of his gloves. "I think you can take these off now; it's not that cold in the Capitol." Sera hopped off the porch steps and waved at the guards in the street. "The S&R should have room for us in one of the carriages, so we'll be back under the dome in no time. I have so much to tell you on the way. You won't believe what we found."

Chapter VII

The Silver River Gorge is quite a sight in the early summer. For days on end the sky will be bright and clear, and I'll sit on my balcony in the mornings and watch the snowline recede. Every year I expect this change to occur slowly, imperceptibly, maybe because the long winters feel like they'll take forever to unfreeze.

And yet the summer sunlight always proves me wrong. It erases those layers of ice on the mountains with remarkable speed. With warmer light to aim for, the flowers and trees fight back again, and almost overnight the valley turns deep green.

I must admit, however, that not all summer days in the Gorge are calm and clear. Case in point, I have been locked in the Capitol over the last few days by a storm that moved in with the warmer weather. The wind has been too fierce for taking in views on my balcony, and the constant rain has made hikes into Shoulder Ridge impossible. Without much else to do until the storm passes, I have been spending most of my time here in the library—which is just as well, considering how much work I have left to do.

I have tried to stay out of this story so far, but it's becoming increasingly difficult to keep my thoughts to myself. These long days are wearing an old man thin. My hand shakes from the countless hours spent recording everything I see. Sometimes my confidence shakes too when I think about all the pages left to compose.

I hope you don't find this unprofessional, by the way, but I desperately needed someone to talk to. Even though I can visit so many different people through the Grand Fireplace, nobody can see me or hear me, which is an awful kind of loneliness. That's where you come in. Someone to talk to. Sort of.

The hardest part of the whole project is seeing where and when things went wrong. I was there when it happened the first time, and I wasn't able to make much of a difference. Now I have to relive it as the Philosopher, and I still can't change a thing. I'm here to write it all down before I run out of time. Before we can't go back again. Before another gate closes.

And everything is about to get much worse. I'm coming to a part of the story that's too close to home, especially since I'm trapped in this basement again, listening to the rain outside. Oh, you'll see what I mean soon enough. As for the rest of them, they were talking in this same room in front of this same fireplace. By the owl, Vesu was reclining on the same couch that I am now . . .

"Mr. Wrinn, did you think it would come to this?" The Philosopher was lying on a long velvet couch in the library, a damp towel resting over her eyes.

"It's quite unprecedented, madam." Ozar was sitting on a chair across from Vesu, his hands folded in his lap. He watched her lean over and wring out the towel. The last few drops of warm water splashed into the washbowl on the floor. *But you should have seen this coming*, he thought. "Should I ask Palo to bring you more hot water?"

"No, no, I'm fine, but I can't get over it. The council didn't listen to a word I said. And they voted for Taro's motion anyway."

"With due respect, madam, the council members are afraid. The boy is still missing. The outposts have been attacked. With their constituents in a frenzy, the council had to act swiftly."

"Yes, I see all that. But the measures seem drastic in light of everything we know."

"How can you be so sure? Over the last three weeks, we researched the complete history of the Alpinees, inside and out. But we know very little about their intentions—"

Ozar's argument was interrupted by the squeaking hinges of the double doors. He craned his neck over the chair to find Sera entering the library, Zeno and Aris a few strides behind her. Ozar pushed his fists together, forcing all the knuckles in his fingers to pop at once.

"Vesu, is it true?" Sera asked from across the room. "The council passed Taro's motion?"

"I'm afraid so, Sera. The vote was unanimous. The S&R is closing the North Gate as we speak."

"And the lockdown, how long will it last?"

"Until the emergency order is lifted," Ozar answered. "The council made it clear that no one is allowed to leave the city limits."

"Can they do that?" Zeno asked.

"It is certainly within their authority," Ozar said. "The Philosopher and I warned the council about the precedent this would set, but their fears won out. Any violators will receive the most severe punishment."

"I thought that last part was particularly unreasonable," Vesu said, "especially considering what we've learned about the Alpinees. Not one instance of aggression—not one—going back as far as our records show, and as far as that fireplace can take me. But would the council allow me one minute at the meeting to share this information? No, of course not! Ozar, I see your point quite clearly now: the council members' minds were made up when they walked in. They don't care one bit about history." Vesu threw the towel into the washbowl, nearly knocking it over.

"What do we do now?" Sera asked.

The Philosopher's frustration with the council was enough to restore some of her energy. She got up from the couch and started pacing again in her usual spot in front of the fireplace. Vesu always did that when she had a difficult choice to make, so Ozar was used to it. But it bothered him anyway. Her constant footsteps over the years had left a line in the carpet, about seven or eight feet long, where the fibers were fraying and the colors had all but faded away. Ozar wondered why Vesu had to move around so much in order to focus. That was definitely not his style. He preferred to make his most important decisions sitting completely still, in a quiet room, alone.

"If the council doesn't care about history, then we need to get better information," Vesu said. "Something more reliable. We need to go to the source."

"The source? What source? What do you mean, madam?" Sera spoke so rapidly that her questions tumbled out over each other. Usually, she picked up on Vesu's clues rather quickly, but this time she was lost. Ozar, on the other hand, leaned back in his chair, crossing one leg over the other. *I know exactly what she means. Is she really this predictable?*

"Zeno, I would like to accept your offer, if it still stands," Vesu said. "I want you to take me to the Alpinees. I need to speak with them directly."

"Madam Philosopher, you can't be serious." Ozar tightened his grip on the armchair, revealing all the veins running through his hands.

"I'm quite serious. I need to find out what they want from us. And if the Alpinees are looking for me, then this might be our only way to get the boy back safely."

"Best intentions aside, this plan violates the council's order. If you're caught, the punishment—"

"I understand the law, Ozar, but it's a chance I'm willing to take. That is, if Zeno is willing to lead me. What was the scout's name? Isolo, was it?"

"Yes, madam. I'm ready when you are."

"That settles it. I'll meet you by the back exit one hour before sunup. And don't be late—that's when the guards change shifts, so we can slip out unseen."

"I'm coming too," Sera said.

"Same here," Aris added.

"No, I need you both to stay in the Capitol. This is imperative. If anything happens to me, Ozar will need your assistance."

Yes, I will need them, Ozar thought. *They both have very useful skills.*

"Vesu, listen, we can help," Sera pleaded. "I need to tell you about the letters from the ambassador, and what we found in the Mid Quarter, and—"

"That's enough. I've made up my mind. It's very late, and I need to rest. We have a long climb tomorrow."

Ozar sat quietly with his hands folded in his lap while everyone else left the library for their living quarters. Sera was the last to leave, complaining to Aris about having to stay back. When Ozar heard the double doors squeak and slam behind them, he walked over and lowered the bar lock. He pulled hard, twice, to make sure it was secure. Then he sat down at the long mahogany table.

He still had work to do.

From the bottom of a pile of books, Ozar slid out a leather binding with hundreds of papers stuffed inside. These were the letters from Ambassador Elerin that Sera had retrieved from the stacks weeks ago. *She's a clever girl, very observant. Let's see what she discovered.*

He brushed some dust off the cover and opened the leather folder. Ozar turned each page, one at a time, scanning the words. *Well, it's not the handwriting.* He continued to flip faster through the pages. *A change in the writing style? Possibly.* When he reached the end of the stack, he noticed a drop of blood at the bottom corner of the parchment. He held the page up against the flickering light from two lamps over the fireplace. *Ah, that's it. The paper. She's more observant than I thought. I should have been more careful.*

Ozar moved the stack of letters to the side. He took out a crisp, clean, blank sheet of paper and dipped his pen into the inkwell. Then he started with the greeting in perfectly smooth, elegant script.

My Dearest Vesu,

That was as far as he got when Palo walked in.

"Excuse me, sir?"

"Yes, what is it?"

"Your guests have arrived, sir."

"Show them in."

When Palo returned a few minutes later, Ozar was sitting at the head seat, hunched over, busily writing. He didn't look up as his two guests pulled out chairs on either side of him and sat down at the mahogany table. Ozar said nothing; he kept scrawling away. The long silence was clearly making both guests uneasy, but the chief was the first to break. He tossed his cap on the wooden table.

"Well, we set the fires right on time, Councilman," Chief Gaffney reported. "Exactly as we discussed."

"Yes, I know," Taro said, "I was able to see the fires from my terrace. In fact, everyone in Sterling could see them, wherever they were standing. Nicely done."

"We have the Low Quarter boy too, of course," Gaffney continued.

"Where is he now? The location is secure, I trust?" Taro took out his ivory comb and groomed the precise swoop of his hair.

"We're holding him in a jail cell, here in the Capitol. Two of my most trusted men are keeping watch. He'll be safe there, if that's what you're asking." Gaffney coughed and pulled a cigar out of his front pocket. He tapped one end of the cigar on the table and then the other. He brought it up to his mouth and then back down again.

"You know, Councilman, did we really need to take the boy? I didn't feel comfortable with it from the start. His family is assuming the worst, I'm sure, and the boy is terrified. We gave him warm clothes and a blanket, but he still won't stop shaking."

"No harm will come to the boy; he'll be returned to his family soon enough. And the entire gorge will be safer because of it. We had no choice. Without him we didn't have the votes. We needed justification for the emergency order, otherwise—"

"I understand the politics, Taro. And I knew this plan would require compromises. But . . . by the owl, this went too far."

The tapping of Ozar's pen on the table stopped. The silence was subtle, but it was enough to grab Taro and Gaffney's attention. They both turned to hear what Ozar had to say.

"Chief Gaffney, have you ever studied politics?"

Gaffney raised an eyebrow and shrugged. "Not in the formal sense, sir. What I know I've learned on the job."

"That explains why you ask so many simple questions." Ozar clicked his tongue and let his pen drop to the table. The fall was only a few inches, but the thud sounded louder than it should have. "Look behind me. This library is stacked to the ceiling with books and treatises on politics. All the means and methods of kings, councils, courts, and constitutions. I've read every single one of them. So, let me share a lesson, one that might register with you."

"By all means, go right ahead."

"Do you keep a garden at home?"

"Yes, I do."

"What are the three most important things that a garden needs?"

Gaffney didn't answer right away. He tapped his cigar on the table again and lifted it to his mouth. He struck a match and puffed until the end was glowing orange. Then he blew a heavy cloud of smoke across the table.

"I'm not here for lessons in gardening," he said. "I'm here to protect the city."

Ozar slammed his fists on the table. The unexpected boom echoed off the bookshelves.

"Put out that cigar *now*," Ozar commanded. "If you let a single ash fall onto this table, the smoke in your lungs will be replaced by river water before this night is over. Palo, please dispose of the chief's cigar."

Palo appeared immediately and slid the cigar out from between Gaffney's fingers.

"Now that I have your attention, let's return to our lesson. The reason that a politician should always keep a garden is because they both need the same things to survive: soil, seeds, and light. That's how we helped Taro capture the council.

"Your men, you see, the S&R guards, they have been our soil, the foundation for our ideas to take hold. Once we had them banded together, we only needed to plant a couple seeds—the Alpinees, the Royal Army—because the other seeds were already there, buried beneath the surface. Doubt about the Gorge's security. Worry for their own safety. Fear as to whether they could protect their families.

"Those parts of the plan were easy. Waiting for the roots to spread was much harder. That part took time; it simply couldn't be rushed. As the councilman observed from his terrace tonight, our patience has paid off. Those little roots have stretched from one end of the Gorge to the other.

"Ah, I see the way you're scowling at me, Chief Gaffney, but you haven't let me finish. The lesson is not over. You may think this all sounds contriving—cruel, maybe—but don't forget the real reason we're here. The reason *you're* here.

"The garden needs something to grow toward, a source of light to aim at. For too many years Sterling has been going nowhere, sleeping in the shadows of these mountains. And a sleeping city makes an easy target, don't you think? Councilman Taro sees that clearly, and I know you see it too. We need to show everyone else what's possible when we open the armory. We must remind them that the whitefire crossbows have always been the key to defending this city. By rearming the S&R, we will send a clear message to the king that Sterling will stand up for itself again."

Chief Gaffney sat quietly for a moment, tapping his fingertips along the patterns on the tabletop. Then he picked up his hat and set it firmly on his head. "I agree, sir," he said. "I was not suggesting that we abandon our plan. I only wish the armory could be opened some other way."

"We all wish there was some other way," Taro said. "But we can never be too sure how much time we have left."

"The councilman is right," Ozar added. "*This* king and *this* army will leave us alone. I'm concerned about the *next* king, and the one after that. If I have learned anything from the literature, it is this: only a king has eyes to close. The crown never sleeps."

Ozar lifted his pen, dipped it in the bluish-black ink, and continued writing his letter. The guests took it as a sign that they were dismissed.

"Before we leave you, sir," Taro said, "shall we address the other important task of the gardeners? Pulling the weeds, so to speak? Amos Harper largely took care of himself, although the next one will not come out so easily, I imagine."

"I was just getting to that." Ozar finished the last line of the letter and signed the name "Elerin" at the bottom in long, swooping letters. Then he folded the page and handed it to Taro.

"Here's the letter. We will move forward exactly as planned, with one exception. Chief Gaffney, please assign a group of your best men to monitor the Capitol's rear exit overnight. The guards should be instructed to stay out of sight, but to follow anyone who leaves. Anyone. Wherever they go. Is that understood?"

"Not a problem, sir. And then what?"

"Simply enforce the law. Now, you both know what to do from here. Above all else, remember this: Vesu cannot have any reason to doubt my loyalty. She can only pass the

Philosopher's shawl on to me freely. Without those feathers, the entire plan fails. Do you understand?"

Taro and Gaffney nodded.

"Alright. Palo will show you out. I have work to finish."

Ozar waited until he heard the library doors shut and the bar lock rattle when Palo secured it. Then he began clearing off the long mahogany table. Ozar started with the book piles, moving them to the floor, while Palo organized the papers and filed them away on a nearby shelf. Bit by bit they uncovered the intricate patterns on the tabletop. The dark wood of the legs and sides contrasted sharply with the lighter woods on the surface. The cherry, chestnut, and gold pieces did not depict anything in particular, but the abstract design appeared to flow diagonally across the table, from one corner to the other.

When the table was completely cleared, Ozar and Palo moved to opposite ends.

"Are you ready, Palo? One, two, three."

Together they lifted the top, which easily unclipped from its legs. They moved sideways a few steps, slowly and carefully, like the whole procedure was choreographed. Then they flipped it over.

From the table's surface an entire landscape dropped out: two miniature mountain ranges rising up on each side of a tiny, fragile city. A river ran diagonally across the entire scene, connecting forests in one corner to wide open fields in the other. In the center, a building with a dome was carved into the wood, and on either side of it were two arches, four bridges in all.

Ozar and Palo set the model of the Silver River Gorge back on its stand and made sure it was sturdy.

"Can I get you anything else, Mr. Wrinn?"

Ah, you listened to my lesson, Palo, and more closely than my guests, it seems, because you see what's missing. "I could use a glass of water, if it's not too much trouble." *After all, how could one expect a garden to grow without rain?*

"By all means, sir, I'll be right back."

Ozar took the Philosopher's chair and sat with his back to the Grand Fireplace. He tilted his head far to one side, cracking all the tiny bones in his neck. The room was quiet. He was alone.

◉

"Holy ocean . . . did the rain always taste this good, or am I just used to that warm, stale well water in the Basin?"

Captain Pearlin cupped her hands together and extended them out from under her tent. The little bowl formed by her fingers was immediately filled by the wall of water gushing from the tent's slanted roof. The storm had started the night before, but at sunrise the rain was still coming down hard. In fact, Pearlin assumed the sun was up because of the time; the sky was one giant cloud. She didn't mind a stormy morning once in a while. The chilly air was refreshing compared to the dry heat of the Basin. She lifted her hands to her lips and slurped the cool, clear rainwater.

"If you think that's good, imagine the first sip of beer when we make it to the Gorge," Carolin said groggily from the next tent over. She rolled around in her sleep sack. "I've been having dreams about that moment. I pull a chair up to the bar, take a sip of golden ale, and every morning I wake up licking imaginary foam from my upper lip." Pearlin laughed, spraying the rainwater out of her mouth. "Honestly, if the colonel would let me, I'd skip all the welcoming ceremonies and disappear into the first tavern I see."

"The first round is on me."

"In that case, I better get up so we can get moving. We have a lot of ground to cover before we're served a proper pint."

Carolin threw on her red-and-white uniform and laced up her boots. Then she reached into the downpour, splashing her face and neck. The fresh water, combined with the early morning air, sent a chill down her spine. "Ha! That's the first time I've had goosebumps in years. I feel like that sticky layer of sweat has finally washed away."

"I think everyone feels refreshed," Pearlin said as she combed her hair. "Especially the Prairie Riders. As soon as we left the Basin, the ivy in their hair sprouted new leaves; did you notice that? And yesterday I saw little orange and red flower buds pop up around their eyes. Don't get me wrong; our troops look stronger too. Healthier, well rested. They almost look like warriors again."

"They better feel well rested. We let them sleep in the last couple of days."

"Easy now, we all needed a break. And we're making good time. How many more days, do you think, until we reach Sterling?"

"Well, I caught the outline of the Cloudhorns last night before the storm blew in. I guess about four more days until we reach the North Gate. Keep in mind, though, that the mountains can be deceptive. They're always farther away than they appear."

"Four days sounds about right to me."

"Speaking of the mountains, did you notice anything unusual about them?" Carolin asked.

"Not really, although I wasn't paying much attention. I had to set up camp and make sure the Prairie Riders got settled in."

"It's probably nothing. But today is the first day of summer, right? And the Cloudhorns are still covered with snow and ice. Do you think that's normal for this time of year?"

"It might be," Pearlin said, putting her comb away. "But it doesn't feel right. And neither does all this rain, despite how good it tastes. Take a look at the river over there, where it bends. See how much it swelled? Thankfully, we didn't set up camp any closer, or we would have flooded."

Carolin walked out of her tent to get a better view. The Silver River hadn't simply overtopped its banks; the current was halfway up the tree trunks at the edge of their makeshift campsite. The bushes where Carolin picked blackberries the day before were totally submerged. She looked around for the Prairie Riders and found their bison resting under a tunnel-like shelter held up by curved branches. Water slid right off the waxy leaf-and-vine roof. *Another new shape?* Carolin thought. *I swear, every day we travel together these creatures find new ways to amaze me.*

It took Carolin a minute to figure out how they did it, but once she did, it was unmistakable. The shelter that the Riders had built during the night was clearly not made of gathered materials—those dense, wiry plants didn't grow around there. *Ah, another reason why the bison keep them around. This shapeshifting would be very useful.* Starting at the base, Carolin noticed roots dug into the soil in the shape of feet and toes. The woody columns had to be their spines, branching out over the bison to give the structure its stability. As for the roof, evidently it was formed from nothing more than the Riders' arms and fingers spread out in every direction. Multiple layers of thick, leafy foliage made a perfect barrier against the elements, so the bison stayed dry despite the unusually long storm. Carolin shook her head as the bison swished their tails without any concern for the weather. *If only our troops could work together so well.*

As for the four hundred South Branch soldiers scattered about, they all seemed equally oblivious to the rising water. Most of the regiment was still asleep. Only a few groups in the larger tents had started their day, building small fires under their canopies to brew coffee and cook breakfast. From crackling cast-iron pans, the smell of burnt boar bacon wafted through the air, a delicacy compared to savanna rats. *I'll never eat those little monsters again if I can help it,* Carolin thought.

Facing south toward the Gorge, Carolin tied back her long hair, which had become curly in the rain, to get a clearer view of the mountains. No luck. Too many layers of fog and sheets of rain. Lightning flashed overhead, followed by thunder that snapped and roared. Carolin noticed that the rumbling in the sky lasted far longer than it should have. It rolled on and on, like a bear crashing through the woods, chasing something.

The bison apparently noticed it too. Inside the tunnel-shelter they huddled closer together. Carolin got the chills again but not the same kind as before. Not the good kind. She stepped into Pearlin's tent for cover.

"You're right; this storm doesn't feel natural. How could it rain here for a full day when we didn't feel a drop in the Basin for months? It's like someone sucked the prairies bone dry and then dumped all that moisture in the Gorge."

"Let's talk to the colonel about it when he wakes up. He should say something to the Philosopher when we get there."

Pearlin opened the canvas flap wider so they could check on Colonel Orowin in his tent. Apparently, he wasn't bothered by the thunder because he slept right through it. With one leg crossed over the other and his hands folded together on his belly, the colonel was snoring peacefully under his cap.

"He looks so comfortable, I'm afraid he won't wake up," Carolin joked. "Should I go tell him what time it is?"

"No, let him rest a while longer. He's earned it."

"I bet he's dreaming about the plush bed he'll get in the barracks when we return to Imperial Bay. Or the roasted whitefish they'll serve him for dinner. Or the lemony turmeric cakes for dessert. Or the bottomless bottles of royal wine . . ."

"Yes, I'm sure he misses everything about home," Pearlin said. "After this assignment is over, we need to make sure he gets back to Imperial Bay. For the last six years he's taken care of us, so now we need to look out for him."

"Of course, I'll be with him every step of the way." Carolin took her bow and arrow off the hook in the tent. She aimed a pretend shot at the center of the cloud stretched across the sky. "I swear, if anyone stands in the way of our colonel and his royal wine, they'll find my arrow between their eyes."

"Madam Philosopher, are you alright? Here, take my hand."

Zeno reached out to Vesu as far as he could, clutching a tree branch with his other hand to keep from sliding down the embankment. They had been hiking up the forested trail in the Cloudhorns for several hours, since before the sun came up, and the rain still hadn't stopped. The downpour was so heavy that a few sections of the footpath had washed out while other stretches, like the one they were currently on, had completely caved in.

"Oh, I'm fine, I'm fine," Vesu said, out of breath. "I lost my footing for a second." She took hold of Zeno's hand and pulled herself up the muddy slope. Her silver dress was soaked, and her legs were covered in sludge and grit up to her knees. Even the intricate braids that were pinned up in her hair had unraveled. Zeno barely recognized her. "Let's take a short break, if you don't mind. I'm not in the same shape that I used to be. I need to let my lungs catch up."

Vesu and Zeno took a seat on the ground under a giant red cedar tree. For the first time that morning, Zeno didn't feel cold rain stinging his eyes. The lower branches of the cedar, drooping slightly with their flattened leaves, provided decent shelter from the storm.

Zeno gazed up into the canopy. The waxy, moss-colored leaves swished around in the wind. They reminded him of the pine-green jackets that the Alpinees wore. Zeno desperately hoped they would find Isolo soon. This trek into the mountains was taking far longer than he expected. On a normal day the climb was strenuous, but in the driving rain, it was dangerous.

Zeno was confident they were getting close; they had to keep pushing. The route was familiar because it was the same trail that he had taken home after the Alpinees rescued him. The same trail he hiked down the night that . . .

The snake, the storm, the slide. The rope, taut. The black void of the crevasse, bottomless. Zeno's stomach flipped over. *I should have turned around.*

As these memories flashed by, another wave of doubts flooded in. *Wait, did I take a wrong turn? Have I put the Philosopher in danger? What if we don't find Bimo?*

"Zeno, are you listening?" Vesu whispered. "Do you hear that?"

His thoughts still racing, Zeno didn't catch the question at first. "I'm sorry, madam. The thunder? Yes, it's been growling at us all morning."

"No, listen closer . . . the gentle music above us. Apparently, we're not the only ones hiding out in here."

Music? Zeno closed his eyes and pushed away the voice inside his head. Then he heard it. Against the backdrop of the storm, the slurred warbling of a songbird floated through the branches, followed by rustling feathers. A choir of baby birds chimed in, twittering. Vesu was right; it was nice to know they weren't the only ones waiting out the weather.

For several minutes Zeno and Vesu simply sat there enjoying the bright, cheerful chirping. Then a tiny feather landed in a puddle at the Philosopher's feet. Vesu's eyes lit up. She snatched the feather from the murky water and used her sleeve to wipe the fog from her glasses. Vesu examined the quill, twirling it around in her fingers. Although wet, the feather kept its color and sheen: ripe raspberry-purple on the edges and ochre-brown in the middle. Vesu showed it to Zeno, pulling the fluffy part through her fingertips.

"It's gorgeous, isn't it? I wonder what kind of birds are serenading us."

"I'm sure Sera could tell you. She's an expert on all that stuff."

"Ah, yes, you're right. I'll have to ask her." Vesu tucked the feather inside the pocket of her dress. As she did, a smile snuck in at the corners of her lips. "She's a brilliant girl, don't you think?"

"Who? Oh, Sera? Um, yes, of course."

"And very beautiful, I might add."

Zeno looked down and around, anything to avoid eye contact. He fumbled with his boots, pretending to lace them up, though they were already tied.

"It's clearly none of my business," Vesu said, "but Councilwoman Veti hosts a dance at the Capitol every summer. It's quite an elegant affair, I must say. You should invite Sera, if you're interested in attending."

Zeno let go of his shoelaces. "She probably thinks I'm dumber than a beetle. Plus, I'm a worthless dancer. You really think she'd go with me?"

"As a matter of fact, she has a peculiar fondness for beetles," Vesu said, laughing. "And Sera isn't so graceful herself. As you know, she's more of a bookworm—which is partially my fault, I suppose. Too much time in the library. But I think Sera would go if you asked her. I know you weren't seeking my advice, but I'm the Philosopher, remember, so I'm allowed to give it anyway. When you love someone, Zeno, keep them close. Don't make the same mistake I did, falling for someone a world away."

Zeno sat quietly for a moment, pondering Vesu's words. Up there in the Cloudhorns, he already felt too far away from Sera and Aris. He worried about the letters that Sera found, and the weatherbox in Mr. Marcel's shop. They had to be connected somehow.

"Speaking of Sera, I think she found something important. What she was trying to tell you last night in the library is that—"

"Shhh, do you hear that? The rain stopped."

Through the cedar's crown, yellow beams broke through at last. A sparrow-sized bird burst out of a nest in the upper branches, fluttering into the warmer air. The pinkish-purple plumage around its head and breast was easy to spot against the patches of clear blue sky.

"I think that's our sign to keep climbing," Vesu said. "I feel better after a little rest, but we need to find the Alpinees scouts soon. We don't have much time before the S&R guards start wondering where I've wandered off to."

Zeno and Vesu continued trudging up the mountainside. Zeno led the way, warning her about loose rocks and roots along the path. With more daylight to track the trail through the forest, Zeno was sure they were headed in the right direction. But he wondered why the Alpinees hadn't come to meet them yet. *I know they see us coming*, he thought. *They can see everything from up there.*

About an hour's hike from the cedar tree, the narrow trail opened up into a wider glade. The flat rocks and grassy areas made it a perfect location for another short break, if Vesu was ready for one.

"Madam Philosopher, would you like to stop here for . . ."

Zeno didn't finish his question because Vesu had veered off the path and was standing in the center of the glade, staring up at the sky with her hand over her eyes to shield the glare. *What in the Gorge is she looking at?*

Then Zeno saw the shadows racing across the ground: dark outlines of six long bodies, arms spread wide. *They found us. Finally.* He sprinted across the clearing to Vesu's side, reaching her just as the Alpinees scouts touched down. Their feet skidded on the gravel as they landed, scratching to a halt on the stones directly in front of her.

The six scouts towered over Vesu, their razor-sharp axes glinting a few feet from her face. In the direct midday sunlight, Zeno could see the threadlike ice-blue veins running under the Alpinees' nearly transparent skin. Vesu stood firm in her soggy, tattered dress. As filthy as it was, the material still glittered where the daylight struck her shoulders. Unfazed, she calmly and confidently addressed the lead scout.

"You must be Isolo. My name is Vesu, the Philosopher of Silver River Gorge. Mr. Harper brought me to see you so I could ask about a missing boy."

"Madam Philosopher," Isolo said in an urgent whisper. "I'm sorry, but we don't have much time." His mirror-like eyes flashed across the tree line behind her. "You have been followed."

"I beg your pardon, sir, but you must be mistaken. I have come here alone to ask you—"

"You have not come alone, whether you know it or not. S&R guards have been tracking you. About a dozen of them. The thunder masked the sound of their movements. They're climbing quickly, so we have only a minute or two. May I begin?"

Vesu was speechless. *My own guards? How did they know to follow us?* The thought was paralyzing. She scanned Isolo's eyes, searching desperately for a trick, a trap, or a lie. Any of those would be preferable to the truth. *My own guards.*

But Vesu found nothing sinister hiding in those two tiny mirrors. She saw only her own reflection; her tired eyes and her snarled, wet braids. She nodded for Isolo to continue.

"We don't have the boy. Yesterday the S&R seized him from a field near the Low Quarter, and then they set the outposts ablaze. I suspect your council accuses us of these crimes."

By the owl, I knew it! Zeno almost said it aloud but caught his tongue in time. He was relieved that his trust in the Alpinees had been affirmed, although he shuddered to think that the S&R had taken me.

"I hope you find the boy soon, although we are also in desperate need of your assistance." Isolo dropped to his knees so he could speak with Vesu face to face. "My dear friend, Amos Harper, told us that one of your predecessors designed a device that's capable of stirring up storms. Before we lost him, he said you were searching for it everywhere. Please, madam, tell us: what did you find?"

"Isolo . . . I can't . . . I don't . . ." Vesu was at a loss for words. The truth was that she had never helped Amos search for a weatherbox herself—not directly, at least. Once the council accepted the severity of his weather reports,

Vesu instructed Ozar to research the matter exclusively. For months on end, he barely left the library. He often stayed late into the night, hunched over the mahogany table, filling journal after journal with notes, maps, and charts. Vesu largely left him alone, and she asked Sera to do the same. She knew that Ozar preferred to work by himself.

When Ozar informed her that he had exhausted all possible sources, he handed over his papers for Vesu to review. As always, Ozar's work was a meticulous maze. The reference list was a volume in itself; even the footnotes had footnotes. In the end, however, his ultimate finding was compelling and straightforward: there was nothing to find. Every attempt to design a weather device had failed. *The sky will give and take as it pleases, seeking its own balance.* That's what Vesu had told herself at the time. *The cleverest Philosopher could not control nature's chaos, try as they might.* Thus, Vesu had called off the search.

As Vesu stuttered, struggling to explain it all, Isolo reached into his pine-needle jacket and pulled out a bundle of flowers, holding them gently so as not to ruffle the petals that dangled like icicles from the stems. Zeno's lower lip tingled. He hadn't yet seen the flowers that the Alpinees used to heal him, but he remembered the taste. He was surprised to see that instead of a smooth surface, the teardrop-shaped petals had a crystalline, lattice-like texture. They appeared so fragile, as if any minute they might dissolve. Isolo handed the bouquet to Vesu.

"With the right care and support, these petals will help cure the worst addictions to those seeds. We can bring more, as much as your city needs. Just tell us where we might find such a contraption so we can protect our families, keep our home."

"Isolo, sir, I'm afraid I can't help you. My assistant searched every bookshelf from top to bottom, day and night—"

Swoosh-swoosh-swoosh-swoosh-swoosh.

The whirring sound came so suddenly that no one had time to react. An ice axe flew end over end past Vesu's head, slicing the arm of an Alpinees scout.

"Get down, madam!" Isolo yelled. "Zeno, take cover!"

Vesu hit the ground, instinctively protecting her head. Zeno, however, stood frozen in place. He stared in shock as the scout's ice-blue blood poured from the gash, turning purple as it made contact with the air.

"Zeno, turn around now!" Isolo's second warning hit its mark. Zeno shook himself out of his stupor and spun around. A line of S&R guards was storming out of the forest, axes held shoulder-high. The guards moved fast, spreading out in a circle and surrounding Isolo's crew.

"Scouts, form a wall," Isolo ordered, maintaining his composure. The four other Alpinees crept in closer, positioning themselves in a tight ring around Vesu, Zeno, and the injured scout. "Brace yourselves for battle," Isolo said under his breath. His scouts removed their ice axes from their leather sheaths and held the long weapons defensively across their bodies.

For a half minute, neither side advanced. A strained silence filled the thirty or so yards between the two bands of soldiers. The S&R broke it first.

"Ms. Vesu Doveney, Mr. Zeno Harper," a guard announced, stepping forward. Zeno didn't recognize him, but knew he was a sergeant by the silver medallions pinned to his front pocket. "You are both under arrest for failure to comply with council order number—"

"How can they be under arrest if you do not yet hold them?" Isolo asked.

The sergeant pretended not to hear him. "The violation of said order is treason, punishable by death. Therefore, in the name of the council—"

"You cannot kill them while we stand between you."

The sergeant gritted his teeth at Isolo's words. "Go ahead, savage. Try to stand your ground. Your group is outnumbered, two to one."

"In that case we're evenly matched. Each of my men is twice the fighter." Isolo slammed the shaft of his axe into the ground in a steady rhythm. The other scouts joined him, pounding the rocks in unison. As the menacing rhythm accelerated, the Alpinees rotated in place, sizing up the guards and staring them down.

The S&R shifted uneasily in their boots. While they waited for orders—to stand by or strike—the sergeant sensed their apprehension growing. The intimidation spread like poisonous air: his own heartbeat quickened along with the cadence. He realized that every second he waited, the Alpinees gained an advantage.

"For the Bridges!" the sergeant howled.

"For the Gorge!" the S&R guards screamed back, charging at the inner circle of scouts.

The Alpinees spiraled out from the center, each taking on two to three guards in close combat. Iron clanged against iron. Wooden handles split and cracked; spikes squished through soft flesh. With the sounds of war all around him, Zeno resisted the urge to join the fray. He remained at Vesu's side, ready to defend her and the wounded scout if any guards broke through the wall.

Fortunately, Isolo's words were not an empty threat. The scouts effectively held the line, and then began to pull ahead. Zeno counted the gray S&R uniforms as they collapsed lifelessly to the ground. *Three, four, five . . .*

Then, to his right, an Alpinees scout groaned in extreme pain. The stinging cry creaked like a tree toppling over, and the scout fell onto his back. Purple fluid pooled on the rocks. Two S&R guards trampled over his body, heading straight toward Vesu.

Two at once. Alright, I'll need to fight like the Alpinees then. Zeno lifted the injured scout's axe. It was too heavy to hoist over his shoulder to swing, so Zeno pointed it out like a spear. "Don't come any closer," he warned, jabbing at the air in front of the guards.

The weapon was enough to slow them down. The guards stalked back and forth like wolves, staying out of reach. Zeno expected Isolo or another scout to come to his aid, but they had not yet noticed the breach in the wall, still tied up in their own skirmishes. The guards saw it too and seized the advantage. They spread apart, forcing Zeno to protect the Philosopher from multiple angles.

"I see you've chosen a side," the sergeant said. His silver medals flapped as he moved sideways, dodging the spearpoint. "And to think that your father was one of us. What would Amos say if he saw you now?"

Zeno stopped waving his weapon. His eyes locked in on the sergeant's flashy, silver badges. Surging forward, Zeno thrust the spike at the sergeant's chest. The blow landed right where he intended: an inch below the badges, straight through the sergeant's heart.

The other guard stopped in his tracks, stunned by the quick strike. Zeno tried to yank out the spear to go after him too, but the shaft wouldn't budge. The sergeant had fallen backward after impact and was pinned to the ground. Zeno pulled harder, twisting, swiveling . . .

That three-second delay was all it took. The other guard made a break for Vesu, yanking her off the ground by her braids. He pressed the tapered blade of his axe against her neck.

"Stop, everyone. Let your weapons fall!" His command caught the Alpinees' attention, and the fighting abruptly ceased. The guard applied more pressure to Vesu's throat. "Leave us be, or I will carry out the traitor's sentence right here on these rocks."

The Alpinees lowered their axes and slowly backed away. Zeno, however, couldn't let go. He found his own hatchet lying at his feet, so he raised it up, preparing to hurl a shot at the guard's forehead.

But Isolo came up behind him before he could make that mistake. He grabbed Zeno's forearm and pried the handle from his fingers. "If you throw it, he'll kill her," Isolo whispered. "You defended her bravely. Now come with us."

Zeno's knees were shaking and he could barely walk, so Isolo lifted him over his shoulder. He headed toward the other scouts, who were already scrambling up the mountainside, carrying the wounded soldier. The friend they had lost in battle would stay behind.

As they climbed higher into the Cloudhorns, Zeno watched the six remaining S&R guards converge around Vesu. They locked iron cuffs around her wrists and marched her toward the trail. Even from a hundred yards away, Zeno could see what Vesu was still holding in her clenched fist: the bouquet of flowers with their clear, crystalline petals.

Chapter VIII

I think it's time that I warn you: I might very well be losing my mind.

When I "wake up" in the mornings, my eyes are already open, like windowsills with broken locks that rattle throughout the night. When I descend the marble stairs to the library to continue my work, the stone slabs wobble as though they'll cave in beneath me, or maybe crumble away like mud. And when the silver flames wash over me every time I exit the Grand Fireplace, the sensation lifts me up like a million microscopic bubbles, and I see stars.

So, suffice it to say, I'm not feeling entirely like myself these days. In an attempt to find balance, I often retrace the same worn-out line in the carpet that Vesu used to walk, contemplating everything that I've witnessed through the fireplace before I sit down to write. The pacing and meditating only helps so much though. I feel like I'm floating somewhere limitless—in a dark ocean or a night sky; it's hard to tell which one. Maybe it's both. Wherever I'm drifting, I'm drifting away, and I hope I can find my way back when it's over.

When I started this project months ago, I knew full well that confusion and disorientation would set in eventually. After all, this is not what the Grand Fireplace was intended for. Most Philosophers before me entered the fire only a few times per session, saving the grueling trips for matters of utmost concern to the council. For this assignment, however, I do not have that luxury. I walk through those flames once or twice each day.

The constant journeys back and forth are taking their toll on me. The space between then and now, here and there, has been blurred too many times. I thought if I got more sleep that my dreams would file the past and present onto the correct shelves in my brain, but my feather pillow is not quite the librarian I thought it would be. These days sleeping in late is about as effective as a chalkboard eraser. All the timelines I've drawn out are not really removed; they're just spread around. My own memories have blended together with so many others that they hover around inside my head like a chalk dust cloud.

Back when I started as a Philosopher's apprentice, I assumed it would be easy to see the truth when the shawl was passed on to me. I thought I would be able to rewind history and watch it over and over—a thousand times, if need be—until the answers I was seeking stuck out in time like evergreen trees poking out of the snow.

Once I conducted my first council meeting and presided over my first trial, I immediately felt the full weight of the feathers on my shoulders. It hit me that the truth can't be captured so easily. The Silver River still requires us to decide where to go, how long to stay, whom to trust, and what to believe. Now every time that I go back to watch these events unfold (especially the ones I'm about to share with you), I tear myself apart wondering whether I would have made the same choices. If I had a seat on the council, would I have cast the same vote at the Philosopher's trial? If I were Vesu, would I have chosen the same successor? Would I have had that strength?

Despite the persistent dizziness, writing this down helps me refocus, so stay with me a little longer. I keep finding the energy to move my pen across the page because I remind myself that, in a few days, I'll be the only bridge you have left. My journal will be the last record of Vesu's trial—and everything that came after, of course.

You'll have to forgive me, again, for rambling. I suspect you're tired of all these riddles. I'm afraid I don't have time for them anymore either, so I should probably get straight to the point: after the S&R arrested Vesu in the Cloudhorns, they locked her in a cell at the far end of the Capitol jail, which happened to be the same cage where they had hidden me.

Lying on the stone-cold floor of the jail cell, Vesu shivered. Despite the damp basement air and the cool draft, the S&R guards never offered her a blanket or a change of clothes. She was wearing the same silver dress from her hike with Zeno, and it still hadn't fully dried out. In the corner Vesu's sandals sat stacked together, caked with mud, the leather straps split. She rubbed her bare feet together to keep them warm.

She tried to fall back asleep, but the leaky ceiling was relentless: dripping, dribbling, drizzling. If the droplets had found a rhythm and stayed consistent, she might have drifted off. Instead, water trickled into the drain chaotically, making it difficult to distinguish between seconds, minutes, hours . . .

Vesu gave up trying to sleep. She sat up, rubbed her eyes, and put her glasses on. She couldn't see very far beyond the iron bars because the basement was completely dark. The guards had not yet come by with breakfast, which was when they normally lit the lanterns in the hallway.

I hope the day arrives soon, she thought. Vesu wasn't hungry, but the morning routine was her only way to keep track of the days passing by. She counted the bowls pushed up against the cell door. *One, two, three* . . . Each tin container was filled with cold, congealed oatmeal. Vesu hadn't taken a single bite since she arrived. After three full days, the mush was growing mold, although the guards never bothered to clear away the dishes. I suppose their negligence should come as no surprise. After learning that six of their comrades died taking Vesu into custody, perhaps the guards wanted the rats to come crawling.

Let the rats come, Vesu thought. *I won't be here much longer.* She was not allowed any visitors, and the guards were prohibited from speaking to her. Nevertheless, she sensed that her prosecution was imminent simply by the sounds of the previous night: other prisoners whispering down the hall, more guards shuffling past her cell. *If my trial is today, I better be prepared.*

Vesu acknowledged that all the evidence was against her, so it wasn't her defense that needed preparation. Taro's snare had snapped; his case was made. Vesu could practically hear the councilman's arguments already: "The guiding light of this governing body—our own Philosopher—has conspired with the Alpinees. Not only is that solemn trust forever lost, so are the lives of those brave guards who made the ultimate sacrifice . . ." The council would have no choice but to find her guilty, regardless of the defense she put forward, regardless of her otherwise shining record.

Don't get the wrong impression. Vesu wasn't planning an apology or any type of plea deal. *I'll let Taro's game play out, whatever his motives might be.* Vesu was focused solely on her next move, on what she could control. She was concerned with what would come after the closing arguments, after the council handed down its verdict: her selection of a successor.

Vesu knew the rules of procedure better than anyone. For violation of the order, the council had the authority to strip Vesu of her title, banish her from the Gorge, or take her life as punishment. But that is where its power ended. The council could not dictate who would wear the shawl next; that was for Vesu to decide. I can assure you that the Philosopher's choice in this regard is inviolable, protected by precedent going back centuries. The Grand Fireplace simply won't work if that selection is stolen or coerced.

What is not guaranteed, however, is that every Philosopher will choose wisely.

So, Vesu spent those three days in confinement evaluating her decision carefully.

At first the answer seemed obvious. Ozar had served exceptionally well as her Junior Philosopher, and his attention to detail was unrivaled, along with his work ethic. Indeed, Vesu regarded Ozar as the most meticulous researcher ever to walk the library's aisles. When he delved into a subject, even unchartered waters, few facts or figures escaped his net. Many of Vesu's most important initiatives had passed due to Ozar's investigative work.

As Vesu considered it further, perhaps Ozar's political skills were more valuable than his scholarship. After all, he could read the council members far better than she could. Ozar understood their interests, personalities, and pressures. Vesu would be the first to admit he had a better handle on the political winds blowing through the council chamber.

Considering all they had accomplished together, Vesu never questioned his loyalty; she had no reason to suspect he was keeping any secrets.

And yet, something about the silence down in that lonely cell forced Vesu to rethink everything. *Maybe I need to look closer.* Despite Vesu's experience, and the City of Sterling's entire history at her fingertips, someone had still managed to set a trap that she never saw coming.

Alright, what am I missing? In the fuzzy darkness Vesu had to blink a few times to confirm that her eyes were open. She began pacing across the cell, one brick wall to the other, going over every memory from the last month. She replayed the conversation with Isolo that had been cut short. *What if a weatherbox does exist?* That led her to reconsider the copious notes that filled Ozar's journals about the mountain climate. Notwithstanding her lack of sleep, her memory was sharp. She pictured the weather pattern diagrams, the climate modeling, and the catalog of inventions and contraptions, every single one a failure. *Ozar never overlooks anything.*

"Excuse me, Miss," a shaky voice said from across the hall. "May I ask you a question?"

At first Vesu wasn't sure whether the voice was real or if the echoey basement was playing tricks on her again.

"You wouldn't happen to have any seeds, would you? Any trills, I mean?" Vesu was certain she had heard it this time. In the unlit cell across from hers, the outline of another prisoner shuffled back and forth. The wobbly voice matched perfectly with the man's wiry frame.

"No, I'm afraid I can't help you," Vesu said.

"It's alright, Miss. I had to ask. I'm starting to feel the jitters all over again, if you know what I mean."

No, Vesu thought, *I don't know what you mean. At least not as well as I should.* To be sure, Vesu had known for years that the seeds were a scourge on the lower quarters, tearing apart families and taking countless lives. Looking back on it now, she regretted that she never took the time to walk the streets of the Low Quarter to see the destruction firsthand. She had heard the reports and read all the letters, but she never took any action. Instead, Vesu chased the council's day-to-day crises, all of which seemed so insignificant now as she looked up at them from the Capitol's basement. *By the owl, I should have let those distractions wash right down the drain: drip, dribble, drizzle . . .*

Well, it's too late to do anything now. Vesu shuddered. She wasn't sure if it was the damp cold that raised the fine hairs on her skin or the overwhelming shame that bubbled up as she reflected on her failures. Whatever its source, the chill was becoming unbearable, and Vesu desperately hoped her trial would be held soon. She acknowledged full well that the time to pass on the Philosopher's shawl had come.

Then Vesu realized another hope of hers was slipping down the drain with the rest of the water.

I'll never see him again, will I?

After all these years she still remembered how handsome Elerin looked the day they borrowed a skiff and paddled out into Imperial Bay to watch the sailboats come in. Though his smooth tan skin would be wrinkled by now and his caramel-colored hair salty white, he had not lost his youthful way of looking at the world. She knew that through his letters. *I couldn't have lasted this long without his letters.*

In addition to his formal correspondence, Elerin wrote to Vesu privately to keep their relationship alive. She saved every page. They had always planned to see each other again once Vesu stepped down and the king released the ambassador from his official duties, but now there was no way the S&R would set her free, let alone write another letter.

I'll never get a chance to say goodbye. Wrapping her arms around herself to keep warm, Vesu closed her eyes and listened intently to the background sounds of the prison, waiting for the guards to open the door and light the lanterns.

Wait a second. As Vesu squeezed her arms against her chest, she felt something crinkle inside her dress pocket. *The feather.* She pulled out the raspberry-purple plume that had fallen at her feet under the cedar tree with Zeno. In the dark it was impossible to see the feather's colorful streaks, but her memory of the bright bird songs was so clear that it drowned out the leaky ceiling. From her other pocket Vesu carefully withdrew the bundle of snowrose that Isolo had given her. The pale green stems and brown leaves were smooshed together, although the tiny crystalline petals were still intact. *Maybe not all is lost.*

"Pardon me," Vesu said to the man across the hall. "I apologize for being short with you. What's your name?"

Gobu was surprised to receive a response. The strange woman across the hall had ignored him for days, like everyone else coming in and out of that place. "You can call me Gobu, Miss. What's your name?"

"Oh my, I hadn't thought about that yet. I'm not sure what they'll call me, or if the council will even give me a proper name when it's all said and done."

Gobu wasn't sure what Vesu meant by her remark, and he didn't bother to ask. He was simply glad that he had someone to talk to. "I'm sorry you're stuck in here. The food isn't so bad once you get used to it. The hardest part is watching all the prisoners come and go. You never really get to know anyone. Like the boy, for instance. The boy they kept in your cell. I offered him an extra blanket when my cellmate moved out, but the guards didn't want anyone talking to him. No one, not a word."

"Gobu, whom do you mean? What boy?"

"I don't know. Never got his name. He couldn't have been older than ten or eleven, so I can't imagine what he did to get locked up in here. And two guards watching him around the clock like that?"

"Two guards?"

"The chief escorted him out the day before they brought you in. I hope he's back with his family, sitting by a warm fire. That little man was freezing down here. He couldn't stop shaking, shivering. Yes, I hope he has a fire going by now."

Bimo. Vesu didn't want to admit it, but it had to be. The overwhelming shame percolated up again, prickling her skin. *Bimo was right here while I was searching in the mountains. How did I get so lost?*

As Vesu considered Gobu's story, moments from the past couple of months came flooding back in bursts, like a ship taking on waves in a storm. *Sera noticed something strange about the letters from Ambassador Elerin. What could it have been? Zeno asked me to visit his father through the fireplace. Why didn't I listen? Sera tried to tell me what they found in the Mid Quarter. What in the Gorge was it?* These memories floated by her, out of reach, like splinters of a shipwreck bobbing in tidewaters. Vesu wished she could swim closer, put the pieces back together somehow, but the undercurrent was too strong and her feet couldn't reach the bottom. Vesu accepted that she wouldn't find the answers before the end. All she could do now was pass on the shawl to the next Philosopher, someone who could navigate through this storm.

Thank you, Gobu, Vesu thought. *Now I know who I must choose. But I better do it carefully.*

As she placed the tiny feather back in her pocket, the jail door creaked open and two pairs of boots clicked down the hall. Vesu sensed the guards were moving quicker that morning, hurriedly lighting each torch along the hallway.

"Gobu, I won't have time for a proper goodbye. But I can give you something else that's more useful.

Vesu squeezed her slender shoulder through the iron bars, extending her arm as far as it would go. She gripped the snowrose tightly in her fist, careful not to shake the flowers' delicate petals.

"I don't have any trills, but I'm not sure you'll need them anymore. Press a few of these petals under your lips. They should help with your jitters and sleeplessness."

Gobu grabbed the snowrose as the two S&R guards arrived shoulder to shoulder at Vesu's cell. One guard kicked the bowls of oatmeal out of his way, spilling the gray mush on the floor. The other unlocked her cell.

"Madam Philosopher, come with us. Your trial is scheduled to begin shortly."

"You won't allow me to change my clothes?"

"That's not my decision, madam. The councilman gave us orders to take you directly to the chamber." The guards snapped cuffs around her wrists. Vesu followed their shadows into the yellow-orange glow of the hallway, her bare feet numb against the frigid stone floor. She stopped momentarily outside Gobu's cell.

"Feeling any better?" Although only a minute or two had gone by, color was returning to Gobu's cheeks. His muscles seemed more relaxed, his breathing slow and steady.

"Much better, madam, thank you. You have a soft heart, very kind."

"Will you shut up already, Gobu?" a guard said. "We'll be back for you next."

"I'll be here waiting, taking a little rest." Gobu reclined on his bed and folded his hands across his chest. *What did she say her name was?* He wondered, yawning. *Oh, I'm sure it will come back to me. A kind woman, a soft heart . . .*

His thoughts dissolved into a deep sleep.

⬤

"Ladies and gentlemen, may I have your attention," Councilman Taro said from the Philosopher's podium, tapping his rings on the wood surface. The crowd went silent almost immediately. "The Sterling City Council is gathered here today as a tribunal, called to consider the allegations against Vesu Doveney, the Philosopher. She has been charged with a violation of the council's emergency order that locked the North Gate and prohibited any citizen from leaving the city limits."

Sitting at a side table next to Ozar, Sera watched Taro pause to take a sip of water. The tendons in his neck tightened and flexed. He removed the ivory comb from his pocket and groomed the precise lines in his hair. *By the owl, he doesn't even try to hide it anymore*, Sera thought. *Let's get on with it already.*

"Everyone is aware of the unprecedented nature of these proceedings," Taro continued, putting his comb away. "A Philosopher has never been charged with a high crime. Punishment for such an offense may include demotion, exile, or death, if the council so votes. With so much at stake, let me assure you that the council places the integrity of these proceedings above all else. As councilman over foreign affairs, I will serve as prosecutor for this case. And in fairness to the accused, her colleague, Ozar, will take on the role of defense counsel. We will begin our opening arguments shortly. Mr. Harper, you may play the opening hymn."

Sera shot a glance at Aris, who was standing next to the stage near Councilwoman Numa. As he raised his bow to strike the first note, she could tell his hands were trembling. *Come on, Aris. You can do this.*

Sera and Aris had selected the song, "Hymn to the Swallows," together. They chose the hymn with the hope that its graceful melody would soften the hearts of the council members before they considered Vesu's case. Aris's opening performance was important because they would need every advantage they could get.

Over the last three days, Sera had spent every waking minute in the library trying to build a case. Unfortunately, she didn't have much to work with. Most infuriating was that Vesu herself was off limits. Despite Sera's arguments for due process (and basic decency), the council promptly ratified Chief Gaffney's directive barring any communication with Vesu until trial, including any visits from her defense counsel. Sera briefly considered sneaking in, but the S&R made that impossible: multiple guards were stationed outside the Capitol jail at all hours. Vesu was so thoroughly isolated, she might as well have been locked up in the armory.

Another challenge standing in her way was the code of silence between the S&R guards. None of them were willing to share what they had seen in the mountains, so Sera knew very little about the events leading up to Vesu's arrest. She only knew what was considered common knowledge across Sterling by then: that the S&R broke up a secret meeting between Vesu, Zeno, and the Alpinees, and that the confrontation ended with six S&R guards dead.

After hours of arguing back and forth, Ozar convinced Sera that they couldn't possibly defend the charges head on. Instead, they compiled a list of Vesu's achievements during her tenure as Philosopher, hoping the council would consider her contributions and show mercy at sentencing.

When they started to put pen to parchment, Sera fully expected the list to be long. But after three days of research, the record of Vesu's accomplishments was more extensive than she anticipated. Education, environment, economy—

few aspects of life in the Gorge remained untouched by her leadership. While the shawl rested on Vesu's shoulders she had convinced the council to expand services for the elderly, open food banks in the lower quarters, and fund restoration work on the Four Bridges. Her paramount success, in Sera's view, was that the armory remained sealed, the whitefire crossbows safely out of reach. This was no small feat. Every other year a proposal would surface to reequip the S&R, but Vesu had managed to defeat those initiatives time after time. "Weapons designed for massacres," is how she described them, "not for self-defense." That was where the Grand Fireplace was most useful. Vesu chronicled the firearms' bloody history in graphic detail to convince the council that, no matter the reason, the risk would devour the reward.

As you might imagine, going through Vesu's many accomplishments in such short order left Sera overwhelmed. The list that was supposed to save Vesu was making Sera more afraid to lose her by the minute. And Zeno's absence around the Capitol drained the color out of everything. Sera had never been afraid of heights before, yet now she recognized the feeling perfectly. The simple act of climbing a library ladder made her queasy. At night in her dreams, she found herself trapped at the edge of a cliff, blindfolded, forced to crawl on her hands and knees to stay balanced. Sera's instincts told her that Zeno was safe—he knew his way around the mountains—but the ground under her feet wouldn't feel stable until she had answers.

Through the rush of the past seventy-two hours, Ozar also seemed on edge, absent and apprehensive. Sera had no reason to suspect any secrets, so she gave him space and time alone to process everything. *The pressure must be immense*, she thought. She couldn't fathom following in the footsteps of a Philosopher like Vesu who had forever changed the Silver River Gorge.

Then again, maybe the harder part was taking the reins from a Philosopher convicted, a Philosopher disgraced. If the council shared a fraction of the public's sentiment, the shawl would be thrust upon him. Ozar would be wearing the feathers before sunset, ready or not. Sera tried to stay hopeful. *Vesu's victories won't be sufficient to keep her title, but perhaps they'll be enough to save her life.*

With all of this in mind, you can see why Sera counted on Aris's performance to be nothing short of spellbinding. She needed him to conjure up the same level of emotion that, weeks ago, had helped delay Taro's motion.

As the hundreds of spectators in the council chamber took their seats, Aris began to play. "Hymn to the Swallows" started off with a swift series of notes that danced, flute-like, up the stadium rows of the council chamber and then collected, cloud-like, along the domed ceiling. The airy refrain was reminiscent of an innocent breeze lifting dandelion seeds into the sunlight.

Yes, Aris, that's it!

Holding its collective breath, the crowd gazed up and around in anticipation. It was hard to believe the song would ever fall back to earth. It might simply float forever.

As with everything else, however, gravity took hold. After hovering through the chorus, the hymn cascaded downward in eighth notes, the sound waves refracting into light as they passed through the chandeliers. The crystal and glass gave the illusion that the tempo was accelerating: the eighth notes split into sixteenth notes, the sixteenths into thirty-seconds (or so it seemed to Sera, anyway).

Aris, it's working. Keep going!

Aris pulled back the tempo gradually, preparing his transition into the hymn's second movement. Then his careful fingers, always so precise, slipped. A wrong note. The mistake was subtle, but Sera cringed.

Something is wrong.

Then another errant note, a sharp that should have been a flat.

Aris, what's going on? Are you okay?

Sera scanned the audience to see if anyone else had noticed, to see if the spell had been broken so soon.

That's when she saw it. The entire crowd had risen to its feet, the music forgotten, ignored. All eyes were on the double doors at the far end of the chamber where two S&R guards led Vesu up the stairs to the round stage. Gasps and murmurs buzzed through the room like wasps.

From her chair on stage, Sera stood up to get a better view. She immediately regretted it. When she caught sight of Vesu, Sera's skin crawled, and then it burned. The sensation felt like a thousand stinging bees. Now it was clear why Aris had lost his composure. Vesu's silver dress was spotted with mud, fraying at the edges, and her braids were twisted, tangled. She squinted behind her ivory-framed glasses as though the light from the chandeliers was blinding.

Near the top of the stairs, Vesu yanked her arms away from the guards so she could climb onto the stage under her own power. Aris's violin faded away. "Hymn to the Swallows" sounded too shrill now. Even Taro was apparently startled by the Philosopher's appearance. He coughed to clear his throat.

"Ms. Doveney, please take a seat at the defense table. I will begin with the prosecution's opening arguments."

Vesu sat in the chair between Ozar and Sera. Without the slightest sign of nervousness, she adjusted her silver dress and cleaned her glasses with her sleeve. Sera, by contrast, couldn't hold still. Her feet twitched restlessly, her heels tapping on the floor. She could barely hold herself back. Sera's instinct was to wrap her arms around Vesu and squeeze as hard as she could. She wanted to whisper that everything would be fine, that they would defend her, that the council would show mercy. No, better yet, she would stand up before the council immediately, before Taro twisted her words, and ask Vesu what really happened in the Cloudhorns. She would scream for the S&R to bring the Philosopher her proper clothes, shoes, and shawl, or else . . .

Right before Sera burst, Vesu took her hand under the table where the council members couldn't see it and pressed their palms together, interlocking their fingers. The simple gesture was enough to send her message clearly: *Zeno is safe somewhere, and I'll be alright. Don't put yourself in any more danger.*

I won't repeat here what you already know (it's painful for me to write out anyway). I will only say that Taro presented exactly the case you would expect. He called as witnesses every S&R guard who followed Vesu into the Cloudhorns that day. Each one told the same story, which Taro spun into an unambiguous act of treason: Vesu and Zeno refusing to obey the S&R's orders, and the Alpinees rising to their defense. Taro closed his case with a moment of silence for the six guards who had perished. "The Four Bridges will hold them in our history forever, but let us show our respect by calling out their names once more in this chamber."

Against the backdrop of this heavy silence, Ozar took the podium to present Vesu's defense. Sera handed him the scroll with the list of Vesu's accomplishments, which nearly touched the floor when it was unfurled. In a measured voice, Ozar offered his entreaty. "Fellow citizens, council members. Sterling is a remarkable place. One of a kind, we would all agree. At the same time, we readily acknowledge that this city is not without its faults, its vulnerabilities. We have made our fair share of mistakes.

"And so it is with each of us as individuals. When the time comes for your name to be inscribed into the Four Bridges, how do you want to be remembered? Only for your lowest moments? Or for your life considered as a whole?

"With these questions in mind, I urge the council to consider the evidence against Vesu Doveney with mercy. Look beyond the darkness of recent events, and consider her brilliant tenure as Philosopher in its entirety. Let me take this opportunity to remind you of everything that she has accomplished."

As Ozar went on to describe Vesu's successes at length, Sera gauged each councilmember's reaction. Veti, Rolu, Numa . . . She was looking for any subtle sign—an eye twitch, a head nod, a shoulder shrug—that might reveal their vote. For the council to hand down a death sentence, the decision had to be unanimous. *We only need one to save her*, Sera kept telling herself, *just one*.

An hour passed and then another. Ozar didn't reach the end of his list until the chamber's clock struck seven; Vesu's trial had lasted a full day. Sera was sure the council members were moved to some extent—their initial shock during the guards' testimony was showing cracks—but she couldn't tell if it would be enough to demolish Taro's case. She gave up trying to guess, bowing her head as Ozar concluded his remarks.

"Council members, in light of everything you've heard today, please take this to heart: while we expect our Philosophers to guide us through storms, remember that they cannot always predict the weather. Such a life should be evaluated in full, from cover to cover. And Vesu Doveney's story shows that she cares deeply for the City of Sterling. Indeed, she loves nothing more."

Those closing words were Sera's cue. She knew the routine well. With hundreds of spectators watching in silence, Sera carried a straw mat and wooden bowl to center stage. Vesu rose from her seat and followed. After rolling out the mat, Sera set the bowl beside it, careful not to spill its contents. A hundred trillium seeds, maybe more, were piled up inside. *Such a cruel disguise*, Sera thought as she returned to her table. *That benign light-green, that shiny-smooth skin . . . no marks of any poison. No warning at all.*

Vesu fell to her knees on the straw. If the council voted to convict her, the sentence would be imposed right then and there.

Councilman Taro took to the podium. "The time has come for us to cast our votes. Where I stand on the matter, you already know. Vesu Doveney is guilty of this high crime, and I propose the law's highest penalty. Councilwoman Veti, do you concur?"

With her head down and her hands cupped over her mouth, Veti's response was barely audible. "Yes, I do." She buried her face in her silk scarf.

"Councilman Rolu, do you concur?"

"Aye," he said, tugging on his black beard.

"That leaves the councilwoman from the Low Quarter, the last voice to be heard. Do you agree with your colleagues?"

Councilwoman Numa stood up and buttoned her coat. The chamber was so quiet that Sera could hear the mob chanting outside as they awaited the verdict.

"Yes," she said, "I find the Philosopher guilty of these charges." As the significance of her words spread up the chamber's rows, the audience was on the verge of erupting, but Taro raised his arms immediately to silence the room. His rings flashed under the light of the chandeliers.

"Ms. Numa, you failed to comment on the punishment. How do you vote?"

"I am not convinced, Councilman, that this crime warrants execution. Under the circumstances, I believe the more appropriate—"

"Ms. Numa," Taro interrupted. "I hoped it would not come to this, but I must disclose another matter to the council."

Sera choked; she had to remind her lungs to breathe. *What in the Gorge . . . ?* She swiveled toward Ozar. He appeared to be unfazed, his hands folded in his lap. *Are you not hearing this?*

"Normally, I would never hold back information of such consequence from my colleagues," Taro said, sliding the rings on and off his fingers. "I did so here in an attempt to preserve the position, to protect the Philosopher's honor. Councilwoman Numa intends the same, I believe, in seeking to spare the Philosopher's life. But she deserves to know the full story. Guards, please distribute the letters."

The S&R brought out a stack of papers to each desk. The council members flipped through the pages as Taro gave his report. "You are reading a series of letters intercepted by the S&R. Without the council's knowledge, the Philosopher communicated with Imperial Bay through Ambassador Elerin. Mr. Wrinn must have misspoken a minute ago when he said that Vesu loves nothing more than our city, for we've uncovered a love affair, or so it appears. Take a look for yourself."

Any ounce of sympathy that the council members had shown earlier evaporated. The proof was laid out right in front of them: intimate messages, by the hundreds, exchanged back and forth between Vesu and Elerin. It only took a few sentences to see the relationship was more than a recent fling. The letters referenced private moments that the two had shared many years ago.

The chamber grew foggy as Sera fought back tears. For a moment, amidst the commotion, her eyes connected with Vesu's. *Madam, is it true?*

Vesu nodded.

Sera slammed her notebook shut, and the gust of air sent a few pages flying off the table. *Her long-lost lover in Imperial Bay was Ambassador Elerin? Why would Vesu keep this a secret from me?* Through hot tears Sera couldn't read her own notes anymore. The outline she had prepared of Vesu's accomplishments was a blur. The white papers scattered across the table looked like snow melting into slush.

"Of course, the romance itself is not the real danger," Taro continued. "Another letter for Vesu arrived this week from Imperial Bay. The message reveals that the king is marshaling troops to reinforce the Royal Army's South Branch." Taro marched over to Numa and tossed the letter onto her desk. "Would you like to examine the signature, councilwoman?" Of course, the ambassador's swooping script was unmistakable; Ozar had made sure of that. "Do you want to reconsider your vote?"

"Taro, would you give it a rest?" Vesu barked from center stage. She had kept so quiet throughout the trial that her outburst caught everyone off guard. She pushed her braids away from her face, and her eyes flashed silver in the light. "Before you make the councilwoman choose, I believe we have another item of business. The council rules still allow for my selection of a successor."

Caught by surprise, Taro faltered through a few words. He stole a glance at Ozar and then tidied a loose lock of hair. "Go ahead, madam, but make it quick."

"Fellow countrymen and friends, I kneel before you today knowing that I let you down. Every single day as your Philosopher, I searched the Silver River for the truth. I trusted that its light and its warmth would keep us together through the long, cold nights that always come. And I have never lost that trust.

"But what I failed to see, until recently, is that the truth vibrates in the sound around us. So, let me share one last bit of advice: listen to those who love you, even when the words are hard to hear."

Vesu pushed up the threadbare sleeves of her silver dress. "As for my selection of a successor, that decision became self-evident once I heard what Sterling needed most. In fact, my appointment has already been made."

With that, Vesu reached out and cradled the wooden bowl with both hands. *No, Vesu! No!* Sera screamed to herself as the Philosopher tilted her head back as far as it would go, her eyes looking past the chandeliers, beyond the sparkling blue stained-glass dome. Then Vesu swallowed the seeds, all of them, all at once.

🜊

Ozar sat relaxed in his chair at counsel's table and looked up and around the chamber. Chaos was unfolding in every direction. Three hundred and sixty degrees of shouting and cursing and yelling about what Vesu's parting words could possibly mean. *Well, this is not how I expected my first few minutes as the Philosopher to begin.* Ozar waited patiently until the S&R carried Vesu's body offstage. Then he stepped up to the podium.

"Order in the chamber, please. Ladies and gentlemen, come to order."

No one was ready to listen. Ozar rang the Philosopher's bell a few times, but it wasn't enough. *I'll have to try a different approach.* He crumpled up one of Vesu's letters to Ambassador Elerin, struck a match, and lit the parchment on fire. The red-orange blaze at center stage caught everyone's attention. As the smoke curled up into the chandeliers, the crowd hushed, and Ozar stomped out the flames, leaving streaks of black ash across the marble floor.

"Thank you. That is much better. Now that I can hear myself think, we should get back to business."

"But Mr. Wrinn," councilwoman Numa said, "who will preside over the council?"

Ozar bent back one wrist until it popped and then the other. "I thought Vesu's directions were obvious."

"Obvious? She didn't name her successor," Veti said.

"I understood her decision quite clearly, sir," Taro broke in. "Vesu said her choice was 'self-evident,' that the new Philosopher has already been appointed. That could only mean Mr. Wrinn is the lawful heir. For hundreds of years the custom and practice has been for the shawl to be handed down to the Junior Philosopher. And Mr. Wrinn has served Vesu loyally for the better part of two decades, defending her record before this council up until the very end."

Easy, Taro, no need to overplay your hand, Ozar thought.

"Thank you, Councilman," he said. "That is also my understanding of Ms. Doveney's final wishes. For the sake of completeness, we should hear from the Philosopher's apprentice. Ms. Avery, do you have any reason to doubt Vesu's intentions?"

"No, Ozar. No *sir*, I mean," Sera said. Her eyes were still red with resentment. "Vesu didn't say a word to me about any of this."

"Thank you, Ms. Avery. Does the council have any evidence to the contrary? Any objections to my appointment?"

Veti, Rolu, and Numa shook their heads. They knew Taro was right; the Junior Philosopher was next in line for a reason. If Vesu meant to designate someone else, she could have simply announced another name. After a long day of revelations, the council was eager for certainty. They wanted to go home with the reassurance that their new leader would be someone familiar, someone with experience.

An S&R guard brought out the Philosopher's black-and-white speckled shawl. Veti, as the senior councilmember, met Ozar on stage to administer the oath. "Mr. Ozar Winn, do you swear to protect the Silver River Gorge and every citizen inside?"

"On my honor, until the river runs dry," he answered. Veti draped the shawl over his shoulders and then fastened the clasp. Standing at the podium, Ozar fidgeted for a moment, adjusting the collar around his neck. The snowy owl feathers fit awkwardly, like they were one size too small. *A minor discomfort,* he thought. *I'll have it altered soon enough.*

"Ladies and gentlemen of Sterling, let me start with a promise. I will be a different Philosopher than all those who came before me. The Silver River is not merely a bridge to the past; it is also the map to our future. For too many years we have relied on our remote location, on our mountain geography, to keep us safe from our enemies. I'm here to warn you that a thousand miles won't be enough to protect us from Imperial Bay. We need a stronger defense."

The audience rumbled in agreement. Ozar opened the drawer of the Philosopher's podium and removed a leather-bound book, which he held high in the air. "Orso the Bold, a former Philosopher whom I admire greatly, said it best: 'Every raindrop that falls in Imperial Bay will flow through the Gorge eventually.' What he meant was that the troubles, the greed, and the ambitions of kings and queens will find us here sooner or later. The City of Sterling cannot play dead and expect death to leave us alone."

"How will we defend ourselves?" Rolu asked. He held up the page that Taro had tossed on Numa's desk. "The ambassador's last letter indicates the Royal Army is building up the South Branch."

Very good, Rolu, Ozar thought. *Now you're seeing the world the way I do.*

"Vesu's betrayal has set us back. Indeed, her position on these matters has left us vulnerable all along. However, we are not helpless, and we never have been." Ozar tossed the book to Rolu, who caught it easily with his giant hands. "For those of you who may not remember, Orso was the same Philosopher who invented the whitefire crossbows. He built them using the embers from the First Fire, which burn so hot that they glow bright white, even to this day."

"Excuse me, Ozar," Veti said, "but are you suggesting that we unlock the armory?"

"Please use my proper title, councilwoman. And no, that decision is one the council should consider carefully. But I think you would agree that we must act soon, perhaps at the next council meeting. It is impossible to predict when those red-and-white stripes will come marching across our fields. Six months from now? A year? The only thing we know for sure is that they will come eventually."

The council members talked amongst themselves for some time while Ozar organized his papers and collected his thoughts. *My garden is blooming at last. By next month the fruit will be ripe enough to harvest.*

Sensing the excitement was over, members of the public began filing out. Ozar took care of a few formalities, appointed Sera as the Junior Philosopher, and then prepared to adjourn his first meeting.

"Mr. Philosopher, sir!" Chief Gaffney's voice shot through the chamber like a cannonball. Taking two stairs at a time, he bounded down the aisle from the balcony toward the stage. "May I speak with you alone in the library?"

"Chief Gaffney, I was about to end our session. Whatever it is can wait."

"I'm afraid it can't, sir. The matter is urgent."

Ozar scowled at him. *What could possibly be more pressing than our plan? With Vesu out of the way, your guards will be holding those crossbows in one month's time. Don't you see that?* "If the subject is so important, then the council should hear your report directly. Unlike my predecessor, I will not keep secrets from the council."

By the time he got up on stage, Gaffney was winded. He gave his report with his hands on his knees. "Mr. Philosopher, the guards stationed at the North Gate towers spotted hundreds of flickering lights about three miles northeast, where the shortgrass fields meet the forest. They appeared to be campfires, but with the sun setting behind them, the guards assumed it was merely an illusion caused by the glare." He paused to catch his breath. Beads of sweat collected in his grayish-yellow mustache. He wiped them away with the back of his sleeve. "At any rate, I thought it was worth investigating. When I arrived at the towers, the sun had set over the Cloudhorns, and we got a better view. The South Branch has entered the Gorge, sir. Several hundred soldiers."

"The Royal Army?" Taro asked. "That's quite a conclusion to draw at that distance. At dusk, no less. I'm sure it was a trick of light or shadow over the mountains. This valley is full of those."

"The councilman is right," Ozar said as he continued to pack up his papers. "I appreciate your vigilance, but you must be mistaken. The letters we intercepted from the ambassador make no mention of any immediate advances."

You must let this go, Ozar thought. *I have read the true letters from Ambassador Elerin. The South Branch has been instructed to stay far away from the Gorge.*

"With due respect, I know a proper military formation when I see one. If you don't believe me, I'll take you to the tower now. The council members should come too; we have carriages waiting outside. If the Royal Army attacks, I'm not sure how long the North Gate will hold."

Ozar wasn't persuaded. If it were up to him, he would have stayed back. He was ready to hunker down in the library and get to work on a motion to unlock the armory. After all, it was only half past ten. There was still enough time for Sera to light the Grand Fireplace so that Ozar could feel those silver flames for himself. He had waited so long for that.

However, his first step back in time would have to wait. The council followed Chief Gaffney to the carriages, so Ozar was obliged to go along for the ride. He boarded the last carriage with Sera.

The drivers whipped the horses through the Up Quarter's cobblestone streets. The rattling carriage, combined with the winding roads, made Ozar nauseous. It had been quite some time since he had ventured out of the Capitol building. In fact, Ozar couldn't recall the last time he had paid a proper visit to any of the neighborhoods. Usually, Sera volunteered for Vesu's assignments at the Four Bridges, and Palo ran all of Ozar's errands.

Ozar peeked through the curtains. The Up Quarter's multi-level buildings, with their elaborate timber frames, struck him as exotic. *Were these homes always so opulent?* Ozar didn't recognize any of the faces in the windows watching the caravan whiz by.

After the carriages cleared the Up Quarter, it didn't take long to reach the North Gate, where they parked at the base of the east tower. The guards shuffled the council members to the spiral staircase, sending them up single file. Ozar was the last one to reach the top.

Alright, let's see what has Chief Gaffney so alarmed.

Ozar set his elbows on the stone parapet and peered out into the night. Except for a thin band of clouds, the purple-black sky over the fields was clear. The canopy of stars was so vivid, in fact, that Ozar nearly lost his balance, overcome with the reminder that the planet was spinning beneath his feet. He stared down at the ground to center himself, breathing in the scent of the lands beyond the wall: the rich soil, the moss, the sweetgrass . . . the smoke? Ozar sniffed a few more times to check his senses. Yes, the smell of smoke was heavy, overpowering the regular aromas of the fields and forests. *A forest fire, at this time of year?*

Then he caught a whiff of boar meat cooking at high heat. Surveying the horizon a few miles out, Ozar spotted hundreds of flickering orange dots, too many to count. Against the orange glow, he saw tents. *How in the Gorge . . . I don't understand. The ambassador's letters to Vesu said the South Branch would remain in the Basin.*

"Now that you've seen it for yourself, sir, we need a plan." Gaffney approached Ozar at the tower's outlook. The four council members were standing in a row behind him, Sera off to one side and Aris behind her. "As far as I can tell, the South Branch has set up camp for the night. I don't expect them to attack over unfamiliar ground in the dark, though they could reach the gate before noon tomorrow if they leave at first light."

Ozar straightened out the shawl, which rested somewhat crookedly on his shoulders. He tugged on his chin, and his jawbone clicked. *I never doubted they would come for us, but I didn't think it would be so soon. No matter. The plan is merely accelerated; that's all.*

"The whitefire is our only choice. Opening the armory, though, requires all of us. Does everyone agree?"

Veti, Taro, Rolu, and Numa nodded.

"Mr. Philosopher, sir," Sera said. "Don't you think we should find out why they're here first?"

By the owl, she sounds like Vesu. I'll need to get that voice out of her head.

"If Vesu had not betrayed the council's trust, Ms. Avery, perhaps we could take that chance. But why would the South Branch arrive at our doorstep, armed and unannounced? We must assume the worst; otherwise, we are putting Sterling and its citizens at risk."

Sera squinted at the line of campfires blinking along the horizon. The orange glow was ominous. She clasped her arms behind her back and bowed her head. "You're right, Mr. Philosopher. We must be ready."

"Let's get moving, then," said Taro. "Mr. Philosopher, how do we open the armory?"

"I don't know, exactly," Ozar admitted. "The Philosophers who built it wrote that, upon a unanimous vote, 'the Philosopher will find the key in the Silver River.' Chief Gaffney, why don't you send a few guards down to the Four Bridges—"

"It's the river! The water!" The words gushed out of Sera's mouth.

"Yes, Ms. Avery, that's what I'm suggesting. We will search the river immediately."

"No, the river *is* the key! Do you remember the texture of the armory's walls? They're rock hard, but they're also gritty to the touch, like sand. An axe or hammer is useless against them, but water should wash away the surface. No, it *will* wash it away. I know it will, Mr. Philosopher."

Ozar grinned. *A very bright girl. I knew she would make the perfect assistant.*

"Chief Gaffney, you heard the Junior Philosopher. Send your men to the river at once with as many buckets as they can carry. Have them meet us at the armory."

Ozar turned back to gaze out at the fields, the tree line, and the sky. In his imagination he followed the Silver River north, flying like a bird over the Royal Army, past the Basin, through the midland forests, and across many miles of meadows until he landed above the white-sand beaches of Imperial Bay. He envisioned the view of the ocean and the royal gardens through the castle's stained-glass windows. *I'll rule it all with reason, not the randomness of bloodlines.*

Ozar was so deep in thought that he bit his lip too hard, and his canine tooth broke the pink skin. The blood tasted metallic . . . and sweet.

Chapter IX

It struck me this morning when I sat down to write that the ink-filled pages in my journal far outnumber the blank ones at the back. Counting the empty sheets until the end was quite encouraging, and by the owl, I needed the push. This small task gave me hope that I will finish this history soon, as I set out to do from the start, even though so many moments are excruciating to relive. I measured the height of the candles too, the ones lining the hearth, and there will be just enough light left to guide me.

If you visit Sterling before I'm gone, the route most people take is the gravel road along the river, which is a fine choice in any season. Coming in from that direction, you'll hear the singsong splashing of the rapids, and your clothes will smell pleasantly of sweetgrass for several days. Stop on occasion to peer through the reeds and you may spot a dragonfly, blinking blue, in broad daylight.

For my closest friends, however, I recommend another path. Instead of following the riverbank, head toward the middle of the meadow where you'll find a long, narrow garden overflowing with flowers. As your carriage moves closer, you'll see that the garden is a covered passageway—a tunnel of sorts—that leads directly to the North Gate. With sidewalls the height of almond trees, the tunnel is tall enough for a carriage to pass through, but I suggest you walk, if the weather is nice, to fully appreciate its beauty. Look up and you'll see that its canopy is a lattice of dense vines that provide perfect shade from the sun. Dangling from the ivy ceiling will be a million tiny flowers, bursting above you like fireworks frozen in time. The grapefruit-red and apricot-orange blossoms smell like citrus, as if you're walking through an orchard.

If you choose this path, keep in mind that the multicolored garden wasn't there when the walls of the armory washed away with river water, as Sera expected. The tunnel of flowers had not yet grown when Colonel Orowin arrived at the Gorge with his troops waiting in formation behind him.

No, as Orowin kicked Una into a trot toward the North Gate towers that afternoon in early summer, the northern meadows were still fields of plain, pale-green grass. It wasn't until an S&R guard fired the first whitefire blast in over a century that the landscape beyond the gate flared into red and orange, setting off a blaze that would spread across the continent.

Come to think of it, that spark would reach the ocean. Eventually.

Scribbling on a parchment page pressed against the back of one of his soldiers, Colonel Orowin finished his short letter and then signed his name at the bottom. Normally, he composed his letters at the table in his tent, but it was mid-morning, and the equipment had already been packed up. So, the young lad was the next-best option. *He'll get over the embarrassment on the ride home. And my cousin will forgive the poor penmanship.*

After folding the letter into an intricate star shape to protect it from prying eyes, Orowin spun the soldier around. "Take this letter directly to Ambassador Elerin at Imperial Bay. If the paper is unfolded before he receives it, you'll be tossed out to sea with a bloody baitfish around your neck, do you understand?" The young soldier nodded. "It's a long journey to make alone, so be careful," Orowin continued. "Consider yourself lucky that you'll see your family before the rest of us."

Orowin sent a single messenger hoping it would speed up the delivery, although he knew the letter might not reach Imperial Bay for a few months. *That should be quick enough*, he told himself. *As long as it gets to Elerin before any other news about our movements.*

With the message on its way, he surveyed the campground, looking for his captains. Una was ready to go, and it was time for Carolin and Pearlin to saddle up their horses too. They would depart together at noon for the North Gate.

Orowin felt confident about his plan despite Carolin's reservations. Over dinner the night before, he shared his decision to keep the first envoy small—only Carolin and Pearlin would ride with him to the S&R towers. The rest of the troops would stay a mile behind, maintaining a defensive formation until they received the signal to follow.

Carolin pushed back immediately. She insisted that the colonel bring additional men, a line of archers, at least, even if their only job was to stand there holding banners. "In case the welcome isn't as warm as we expect, sir," she said.

I share your fear more than you know, Orowin thought at the time, rotating a spear of boar meat over the campfire. He didn't dare say that part out loud though. His two captains still believed, as did the rest of the army, that the king had sent them to the Gorge to protect it. Every soldier in the South Branch took the mission seriously, along with Orowin's directive to safeguard the Prairie Riders. They finally had a reason to serve.

The real orders, of course, Orowin had shred into a thousand pieces. "Remain at your current location . . . Hold your position for the time being . . ." Elerin's sentences were now blowing around the Basin somewhere, indecipherable dust like all the rest of it.

I don't regret it for a second, Orowin told himself, although at times he did regret holding back the truth from Carolin and Pearlin. It wasn't that he didn't trust them; indeed, he had more faith in his two captains than anyone else on the continent. With that rare balance of head and heart, Orowin expected them to accomplish great things. More than he ever had. *That's why I must keep this to myself. The decision to disobey orders was my own, and I will accept whatever consequences may come.*

With his mind made up, you can see why Orowin had to disagree with Carolin delicately: she was right. Moving in without reinforcements would leave them vulnerable, but Orowin simply could not risk the alternative. Approaching the North Gate with too many men might set the S&R on edge. If one axe or one arrow was released too soon from either side, it would be impossible to pull back the rest.

So, Orowin raised every other argument he could think of. He relied mostly on the detailed briefings that Ambassador Elerin had provided before they left Imperial Bay. "My cousin said relations with Sterling have been better than ever, remember? And he spoke very highly of this Philosopher—Ms. Vesu Doveney, if I'm pronouncing that correctly. The adjectives he used were 'gracious' and 'wise.'" He paused while Carolin considered his case, washing down her dinner with a swig of rivershine. "The S&R don't concern me either—those axes are useless from a distance. In all likelihood, the Philosopher will welcome us at the gate with glasses of wine."

Carolin didn't say anything in response, but she also didn't object any further. The thought of that sweet purple drink must have been persuasive enough.

As the morning sun cleared Shoulder Ridge, Orowin realized that locating his two captains in the busy encampment before noon would be harder than he expected. The campgrounds were bustling with more activity than a track-and-field competition. The soldiers had already dressed and packed their belongings; in fact, most of them had their chores done before breakfast. The excitement of seeing snow-capped mountains after living in the Prairie Basin for so long was hard to hold back.

And to visit a city they had only heard about in stories? No wonder the regiment was full of energy. As Orowin passed through the rows of tents, he watched soldiers folding their clothes, grooming their hair, and restringing their bows, anything to keep busy while they jabbered about (and bet on) what Sterling would really be like. Out of respect they lowered their voices when the colonel passed by, but he picked up the substance of their conversations nonetheless. Bakeries, taverns, shops—all the little luxuries from home that they missed. To be fair, most of the soldiers were simply excited by the prospect of sleeping in a real bed, depending on how many troops the city would be able to quarter comfortably. Orowin couldn't help but grin as he listened to a group argue over how much they'd pay for the last room at the inn, if that's what it came down to.

After finding the captains' tents empty, Orowin led Una to the temporary stables, where he spotted Pearlin tending to the bison. She was using a hard-bristled brush to remove dirt and burs clinging to the animal's thick fur. The sight of Pearlin standing so close to the colossal creatures still made him nervous, though he was certain the bison wouldn't harm her. Every week that he traveled with the bison and the Prairie Riders, his respect for them grew, as did his curiosity. The creatures were opposites in almost every way: one round and rigid, the other long and flexible. One heavy as a boulder, the other light as a leaf. Yet, the way they worked together so naturally, covering for each other's weaknesses, fascinated him.

On some nights Orowin lost sleep over it, staying up late to jot down notes about their traits and behaviors. He was willing to put up with Carolin's jabs about sleeping in because it was worth it. In fact, he had developed a new idea to take his interest further. After making his acquaintance with the Philosopher, he would ask if he could search Sterling's renowned library for more information about the Riders. He marveled at how they moved and how they transformed into various shapes: soldiers, shelters, bridges, ladders. That inevitably spurred other questions: *Where did they come from? How do they eat, breathe, and think?* Perhaps when he retired, Orowin would give lectures about the Prairie Riders or write a book about them. He had never been much of an academic, but he was starting to realize that casting for rockfish in Imperial Bay would only hold his interest for so long.

Orowin was tempted to mention the Riders in his last letter to Ambassador Elerin. Always one for novelty, his cousin would have enjoyed a detailed description of the strangely elegant creatures. Ultimately, Orowin decided against it. He couldn't distract from his main message, captured succinctly in the letter's last two lines: *My soldiers are following my orders. Promise me they will not be punished.*

His curiosity notwithstanding, Orowin was getting ahead of himself. Before he wandered around any libraries, he had to discuss another important matter with the Philosopher: the weather. He had promised Pearlin that he would explain how the climate had changed so dramatically during their tour in the Basin. The persistent droughts were unnatural, the temperature unbalanced, and the river erosion unheard of. And it was only getting worse. For the Riders' sake, he hoped the Philosopher would have answers. *These creatures were born in the Basin. They belong there.*

Orowin wrapped Una's reins around the fencepost where Pearlin was working. "I had a feeling I'd find you here. Where's your coconspirator?"

Pearlin pointed to the field behind the stables where Carolin was conducting target practice. A group of archers stood behind her, watching every movement in awe. She tucked her wavy black hair behind her ears, aimed her aqua-blue eyes downfield, and pulled back the recurve bow as if the fifty-pound draw weight was merely ten. Smooth and effortless, she must have been holding her breath because her posture was perfectly still.

She never misses, Orowin thought. *Wait a second, what is she aiming at?* His eyes flashed to the field, and he almost swallowed his tongue in surprise. Carolin was aiming at a Prairie Rider, whose tree-like arms and legs had morphed into an archery target. Orowin's breath returned when he realized that the Rider was in on the contest, its green ivy curled into a circular shape for the bullseye.

Barely a half-second after the *twang* and *thwish*, the Rider opened its leafy vines, and the arrow passed straight through—a clear miss.

The archers behind Carolin burst into laughter, except for the few soldiers handing over money in a lost bet.

"Let me have one more shot!" Carolin yelled, nocking another arrow.

The Rider was having fun too, apparently. Its ivy regrew instantly into a perfect circle, but this time rings of red and orange flowers bloomed around the center.

Carolin let another shot rip. Rather than dodge it, the Rider snapped out one of its branches like an arm and snatched the projectile in mid-flight. With the arrow in its grip, the ivy extended and curled around it from tip to fletching. The vines tightened until the shaft cracked into pieces.

The archers couldn't contain themselves. Carolin had finally met her match. Orowin laughed too, his belly shaking. *I must remember to write this down before bed. It will be a perfect anecdote for my book.*

"Captain Carolin, I think you've had enough practice," he said. "Come to the stables. We're almost ready to ride."

With the help of a few eager stablemen, it wouldn't take long to equip the captains' horses with the same style of harness and breastplate that Una was wearing. While they waited, Carolin grabbed a stool. "Are you really going to meet the Philosopher looking like that, Colonel?" she asked. "Get over here."

Carolin dusted off Orowin's uniform and snipped a few loose threads near his collar with an arrow's broadhead. Meanwhile, Pearlin performed a quick clean and polish of his boots.

With his clothing set, Pearlin used a pair of scissors to trim his sideburns and beard. When she finished, Carolin poured a few drops of almond and sunflower seed oil onto Orowin's hands. "Don't give away my secret, but this mixture gives me a smoother release on the bowstring. It should work equally well as beard oil, I believe." Orowin ran his fingers through his whiskers. In the sunlight, the reddish-blonde streaks nearly outnumbered the gray.

"That's much better," Carolin said. "Now you look like a dignitary. Let's go introduce ourselves."

Before Orowin stood up, however, two sinewy branches stretched over Carolin's shoulders. The arms of a nearby Prairie Rider were reaching for him. Its vines spread out like fingers, poised, it seemed, to wrap around Orowin's neck. Instead, the Rider had caught a detail that Carolin missed: the colonel's top button was undone. The twisting vines pinched the button and fastened it in the proper loop.

"Why thank you, Ms. Rider, ma'am," Orowin said, blushing. He still wasn't sure how to address them properly. "Your company on this journey has been quite a pleasure."

Orowin and his captains took off toward the towers, their horses passing swiftly through the meadow's knee-high grass. Confident that he had made the right choice, Orowin savored the wind on his face and the subtle cherry-like scent of the beard oil.

With only a few miles to cover and the horses galloping at a steady clip, the North Gate came into view in a matter of minutes. Enormous panels of sturdy oak connected the two sections of rock wall that spanned the mountain gap. *That's strange*, Orowin noted. *The gates are closed.* Another fact he recalled from Elerin's briefings was that Sterling rarely closed its gates to visitors. *I'm sure they're being cautious, that's all. We are arriving without an invitation.*

Una, however, was not so relaxed. Orowin could feel through the reins that she was growing tense as they approached. "Stay calm, girl," he whispered, patting her neck. "I'm right here with you."

About three hundred yards from the North Gate, Orowin pulled back on his reins gradually to slow Una down. Carolin and Pearlin did the same. Even with a small squad, he didn't want it to appear like they were charging in. The field in front of the towers was empty and quiet. The burbling rapids from the Silver River created the only sound in the afternoon air.

The silence was shattered by a *boom*, followed by a *crackle* louder than a thousand firecrackers. Una froze, unsure whether to move. Orowin was stunned too. He yanked Una's reins, searching for Carolin and Pearlin as he turned his horse around, but they had already darted off in different directions. "Move, Colonel! Move!" Carolin shouted. "I think they shot something at us!"

But Orowin's reaction wasn't quick enough. A wave of intense heat washed over him from above. Then the ground ignited into flames in a circle around him. The ring pulsed and shimmered pure white.

The fire crept inward, the grass hissing as it burned. Orowin was trapped in the center. Instinctively Una took a few steps back, trying to build up enough speed to leap over the white wall, but there wasn't enough room. The flames were too hot and closing in too quickly.

Carolin and Pearlin screamed Orowin's name over and over. They whipped the reins and kicked their heels into their horses' ribs, trying anything to push them forward. But the horses refused to budge. The white heat was too much, and the black smoke stung their eyes.

The two captains were forced to watch from a distance as the bright white flames filled in the circle completely. They had to shield their eyes; looking at the fire directly burned fuzzy blind spots into their vision. They continued to call out Orowin's name despite all the evidence that no answer would come. Nothing inside the ring stirred.

Out of stubbornness and disbelief, Carolin and Pearlin waited in the field until the whitefire died out. They rode around the charred circle once more, watching as a final burst of light came from the center, where at last Orowin's uniform disintegrated, floating away as ash and smoke.

Pearlin wiped the tear lines off her cheeks. The drops themselves had already fallen to the ground.

"You think that was enough to scare us?" Carolin screamed toward the S&R towers, her voice strained and seething. She launched an arrow in the general direction of the towers. No one could hear her from that far off, and the shot wouldn't make it halfway to the gate, but neither of those things mattered. She needed to release some of her fury.

Carolin spit to clear the ashes from her mouth. "Whatever the hell that was," she said to Pearlin, "let's see if they can aim it at night, when we come back with the rest of our troops."

⬤

Eb. A. D♯. D♯. G.

Aris sat on the library's velvet couch with his instrument case open before him on the coffee table. The violin rested flat and still inside the bottom half. *Almost like a casket*, he thought. Aris plucked the strings in no particular order. Not a song, just noise. Half the notes were grossly out of tune, so the effect was discordant and a bit jarring.

But Sera didn't seem to notice the eerie tones in the background. Aris watched her pace back and forth frantically before the Grand Fireplace, muttering under her breath. Her words were unintelligible, her breathing shallow and erratic.

"Sera, it's not your fault," Aris said, trying once again to get her attention. She had been unable to complete a sentence since they returned to the library, but Aris could read her racing thoughts easily enough. An hour earlier, standing together on the Capitol's roof beside the silver dome, they heard an awful, unmistakable *boom*—the first whitefire blast in over a hundred years. They couldn't tell whether the shot was a warning or whether it hit any Royal Army soldiers, but that was irrelevant. Sera considered herself more culpable than the S&R guard who pulled the trigger.

"Not my fault?" she said. "In a matter of minutes, I released an arsenal that Vesu managed to keep locked away for decades."

Okay, that's a little better, Aris thought. *At least she's using coherent sentences again.*

"*You* released the crossbows? Don't forget that I was on the tower last night too. When the Philosopher made his proposal, the council members didn't hesitate. You were the only one to speak up."

"Well, I didn't make my voice loud enough. Whatever brought the Royal Army here, it was a mistake to tell the S&R how to unlock the armory. I wish I had kept my mouth shut, but I was so angry at Vesu. I still am. All this time I really thought she trusted me."

Sera stopped mid-stride at the far end of the worn-out path in the carpet. She angled away from Aris and stared at the snowy owl chiseled into the mantelpiece. Unabashed, its glossy yellow eyes stared right back at her.

"If you want to hear the truth, you old bird, here it is. When the key to the armory popped into my head, it was like I had known the answer all along. I couldn't hold it in. And when I saw the Royal Army's encampment on the horizon, I told myself that Ozar was right: without the whitefire, how else could we possibly defend the city?"

Sera withdrew her hands into her long sleeves, balling up the fabric into her fists. "But now I see that was my excuse, my cover to get back at her. With a few words I washed Vesu's victories, so many years of hard work, right down the drain. Part of me knew it was selfish, and the other part knew no one could stop me."

Sera let a full minute pass for the words to sink in. Save for her heavy breathing, the stillness of the library returned. The stone-carved owl wasn't going to say anything, of course, so Sera turned to Aris, anxiously awaiting his response.

Aris had shut his instrument case and was holding it on his lap. On any other day, he would have found words to reassure her, to help Sera make sense of what happened. He would surely have proposed a plan for what to do next. Now, though, Aris struggled to see any light ahead of them. From the moment that Vesu collapsed in the chamber, every hour had grown darker and every minute more uncertain. *No, the shadows started multiplying before that,* he thought. His brother and best friend were still missing. Sterling was under siege. *I can't figure out where all this will end.*

His music was no longer a sanctuary either. After Aris lost his composure at Vesu's trial, he couldn't find the motivation to tune his violin, let alone hold his bow. And playing wouldn't have helped anyway. This disaster wouldn't float away if he discovered the right notes.

So, Aris gave Sera the same response as the snowy owl. He let the silence fill the library until the gurgling beneath the floor became unbearable. The Silver River splashed in the same rhythm it always did, but this time the sound was driving Sera mad.

"Are you going to say anything?"

Aris stood up. "You're wrong."

"I'm wrong? Wrong about what?"

"For one thing, Vesu accomplished more in her lifetime than you, Taro, or anyone else can destroy in a day." Aris moved in front of the coffee table, standing over it defensively. The surface was covered with the books and papers that they had used to prepare Vesu's defense. "Second, Vesu trusted you with everything. That was clear from my first week here, racing after you down these aisles, trying my best to keep up. No one sees the beauty in this library better than you, Sera. Without your help, this list of Vesu's achievements wouldn't be half as long. She needed you."

Sera's soft brown eyes dodged from side to side in search of an exit, an escape, any excuse to prove Aris wrong. She was afraid that if she couldn't, the guilt would consume her completely.

"If Vesu trusted me, why did she keep her relationship with Ambassador Elerin a secret? Why wouldn't she listen to me about the weatherbox? Why did she leave us?"

"I . . . I don't know."

"That's right, you *don't* know what you're talking about. If Vesu trusted me as much as you say, she would have chosen *me* to be the Philosopher, don't you think?"

With Sera's question left hanging, Aris suddenly felt light-headed. He let go of his violin case and grabbed the couch with both hands to keep his balance. He felt like the library floor had transformed into the deck of a sailboat, the whole room rocked by an ocean wave. His legs teetered unevenly as he waited for the world around him to steady itself or flip upside down.

Sera caught the distressed look on Aris's face. His lips formed familiar shapes, but no sound came out. She felt shameful and embarrassed; she had lashed out at the kindest person she had ever met.

"By the owl, Aris, I'm so sorry." Sera rushed over and wrapped her arms around him, hugging him so tightly that the blue sleeves of her dress bunched up around her elbows. "I didn't mean any of that. I miss Vesu deeply, I'm worried Zeno won't make it home, and I'm upset at myself for— Aris, are you okay?"

"I think . . . I might . . . I need to sit down for a second."

With her arm over his shoulder, Sera led Aris back to the couch. While he collected his thoughts, Sera brought him a glass of water, which he guzzled down. *If I'm right about this,* he thought, *I'm going to need a stronger drink.*

"What's going on?" Sera asked.

Aris cleared his throat. "You've listened to hundreds of Vesu's speeches, right?"

"Yes, of course. I helped her write most of them."

"Vesu was careful with her choice of words, wasn't she?"

213

"Come on, you know the answer to that. She was so meticulous that our speechwriting sessions were practically insufferable."

"Well, I was thinking about her final words at the trial. Vesu never said the name 'Ozar Wrinn.' Did you notice that?"

"Right, but Vesu made him her Junior Philosopher several years ago, so that's obviously what she meant."

"No, that's obviously what everyone *assumed*. How can we be certain if she didn't say a name?"

"Alright, I agree that Vesu's instructions could have been clearer. Keep in mind, though, she had been locked in a jail cell for three days. I'm sure she was sleep deprived and starving."

"I don't buy it. Taro and the S&R were beyond cruel, but they couldn't break Vesu so easily. Even at the end, when the council's verdict was imminent, she didn't back down. It was her chamber and she left on her terms."

"Okay, let's go with your theory. If Vesu didn't appoint Ozar, who did she choose instead?"

Aris paused, rolling the crystal drinking glass between his hands. He tilted his head back to take another sip, and waited expectantly—for what felt like an eternity—for any liquid to hit his tongue. No relief came. Not a single drop. Through the translucent bottom of the empty glass, however, Sera's yellow hair diffused the library's candlelight like the first few minutes of a sunrise. *This has to be it. She's our only hope.*

"There's another phrase I wanted to ask you about," he said, lowering his glass. "Up on the tower, after the vote to open the armory, Ozar said '*The Philosopher* will find the key in the Silver River.' That line comes directly from the old journals, right?"

"I thought this might be where you were going with all this," Sera said. "And really, I'm quite flattered. Yes, the answer to the riddle came to me first, but I promise you: Vesu didn't say anything to me about the appointment, and she had plenty of opportunities to do so. During the trial she sat right next to me at counsel's table!"

"That's the part I can't explain." Aris lowered his head and absentmindedly flipped through a notebook on the coffee table. "I thought Vesu was trying to protect you; to buy you time, maybe. But if that were the case, she would have said something, or left you a message . . ."

Aris reached the middle of the notebook, where Sera's notes stopped, and a vivid streak of purple caught his eye: a feather was poking out between the pages.

"What's this? A new bookmark?"

Sera sprang off the sofa like a bird from a branch and snatched the feather. She held it up to the light, examining the colors. "Aris, where'd you get this?"

"You tell me. It was in your notebook."

"I've never seen it before."

"What do you mean? This is your notebook from the trial yesterday, right?"

Sera didn't answer. She returned to the line in the carpet and walked along it slowly, twirling the feather in her fingers. The way she moved reminded Aris of a tightrope walker. He feared that with one false step she might fall forever.

"Sera, what is it?"

"You were right," she said, smiling for the first time in days. "It's a message from Vesu."

"How do you know?" he asked nervously. He was so accustomed to dead ends that he braced himself for another.

"This feather is from a purple finch; I can tell by the markings. And purple finches nest in the cedar trees on the eastern face of the Cloudhorns, which is the route that Vesu and Zeno took to meet the Alpinees. Vesu must have slipped this into my notebook when I wasn't looking."

"So, does that mean . . ."

"We're about to find out. Grab the tinder box and help me light the candles. We have to hurry; Ozar and Chief Gaffney could return from the towers any minute."

Following their usual routine, Sera started at one end of the hearth and Aris at the other. By the time they met in the middle, the flames had grown tall, melting together into a smooth silver wall. Reddened by the intense heat, Aris's freckled cheeks felt extremely hot. He backed away from the fireplace to cool down. *What if we're wrong? When she walks through that fire, she'll disintegrate.*

Sera retrieved the shawl from its hook. Bowing her head, she placed the black-and-white garment over her shoulders. Then she turned around, lifting her ponytail out of the way. "Would you like to do the honors?"

"Are you sure about this?"

"More than anything. I let down Vesu once already. I won't do it again."

Aris reached forward reluctantly and fastened the clasp. The feathers fanned out perfectly as Sera spun around.

"The shawl feels different than before," she noted, running her fingers over the speckled feathers. "It's heavy around my neck, but I feel lighter on my feet."

"Do you know where you're going?" Aris knew the answer, but that didn't make it any easier to ask the question. He retreated a few steps. The flames were at full strength, and the pulsating heat was harsh.

"Yes, I decided some time ago, I think." Sera removed the scrap of parchment from her pocket. As she unrolled it, Aris could read the charcoal letters clearly from where he was standing. *Amos Harper.* Sera tossed it into the flames, and the paper sizzled on contact.

"I'm sorry I can't take you with me," she said as the smoke curled around her. "I know how terribly you miss him."

"Tell me everything when you get back. I'll wait for you here."

Clenching his teeth, Aris steeled himself for Sera's next move, yet she still managed to startle him. Instead of reaching out with a hand or a foot to test whether the shawl would protect her, she took a full stride forward.

The fire wrapped around Sera as gently as a waterfall, her golden-blonde hair the last thing to disappear beneath the silver stream.

⬤

"How long was I in there?" Sera asked, plopping down on the velvet couch. Color flooded back to her cheeks as she threw off the quilt that Aris had wrapped around her.

Was it five minutes? Fifteen? Fifty? Aris shook his head. "I'm sorry, I lost track of time too."

"By the owl, you look so much like him." Sera studied Aris's face. "Your lips, ears, nose—even the freckles." The remark made Aris blush, but he certainly didn't want her to stop. Sera's description was helping to repaint his father's portrait in his memory. *Keep going. Tell me more.*

"Zeno got his eyes, though," Sera said. "The same glacier blue. And the way he carried himself, the way he climbed—for a minute there I thought I was following your brother in the mountains."

"What was it like . . . traveling through?"

"I'm not sure it can be put into words. I imagine it's like trying to share a song with someone by reciting the musical notation. It will never come close to an actual performance, never capture the real feeling."

Aris nodded. He understood completely.

"Until you have the chance to experience it for yourself someday, this description will have to do: passing through the flames felt like a wall of champagne washed over me. It didn't ask for a destination; the fire lifted me into the air and carried me away to all the places I needed to go."

Sera stood up, spread her arms, and moved around the library as though she were flying. "First, I watched your father chase storms with the Alpinees, soaring above him like a bird. Then, perched on one of the chamber's chandeliers, I listened to his speeches before the council. I saw the blizzard from nowhere, the one that buried him in the Cloudhorns."

Aris felt his skin tingle as though a draft had blown through the room.

"But before Amos set out on that last climb, he came here."

"To the library?" Aris asked. "What was he doing here?"

"He was looking for something. Come with me, I'll show you."

Sera led Aris to the mahogany table in the library's main room. Together they lifted up one end so that the stacks of books and papers slid off like an avalanche.

"Your father was standing here, where I'm standing now, arguing with Ozar. In fact, I'm surprised no one heard the shouting match that night."

"What were they arguing about?"

"Amos had been waiting for months for Ozar to finish his research on the storms in the Cloudhorns. On this particular night, Ozar called off their search. He insisted that any weatherboxes had been destroyed long ago—that is, if they ever existed in the first place." Sera knocked on the table, and the sound echoed through the library. "Your father refused to give in. I could practically read his thoughts. He vowed to continue searching on his own. He sensed Ozar was hiding something, but he never guessed it was right here in front of him. None of us did."

Right in front of us? I don't see anyth—

At that moment the pattern on the table's surface jumped out at him. Once Aris recognized the overall shape, it was impossible to see anything else: the colorful wooden inlays cut across the tabletop at an unmistakable angle. In fact, he could suddenly read the abstract design as if it had transformed into a detailed map. *By the owl, I missed it too.*

"It's a weatherbox," Aris whispered. "Of the entire Silver River Gorge."

"Ozar found it on one of his research assignments. He kept it hidden from Vesu and started testing it in the mountains. When he learned to control the clouds well enough, he aimed the storms at the Alpinees, using snow and ice to force them into the Gorge. Ozar thought he was being careful, keeping the storms in the Cloudhorns, but your father caught on. Amos wouldn't stop searching, asking questions, and eventually Ozar ran out of excuses. He used this table to make sure that Amos wouldn't return from his last trip into the mountains."

"Vesu was trying to protect you after all."

"She was trying to protect both of us, I think. Although I'm not sure that she knew what she was protecting us from. And she certainly didn't send us any messages about what to do next. Any ideas?"

Aris folded his hands behind his back. To help himself focus, he whistled "Hymn to the Swallows," the song that he had learned for Vesu's trial. This time, though, he didn't miss any notes.

"I have a plan to deal with Ozar," he said slowly, as if each word stung his lips. "But for it to work, we'll need to put everything back. The shawl, the candles, the papers . . . every little detail. This room must look *exactly* the way we found it this morning."

⬤

Set inside of an ancient crater, the Alpinees' mountain village was oval-shaped, just like the lake at its center. Every structure was forged of ice and snow, formed to fit the natural contours of the rocky bowl. One main road started at the bottom, near the lake, and spiraled up the steep rock face in between the homes and buildings—a corkscrew connecting the whole community. Serrated and snow-capped, the ridgeline at the crater's top was like the rest of the Cloudhorns but with one major difference: no peaks were higher than these. Only clouds, sky, and stars.

From the dock on the lake's eastern shore, Zeno admired the vertical village surrounding him. He had come to that spot many times over the last few days because it was the only place where the water wasn't frozen. "Another side effect of the persistent storms," Isolo had explained. For centuries the dormant volcano churning deep inside the strata somewhere had been sufficient to keep the lake alive. Now, the Alpinees had to crush and stir the surface constantly to save their single source of fresh water. *If the next storm is any worse,* Zeno thought, *this lake will lock up completely.*

Leaning over the dock's edge, Zeno dipped his mug into the mountain pool. The cloudy teal water was mostly slush, definitely not safe for him to drink. A few sips would drop his core body temperature dangerously low. "The only way you'll stave off mountain sickness," Isolo sternly instructed him the night they arrived, "is to brew glacier milk every six hours. My friend, Esili, will show you how. It doesn't matter whether you feel thirsty or not; you need its heat and the extra oxygen in your bloodstream."

Zeno had the brewing method down to a science. First, he crushed a handful of reedgrass, which grew along the lakeshore, into a fine reddish powder (the Alpinees called it volcano grain). Next, he cracked a rubble root that Esili had given him, twisting it until three drops of bluish sap splashed into his drink.

The chemical reaction took only a minute. Simmering and then bubbling, a purple foam floated to the top as the liquid reached its boiling point. When Zeno felt the hot steam tickle his nose, he knew it was ready to drink. He sat on a bench at the dock's end, sipping the foam while he waited for Isolo to return with a decision. *I hope he can convince the other scouts. We'll need all of them if this plan is going to work.* The glacier milk helped settle his nerves, warming his body better than any campfire.

Now I understand why he came here so often, Zeno thought, reflecting on his father's expeditions into the mountains. *The view of the Gorge is so clear, and the altitude makes it easier to think.* Over the last four days holed up in the Alpinees' village, Zeno had done a lot of thinking—once he got over the nightmares, that is.

The hours following the clash with the S&R were mostly a blur. Isolo had carried Zeno to the nearest shelter, forced him to swallow a glass of glacier milk, and then covered him with heavy pine-scented blankets. In fact, that's about all Zeno remembered from his first night in the village. Exhausted and empty, he fell into a deep sleep before Isolo blew out the lamp.

In the early morning hours, though, when the glacier milk wore off and the cold crept in, Zeno's nightmares began. In the first dream, a pack of wolves circled Aris, yipping and gnarring, but Zeno couldn't pull his spear out of the ground to defend him. In the next he found himself in the concert hall at one of Veti's grand balls, dancing with Sera under the chandeliers. She was wearing a gold dress that radiated light in every direction. As he started to twirl her, the Silver River surged from beneath the building, and the deluge broke down the doors. Sera was carried away upside down in the floodwaters before he could grab her.

In another nightmare, Zeno was back in the glade where the S&R had caught up to him and Vesu. This time, though, the guard who held a knife to Vesu's throat followed through with his threat. Blood oozed from the gash, staining Vesu's silver collar purple as though she had Alpinees' blood in her veins.

After that horrible image, Zeno decided sleep was no longer worth it. He counted the blurry stars through the translucent roof of the ice shelter until they disappeared behind blue sky.

If the following nights had been anything like the first, Zeno wouldn't have lasted long with the Alpinees. Fortunately, when Isolo brought breakfast, he noticed that Zeno looked weary and restless, so he found ways to keep him busy. In the mornings, Zeno helped the scouts break ice at the lake. In the afternoons, he joined the team that cleared snowdrifts from the upper reaches of the winding road. By dinnertime, Zeno was so drained that he craved the warmth of those blankets, ready for a full night of dreamless sleep.

As tired as he was at the end of each day, Zeno never skipped the scouts' evening meal. At dusk Isolo's crew gathered in a chapel-like structure that overlooked the oval lake (they called it "the Cathedral") and ate together in silence around a slab of opalescent rock. Instead of using individual plates, the Alpinees passed large bowls back and forth with various dishes to share. Whenever a bowl was handed to him, Zeno was tempted to ask about the ingredients, but he sensed it would be rude to break the silence. So, he closed his eyes and bravely took a bite of everything.

To be fair, the mashed grains and herbs were flavorful, and what he assumed to be raw fish was satisfying. Nevertheless, Zeno wasn't staying up late for the food; he hung around those dinners for the conversations that followed. Each night after all the common bowls were emptied, Esili brewed tea for the Alpinees scouts. She carried the kettle clockwise around the room until every cup was full. Although it bubbled and foamed in a similar manner, the drink was quite different from the one she had taught Zeno how to make. In the dim dining hall, the effervescent liquid practically glowed, shifting between shades of chartreuse.

That first night in the Cathedral, Esili hesitated before pouring any tea for their young guest. She glanced at Isolo for direction, and he nodded in approval. Esili carefully tipped the kettle, as she had for the other scouts, but pulled back the spout before Zeno's cup was half full.

"That will be plenty," she said, squeezing his shoulder.

Zeno examined the brightly colored tea. With his stomach rumbling after the strange meal, he wasn't keen on trying another strange drink. He waited quietly in the back of the room as the scouts raised their glasses in their nightly ritual. After they swallowed that first sip, Isolo broke the silence to address his crew—but for some reason Zeno couldn't understand a word he was saying. Instead of Isolo's normally smooth sentences, his voice sounded choppy and garbled, like wind whipping through a mountain pass. Zeno moved in closer to the table, but it didn't help. The whistling and whooshing sounds were unintelligible. Concerned that his nightmares were spilling over into real life, Zeno anxiously took a swig from his cup.

Esili's fizzy tea made the room spin. Sounds were distorted too, his ears buzzing like a bronze church bell. Zeno shook his head, trying to clear the dizziness. After considerable effort his ears popped. That's when the room came back into focus, the ringing faded away, and he had no trouble understanding Isolo at all.

"To those of you who fought with me against the S&R, I am grateful for your courage. Alas, we must continue to be brave. The Philosopher was taken by force before we could learn anything more about the storms. I seek your counsel in planning our next move."

Isolo went around the table and asked each scout for their advice, starting with Esili.

"The Philosopher risked everything to meet with us," she said. "And her library may hold the secret to saving our home. We must go to her aid."

The next scout didn't see it the same way. "We waited for this Philosopher far longer than we should have, and she didn't have any answers. Going after her again is beyond foolish; it's reckless. We tried to protect her while we could, but her fate is out of our hands. We do not have the numbers."

"More importantly, we do not have the time," added another scout. "Even if the weather holds off for a week, the red-and-white uniforms are moving quickly through the forests. They will arrive at the Gorge in a few days. We cannot possibly fight the S&R and the Royal Army at the same time. I propose that we leave the Cloudhorns at once, before the next storm arrives."

"The Royal Army?" Zeno asked out of turn from the back of the room. He barely recognized the sound of his own voice, distorted as it was by the intoxicating tea.

Evidently, the scouts understood him well enough. Everyone seated around the table turned their head toward Zeno, their mirrored eyes flashing sharply between blinks.

"Please forgive the outburst," Isolo said to the group. "I have not yet educated our guest about our customs, nor have I shared what we see on the horizon."

Isolo then explained, for Zeno's sake, what the Alpinees had been monitoring for weeks now: hundreds of South Branch soldiers marching toward the Gorge with a tribe of Prairie Riders in their ranks. "We don't know why they're heading this way, although they march with the entire regiment. Their horses, equipment, and weapons too. Whatever brings them here, young Harper, it does not appear that they intend to return to the Basin."

"I don't understand," Zeno said. "The Philosopher is certain that relations with Imperial Bay are peaceful. Perhaps the Royal Army will help us—if we meet them before they reach the North Gate, we can explain that Vesu has been wrongfully detained. We can ask for their assistance against the S&R."

Upon hearing this suggestion, the Alpinees scouts seated around the table shook their heads in disbelief. A few stood up to leave. The consensus was clear: Zeno's proposal was not merely impulsive; it was impossible.

"It's time we retire to our homes," Isolo said. "Tempers have a tendency to flare when tired. Let us sleep on these ideas, and we will resume our deliberations tomorrow."

From that night forward, Zeno kept his mouth shut during Isolo's dinners. To convince the Alpinees scouts to defend the Gorge, he needed a plan: one that would help him return home *and* help the Alpinees keep theirs. So, over the next three days, while working alongside Isolo's crew, icebreaking and shoveling, Zeno mapped out a way back into the city.

"But it's hard to draw a map, Bimo, when you don't know your own location."

That's what Zeno told me years later when I asked him about his three days in the Alpinees' village. It wasn't until I started keeping this journal, taking all these trips through the Grand Fireplace, that I fully appreciated what he meant. "Vesu followed me into the mountains, and I failed to protect her. I went searching for you, Bimo, but I let you down." After the battle with the S&R, Zeno gave up hope of joining their ranks. More importantly, he doubted whether he could call Sterling "home" ever again. *If I get back into the city, how will I reach Sera and Aris?* he wondered. *What will the S&R do when they find me?* Zeno's nightmares had ended, but such worries still followed him everywhere. *What if Vesu was wrong about the Royal Army? They may have come to burn Sterling to the ground.*

On his fourth day in the village, when Isolo's crew broke for lunch, Zeno headed to the dock to brew his tea. He hadn't come up with a feasible plan to get home, and his doubts were close to consuming him altogether. *From here on out, I'll always be running.* The slushy lake water lapped against the platform, daring him to jump in. Zeno might have accepted the challenge if he hadn't noticed that the wrist straps of his leather gloves—the ones his father used to wear—had come undone. As he retied the strings, he saw that the S&R insignia on the back of the hand had worn away from so much use. *I can't believe I ever wanted to wear that uniform. The S&R seemed so different when Dad was here.* The thought reminded Zeno of his father's favorite saying, a piece of advice that he had shared on many of their outings with Erro: "If you ever lose yourself up here, retrace the route that led you astray. Usually, it's the same path that will get you out of trouble."

How did I end up here? Zeno blew the air from his lungs and watched the tiny droplets turn into crystals. He recalled the overcast morning when he left the Capitol through the back exit with Vesu. It had rained throughout the night, so the trail was sloppy from the start. The continuing patter on the canopy drowned out the usual sounds of the forest waking up, like the birds and the squirrels . . . *And the footsteps of the S&R following behind us.*

Then Zeno remembered the conversation he overheard between the two guards in the Capitol jail: "Chief Gaffney makes a strong case that we need those crossbows back." *That's what the S&R is really after: the armory.* His father was against opening that arsenal, and he ended up buried in a snowstorm. Vesu's main priority as Philosopher was to keep the whitefire locked away, and she was captured with the help of wind and rain. *Someone discovered another weatherbox,* Zeno realized, *and they're using it to force open the armory.* That was something the Alpinees scouts might fight to resist.

Zeno took off running down the dock in search of Isolo. Before he reached the spiral road, a bright flash lit up the snowbanks. A half second later, a boom echoed up the crater's walls, the sound eventually spilling out into the sky. With his hand over his eyes to shield the sun, Zeno tried to find the source of the explosion, but he didn't have the same sharp eyesight as the Alpinees. The honeycombed city in the valley below looked quiet and sleepy, the same as it always did.

Thud-thud-thud-thud. Isolo's boots pounded the planks when he landed. He had coasted down to the dock from the Cathedral as soon as he heard the boom.

"I trust you heard it?" he asked.

Zeno nodded.

"My scouts tell me the blast came from one of the North Gate Towers. We can see a ring of fire burning in the meadow beyond the wall. Is that what I think it is?"

"The S&R got the crossbows back."

"How could that be? You said Vesu would never agree to unlock the armory."

"She wouldn't. Not even if her life depended on it."

Isolo understood what that meant. He dropped to one knee so that he was eye level with Zeno and rested his long ice axe on the dock beside them. "You are welcome to come with us, young Harper," he said. "We will find another mountain range, far from here, to build a new home. It won't be the same, of course, but you will be safe."

Zeno didn't respond right away. He reached into his pocket and found the stone that Isolo had given him when they first met, the one that Amos had gifted to the Alpinees scout. The stone's smooth surface reminded Zeno of the centuries of flowing water that it took to carve the Gorge, to sand down this rock into a polished circle. *It's not time to run away yet.* Zeno tossed the stone into the lake where it disappeared into the teal water.

"Isolo, you can't outrun the whitefire forever. That's why Vesu took such great pains to keep it locked away. With the armory opened, conflict is sure to spread across the continent. It will find you in the next mountain range too." Zeno pulled the strings of his gloves tighter. "Come with me to meet the Royal Army. Together we'll show them the real enemy, and maybe they'll spare the rest of the city."

Isolo stood up and attached his axe to its leather strap. "Amos would have given the same advice, and I always heeded his counsel. I will try to persuade the other scouts, but I can't make any promises."

That's how Zeno ended up on the bench at the end of the dock, sipping his tea while he waited for Isolo to return with a decision. With the sun edging closer to the jagged skyline, Zeno realized they had to leave soon. If the Alpinees scouts agreed to his plan, they needed to reach the Royal Army before dark, before the soldiers started fighting back.

Zeno didn't have to wait long. The silhouettes of two scouts coasted down from the Cathedral, arms spread out wide so that their jackets could ride the updrafts of mountain air. *Why are there only two of them? Where are the others?*

Isolo landed on the dock with Esili at his side. "Only we were granted leave to join you," he explained. "The scouts would not risk losing more of us."

Esili watched Zeno bite his lip and lower his chin to his chest. "The news is not as bad as it sounds," she added.

"The others have agreed to wait and to watch in the Cloudhorns. If we can convince the Royal Army to side with us against the S&R, the other scouts will join the fight."

From the leather strap across her chest, Esili unclipped an extra jacket made of the same pine-green material that the Alpinees scouts wore. She handed it to Zeno. "Here, try this on. It's the smallest size I could find."

Zeno slid his arms into the spongy jacket and buttoned it up. The sleeves were a little long, but Esili helped him roll up the cuffs to the proper length. "That should work well enough. Oh, one more thing." She removed a bundle of blue flowers from her leather pouch and tucked a couple of stems into Zeno's front pocket so that the blue blossoms hung there like badges. She did the same for her own jacket and for Isolo's.

"These look like trumpet bluebells," Zeno said. "Why are we wearing them?"

Esili squinted at him with her calm, reflective eyes. "You'll see."

Zeno followed the two Alpinees scouts around the oval lake to a cliff on the other side. Along the curve of the crater, the mountain face below was nearly vertical, a sheer drop into the valley. Zeno's stomach turned as his toes neared the edge.

If I make it, he decided, *I'm not inviting Sera to a dance. I'll take her to the ocean so we can find out if the beach looks anything like it does in those paintings.*

"Listen closely, young Harper," Isolo said. "Even with the jacket on, you won't make it past the wall on your own. You'll need to hold on to us and keep steady. The wind in your face will be fierce, but Esili and I will steer us in the right direction. If we stay low along the ridgeline, we should have enough momentum to clear the North Gate. Do you understand?"

"Yes," Zeno said, closing his eyes. "I won't let go."

Chapter X

This morning it finally happened.

I watched Zeno close his eyes, jump off the cliff, and fall through the clouds, but I couldn't follow him any farther than that. The smoky clouds dissolved suddenly, and instead of soaring over the Gorge I was back in the library, staring through the rectangular hole in the floor at ripples of gray water.

I lowered the iron gate slowly, trying not to let it slam. Then I exited the Grand Fireplace for the last time. All that remained on the hearthstone was a hardened puddle of wax—perfectly flat, iridescent white, and cool to the touch. It seemed strange to simply set the shawl back on its hook, like I normally would, so I folded it under a silk sheet and tucked it away in a storage chest.

When it first hit me that the candles would burn out on my watch, and there was nothing I could do about it, I panicked. How was I supposed to see ahead when I couldn't look back anymore? Why didn't the old Philosophers plan for this? Why didn't they warn me?

In a desperate attempt to buy time, I stole a bottle of wine from the kitchen and wandered aimlessly through the library's aisles. Sipping straight from the bottle, I scoured random texts and manuscripts looking for some secret that every other Philosopher had missed. If I searched the stacks long enough, I thought, maybe I'd find a hidden chapter that would teach me to recreate the candles. Or maybe tucked away between long-lost pages I'd discover a blueprint for building another bridge from scratch.

There had to be another way to keep the Grand Fireplace alive; I was sure of it. After all, if this really was the end, why write all of those books? Why waste all of that perfectly good ink?

Of course, I found the bottom of the bottle before I found any answers. By then the room was swirling around me, so I sat on the floor with my back against a bookshelf and banged my head against it. From the ground the shelving unit looked like a staircase—no, more like a ladder—with its parallel layers of oak rising toward the ceiling. The boards were nailed together seamlessly, like the panels of the Four Bridges, and if I squinted, the wood grains rippled like water.

At my age I'd never risk it, but part of me wanted to climb the bookcase to the top shelf so I could see the entire library from above. Maybe from that vantage point I'd be able to uncover Inka's grand design, finally understand how everything was supposed to fit together . . .

That's when the room stopped spinning.

I realized the Philosophers had seen this day coming all along, it just took me longer to decipher the message. Inka had a backup plan after all.

When I finally figured it out, I didn't waste any more time. I raced back to my desk, grabbed this pen, and started spilling perfectly good ink all over the page. Consider this journal one more rung on the ladder, I guess, although I'm not sure how much further it will help you to see once you start climbing.

If you were worried that I wouldn't be able to finish this story because the silver fire died out, don't run away yet. I measured the height of the candles to estimate how much time in the Grand Fireplace I had left. Lucky for you, I timed it perfectly.

With the help of Aris, Zeno, Sera, and the others, I was able to describe events that I never experienced myself. The rest of the story, however, I can tell you mostly from memory.

Because I was there, remember, when the silver dome came crashing down. And somehow, I walked out of there alive.

◉

"Do you see the soldiers out there, Bimo?" Ozar asked.

I stood next to him on the North Gate's eastern tower. The sun had set behind the Cloudhorns and the sky was an angry red. To my left and right, rows of S&R guards held crossbows positioned on the parapet, facing the field. At ten years old, I was barely taller than the tower's ledge, but I could see the line of soldiers in red-and-white uniforms marching across the meadow, and I heard their drums pounding. I nodded.

"That's the Royal Army," Ozar said. "They came all the way from Imperial Bay to tear down our gate and burn our bridges to the ground. Can you believe the king could give such orders?" Ozar patted the top of my head. "Don't worry; we're not going to let that happen. I wanted you to be here so you could see there's no reason to be afraid anymore. With your help we got the whitefire back, and now we'll send the Royal Army back to the ocean."

Ozar wanted me to feel like a hero, I think, but I didn't feel anything at all. No one had explained why the S&R had taken me from my friends and kept me hidden from my family for days.

"Can I go home?" I asked, but Ozar couldn't hear me. The drumbeat was growing more aggressive by the minute.

"They're three hundred yards out, Mr. Philosopher," Chief Gaffney reported. "Should I give the command?"

With his hands clasped behind his back, Ozar cocked his head to one side so that his neck cracked. "No. Let them get closer."

We waited in silence while the South Branch inched forward. Instead of the standard square units that Gaffney was expecting, the four hundred soldiers marched in a wide echelon formation, their ladder-like lines running diagonally across the meadow. Behind them a herd of bison trampled through the grass, their smooth horns visible in the last bit of twilight.

"About two hundred yards, sir," Gaffney said.

"Not yet," Ozar replied.

The sky was nearly black, but I couldn't see any stars. I started to shiver, and it reminded me of the nights I had spent in the jail, so cold I couldn't sleep. I wondered if the chill in my bones would ever go away.

"Hey, kid, are you alright?" Gaffney asked. "Here, take my coat."

"He's fine, Chief," Ozar said without looking at me. "I'll take Bimo back to the Capitol soon enough. And we'll get the fireplace going, I promise."

Chief Gaffney continued to study the Royal Army's formation, running his fingers back and forth across his mustache. The S&R guards glanced nervously at him, waiting for the signal to shoot.

"One hundred and fifty," he announced. "Any closer, sir, and we'll be within range of their archers."

Ozar slid his tongue over the top row of his teeth. He was staring out at the meadow, or maybe at the trees beyond it. Wherever he was looking, he never blinked. Then he turned to Gaffney, his hands still hidden behind his back, and nodded.

Chief Gaffney got the message. "Marksmen, ready! For the Bridges! For the Bridges!" He shouted in both directions.

"For the Gorge!" the guards yelled back, and the twenty-five or so holding crossbows pulled the triggers.

The sky lit up around us like lightning had struck the tower twenty-five times. (Most people think that hell is hot, but I suspect it's also *loud*.) I ducked and covered my ears; cowardly, I know, but I couldn't help it. In my defense, I wasn't the only one. Ozar also doubled over, clenching his teeth. Although he had read every book by Orso the Bold, he wasn't expecting the shock of so many explosions at once.

As the guards fired round after round into the meadow, the tower began to shake. I crawled to the nearest wall and braced myself against the bricks. No structure could withstand these repetitive, violent pulses for long. I was certain the tower would topple any second.

Eventually, between booms, I heard Chief Gaffney's voice.

"Mr. Philosopher, did you hear me?"

"What's that, Chief?" Ozar asked. With my eardrums buzzing, I didn't hear his question either.

"Should I order the guards to keep firing, sir?"

Ozar cleared his throat and tried his best to sound composed. "Hold your fire; give me a minute to assess their position." He walked over to the parapet and raised his forearm to shield his eyes. I regret following him to the ledge, but I couldn't resist. I had to find out where that impossibly bright light was coming from.

In the field beyond the North Gate, rings of whitefire devoured the grass in near-perfect circles. They roared and hissed as they expanded and overlapped. Once my eyes adjusted to the blaze, which looked unearthly against the black sky, I saw red-and-white striped uniforms scattered in every direction. A majority of the South Branch had broken formation and retreated to the forest, seeking refuge from the horrible heat. Those marching on the front lines, however, didn't have the option to fall back: they were trapped inside the rings. Any soldiers brave enough to run through the fire collapsed on the other side, engulfed in flames. Those who waited in the middle didn't survive long either once their uniforms melted to their skin.

Most horrific, perhaps, were the soldiers who tried to escape the conflagration by diving into the Silver River. When they came to the surface to breathe, they inhaled scalding smoke instead of air, and their choice was to suffocate or drown. I didn't see any people swim to safety, just bodies floating downstream.

Ozar stood at my side, watching the gory scene. "See, Bimo?" he whispered at one point. "No reason to be afraid, right?"

In truth, I was more terrified than I had been before the battle, and Ozar didn't sound so confident himself.

When it was clear that the Royal Army was in full retreat, Ozar unclipped his cufflinks, rolled up his sleeves, and headed for the spiral staircase.

"You can take it from here," he said to Gaffney. "I have work to do at the Capitol. If they make another assault, fire as many shots as it takes to wipe them out. Let's go, Bimo; you're coming with me."

I couldn't stand to be on that tower any longer, so I followed him without hesitating.

At the bottom of the stairs, a carriage was waiting to take us back to the Capitol. The S&R guard in the driver's box waited patiently for us to board, but the two horses wouldn't hold still. They pawed the grass skittishly, their necks arched up toward the Cloudhorns.

As the driver turned the carriage around, I saw what the horses were looking at: floating over the city, far above the Four Bridges, a swarm of blue lights was coalescing in the sky. The points pulsed and flashed like bluefire dragonflies. Ozar didn't seem to notice, or maybe he didn't care, too focused on the next part of his plan.

"On second thought," he said, "I hope Chief Gaffney lets a handful of troops run back to the ocean. The king will hear our message more clearly if it comes from trembling lips, don't you think?"

When we returned to the Capitol, I followed Ozar down the main hall leading to the library. With his long strides and brisk pace, it was hard to keep up. Along the way he rambled on about various paintings and sculptures and ancient Philosophers, but I wasn't listening. An army had been obliterated, and the field beyond the North Gate was burning, so the last thing I needed at that moment was a history lesson. I wanted to be back in the Low Quarter playing make-believe music with Kati, Kevi, and Aris. I wanted to go home.

Although my memory of that walk through the Capitol is muddy, I remember passing by the armory. The guards hadn't cleaned up the area where they doused the rock wall with river water, so the mural that used to enclose the crossbows was a mound of silt, like a washed-out sandcastle. While Ozar had plenty to say about the artwork on the walls, he ignored the sand on the floor, and we marched straight through it, adding our footprints next to those made by the S&R's boots.

As we approached the library's entrance, two guards swung open the doors on cue so Ozar didn't have to break stride.

"I bring good news from the North Gate," Ozar announced as we entered. "The South Branch is in full retreat."

He scanned the room for Sera, but the library was empty and quiet. The seats at the mahogany table were pushed in, the books and papers arranged neatly in stacks.

"Ms. Avery, where are you? The first battle has been won, but the Royal Army will return eventually. For the city to be ready, we must begin our preparations right away."

"We're over here, Mr. Philosopher, by the Grand Fireplace," Sera said, from somewhere behind the bookshelves.

"Stay right there, we'll come to you."

I trailed Ozar through the stacks, holding onto his coattail so as not to get left behind. You must remember that I had never seen a library before, let alone the largest book collection on the continent, so the fear of getting lost was overwhelming. My ten-year-old imagination worried that with one wrong turn I might end up walking in circles forever.

If you told me that night I would learn to love the library and come to know its aisles by heart, I never would have thought it possible. Then again, I never expected to find Aris in the library that night either; yet, when we exited the last row of books, there he was, sitting next to Sera on the velvet couch.

"Bimo?" Aris asked, standing up. "Where did you . . . How did you . . ."

I let go of Ozar's coat and ran into Aris's arms. He lifted me up and spun me around. "I'm sorry I wasn't there to look after you," he whispered. "I won't let it happen again."

"It appears you two already know each other," Ozar said dismissively, "so I'll keep the introductions short. Ms. Avery, I'd like you to meet Bimo. He has played an instrumental part in our plan to protect the city."

"What? Where did you find him, sir?" Sera asked. "I thought the boy from the Low Quarter was still missing."

"I'll explain everything in due time. Right now, though, we must light the fireplace."

Sera desperately wanted more details about where I had been, but she couldn't risk deviating from the plan. *Timing is everything*, Aris had reminded her before Ozar arrived.

"My apologies, Mr. Philosopher," she said. "We'll get on that right away."

I watched Sera and Aris line up the candles along the hearth while Ozar rummaged through the heap of scrolls on the desk. When he found the one he wanted, he held it up to the light, and a faint shadow of cursive writing fell across his face.

"Aren't you interested in where I'm going, Ms. Avery? You always seemed so curious about Vesu's travels when she wore the shawl."

Sera dropped the tinderbox, and it nearly knocked over the candles. *Ozar must have figured it out*, she thought. *We should run while we have the chance.* Before bolting toward the doors, Sera glanced at Aris for guidance. As far as she could tell, he didn't seem fazed; he continued to light the candles calmly, one by one. *You still think this will work, huh?* Sera picked up the tinderbox and placed it on the mantel, keeping her back to Ozar so that he couldn't see her hands shaking. *You better be right.*

"Of course I'm interested, sir," she said, "but we've worked together for quite some time. I trust your judgment."

"Trust is indispensable, although I expect more from my Junior Philosopher than blind confidence. If we are to remake the City of Sterling, I need you to challenge me, to keep me honest."

Ozar lifted the Philosopher's shawl from its hook and made his way over to the faded line in the carpet.

"Take Vesu, for example. Can you imagine if she was wearing the shawl when the Royal Army arrived? If you and I hadn't convinced the council to open the armory, the Capitol would have crumbled by now. If Vesu had listened to my advice earlier, perhaps none of this would have been necessary. Perhaps she would still be here."

Sera tried to stay calm, but her patience was cracking beneath her like the edges of a frozen lake. She couldn't stand to hear Ozar speak about Vesu that way.

"The fire's ready, Mr. Philosopher. Have you decided where you will go? Can I help you put on the shawl?"

No one else noticed it, but I saw Aris nervously tapping a beat on his chest with his fingers. He told me later that he couldn't help it: he feared Sera had asked one question too many, pushed a little too far. If Aris's plan was going to work, Ozar had to believe—without the slightest doubt—that Vesu had truly chosen him to take her place.

Fortunately, Ozar failed to detect the annoyance in Sera's voice. With years of planning coming to fruition, his ambitions overpowered his other senses.

"I will visit Orso the Bold," he said confidently, draping the feathers over his shoulders. "Orso understood better than anyone the machinations of kings and queens. His writings made me realize that the crossbows are capable of so much more than security. If we use the whitefire aggressively enough, we can expand our city beyond these mountains and control every acre from here to Imperial Bay. In fact, I won't stop until we melt the throne itself. This continent should be governed by philosophy, not family. Don't you agree, Ms. Avery? Our leaders should be those most capable, those most just, those freely chosen."

By the end of his lecture, Ozar was still struggling to fasten the clasp on the Philosopher's shawl. The feathers didn't seem to fit him right. "I may need your help after all," he said. "I meant to get this tailored, but I haven't had the time."

Ozar bent down so that Sera could fasten the clip at the back of his neck. When the shawl was properly secured, he approached the silver flames with his hands at his sides. The fire flickered like it normally did, although the hissing sounded more intense, bordering on angry.

"It's hotter than Orso described in his journals," Ozar said, stopping three feet before the Grand Fireplace. From where I was sitting on the couch, I could see sweat dripping down the bumps of his spine. He flicked the scroll with Orso's name on it into the fire. It fizzled on contact and evaporated into ash.

As the smoke swirled around him, Ozar cracked his knuckles one at a time, and only then took a half step forward. *What is he waiting for?* Sera wondered. *Jump in already!* But instead of walking directly into the fire, Ozar slowly reached forward with his right hand, like a swimmer testing the water temperature before diving in.

I wish I had turned my head away sooner, but I saw everything. Ozar's hand, all the way up to his wrist, ignited, sizzled, and dissolved. He screamed something unintelligible and staggered backwards, waving his arm wildly until the flames died out. The skin where his hand had been was bubbling like boiling water.

"By the owl, what have you done?" Ozar howled.

No, no, no, no, no, Sera thought. *He was supposed to walk all the way through . . .*

"Did Vesu put you up to this?" Ozar demanded. "Was this her plan all along?"

Ozar lurched toward us. Aris threw me over his shoulder and carried me behind the couch for cover. Sera was on the other side and couldn't get around in time, trapped between Ozar and the Grand Fireplace.

"Sera, run!" Aris shouted. "Get to the council chamber!"

Sera didn't move. She stood firmly before the silver fire, her gaze as resolute as the snowy owl chiseled into the mantel.

"I know about the weatherbox, Ozar, and I *saw* how you used it. Vesu trusted you. I trusted you. Why did you hide it from us?"

"You don't understand what's at stake." Ozar paused as a pulse of pain shook his body. "Vesu lacked the vision to see what the weatherbox was capable of, like she failed to see the whitefire's full potential. I didn't want to deceive her, but I had no other choice."

"Vesu didn't have the *vision*?" Sera asked. "Look at Sterling now. Is that *your* vision? You provoked the army at our gates, you drove the Alpinees from their home, and you murdered my best friend's father."

"I did what was necessary," Ozar growled. "You think you can do better?" His eyes were tearing up, frothy spit forming on his lips. He ripped off the shawl with his left hand and threw it at Sera, who caught it in midair. "You'll be the youngest Philosopher in history. You really think you're ready for this?"

"Sera, let's go!" Aris begged. "We need to get out of here!"

This time, Sera listened. She took a step toward the doors to the council chamber, but she didn't react fast enough. Ozar lunged forward and pushed Sera so hard that she fell backward into the flames, clutching the black-and-white speckled shawl against her chest like it was a life jacket.

◉

Captain Carolin was so dehydrated that she felt dizzy and nauseous. The skin on her cheeks felt warm and tight, like a bad sunburn. She gripped her horse's reins with both hands, not so much to steer as to stay upright in the saddle. At that point she didn't care where the horse carried her, so long as it was *away*.

The blasts from the North Gate towers had ceased some time ago, but a heavy black smoke still hovered over the battlefield. That stifling fog and the moonless night made it impossible for Carolin to get her bearings or to regroup with her regiment. *If there's anyone left in my regiment*. Without any wind to clear the stagnant air, ashes floated around aimlessly, like snowflakes in a surreal storm.

Well, this isn't the snow we hoped to find in the Gorge, she thought, her mind wavering in and out of consciousness. *And that certainly wasn't the welcoming ceremony the colonel expected.*

Her horse came to an abrupt halt in the middle of the field, jolting her awake. He snorted and moved backward with a few jittery steps. Carolin was lucid enough to see what had disturbed him: charred bodies on the ground blocking the way. More red-and-white striped soldiers, like Colonel Orowin, who couldn't outrun the flames.

What do you want me to do? Go around! Let them rest!

That's what Carolin wanted to scream at her horse, but her voice was completely shot. She had lost it hours earlier during the South Branch's march toward the North Gate.

"Stay in formation!" she had shouted, over and over, cursing out any standard bearers who advanced too far ahead. If they followed her plan exactly, Carolin truly believed they stood a chance. By maintaining an echelon formation across the meadow, she hoped each unit's line of sight would remain clear, giving the soldiers a chance to dodge the whitefire blasts until the archers were within range. Convinced of their precision under pressure, she had assured Pearlin that the bowmen could pick off enough guards along the towers to buy time for the rest of the army, including the Prairie Riders, to breach the North Gate.

That plan was never going to work, Carolin admitted to herself now. *This fight was over before it started.* After watching the flames collapse on Colonel Orowin, she tried to warn her soldiers what the whitefire would look like. But in the end, it didn't make any difference. When the S&R launched that first round, the explosions scattered the South Branch in every direction. Keeping their lines together was impossible; the heat was too intense, the fire spread too quickly. And the shots kept coming. *Holy ocean! Was I the only archer to release my bow?*

After the second or third salvo from the crossbows, Carolin was the lone soldier marching forward. The rest of the Royal Army was already in retreat. Pearlin had fallen back too, ordering her troops to abandon the charge and to reassemble at the tree line with the Prairie Riders. Although Carolin knew she was taking on the entire S&R alone at that point, she couldn't stop herself. In a reckless attempt to taste revenge, if only a tiny drop of it, she whipped her horse into a gallop, heading straight toward the enormous gates that connected the two towers. Trusting her horse to weave between the circular fires expanding across the field, Carolin focused on the parapet, flinging arrows through the white-hot rings at the tiny gray figures in the center. After each shot she paused for a moment, listening for the telltale *thud/crunch* that a human body makes when it hits the ground from a great height.

But that sound never came. Despite her reckless, last-minute sprint, Carolin failed to bring down any S&R guards. Most of her shafts skidded into the dirt or cracked in half against the stone wall. When her quiver was empty, she turned her back on that gap in the mountains, not expecting to make it out of the field alive.

Now her head was pounding harder than the worst hangover she could remember. *And I never even tasted the Silver*

River ale. She tried to swallow, but she couldn't generate enough saliva. That's when Carolin gave up caring whether she lived or died and simply let her horse haul her away. Fortunately, the brown-spotted colt had a little drive left. He found a path around the burnt bodies and was nearing the meadow's end. The smoke was less dense there, and the tree line appeared in the distance—along with several groups of South Branch soldiers.

"Carolin? Is that you?" Pearlin rode up to her, with Prairie Riders and bison trailing close behind. "What the hell were you thinking, charging in alone like that? How did you expect to get out of there without . . ."

Pearlin eased up when she saw Carolin swaying in her saddle as though she were plastered, about to fall off her horse. "Whoa, hold on! Let me help you down."

Before Pearlin could dismount, a Prairie Rider reached out with its long, ligneous arms and wrapped its leafy-green fingers around Carolin's body, lowering her gently into a seated position on the grass. Pearlin dropped to a knee and spun the cap off her canteen.

"You need to drink something."

The stubborn captain refused to raise her head, so Pearlin did it for her. She lifted Carolin's chin and poured a stream of water into her half-open mouth. Small sips were all she could handle at first, most of the water dribbling down her jaw. Once her body began absorbing the cool liquid, though, she couldn't gulp it down fast enough. Carolin grabbed hold of the bottle and swallowed the rest without taking a breath.

"How many soldiers did we lose?" she rasped.

"Don't worry about that now," Pearlin said. "We'll get a final count on the ride back to the Basin."

"I need to know. How many did we lose?"

Pearlin scanned the forest's edge, where the surviving South Branch soldiers were congregating. Several groups had been tasked with breaking down the tents and wrapping the dead in tarps, although they quickly ran out of canvas.

And those were only the bodies they managed to find nearby. Pearlin refused to risk more lives sending troops back in to retrieve corpses, so she didn't have an exact number.

"It's hard to say. Roughly a hundred, maybe."

That's a quarter of our troops, Carolin thought. *They killed a quarter of our regiment.*

"Let's get the rest home safely, okay?" Pearlin extended her hand. "Here, I'll help you up."

Carolin ignored the offer, staring at the snow-capped Cloudhorns, which were still visible against the black sky. For months she had dreamed about seeing those peaks up close, and now she wished she hadn't. In one day, the Silver River Gorge had stolen more life from her than all those years fighting heat and boredom in the Basin.

And yet she wasn't quite ready to stand up. The long journey seemed incomplete, her mission unfinished, important questions unanswered. *When did the S&R get those weapons? Why did they use them against us?* She yanked a tuft of emerald-green grass out of the dirt. *Where will the Prairie Riders go?*

Reluctantly, she took Pearlin's hand and hoisted herself up. Pearlin brushed off the ashes and blades of grass that covered her uniform. "You ready to go home?"

As Carolin was about to answer, she saw something strange over Pearlin's shoulder: a swarm of blue lights in the southwest sky. The individual dots darted around randomly, but together they formed a spherical shape, like a cloud of gnats. *I probably stood up too quickly; I must be seeing stars.* After blinking a few times and rubbing her eyes, the light cluster was still there, expanding as it moved closer. Carolin turned to ask if anyone else was seeing the same thing, and the reply was self-evident: Pearlin, the Prairie Riders, and the rest of the Royal Army were all facing the Gorge, watching the strange lights descend out of the mountains.

While the others whispered about what it could be, Carolin grew anxious and assumed the worst. *This might be another weapon. I won't let the S&R catch us off guard again.* She quietly retrieved her bow from her saddle bag and stole an arrow from Pearlin's quiver.

"Wait, what are you doing?" Pearlin asked. "You don't know what that is."

I don't care what it is, Carolin thought. *I'm not letting it get any closer.* With one eye closed and the other squinting down the arrow's shaft, Carolin aimed at the center of the blue swarm. The curled fingers of her right hand pressed against her cheekbone as she prepared to release the bowstring.

That's when Carolin felt vines twist around her shoulders, crawl down her arms, and squeeze around the arrow. A Prairie Rider had her completely wrapped up.

Without the ability to move or shoot, Carolin was forced to watch as three figures dropped out of the sky and landed in the field. The blue orbs flying around them dissipated into the forest. One of the lights whirred past her head, and she saw that the buzzing creature was some version of a dragonfly, but much bigger and more beautiful than any she had seen in Imperial Bay.

While Carolin squirmed, trying to break free of the Rider's weedy tentacles, Pearlin addressed the three strangers.

"Who are you?"

She was surprised to hear the person in the middle speak first. He was wearing the same green jacket as the other two but stood half as tall.

"My name is Zeno Harper."

"Harper? That means nothing to me," Carolin said. "Give us your title so we know what to do with you." The Rider released its grip on her, but kept the arrow out of reach.

"Title? I don't have a title."

"You're not with the S&R?" Pearlin asked.

"No."

"So, the council sent you?"

"No."

"You must be here on behalf of the Philosopher then."

Zeno took a breath and thought for a second. "I guess I am here on behalf of the Philosopher. She's in trouble and we need your help."

Carolin wanted to laugh, but it stung her vocal cords to speak. "You're joking, right? This afternoon our colonel was torched at your doorstep, and now you need our help?"

"The Philosopher would never use those weapons," Zeno insisted. "Vesu was arrested four days ago and we assume she's locked up in the Capitol—or maybe worse. We believe the S&R has betrayed her."

"That's it? That's your story?" Carolin tossed her bow to the ground. "The funny thing is, we actually came here to lend a hand, and look how that turned out. We lost a hundred loyal soldiers and the Prairie Riders still have nowhere to go. If your Philosopher needed our help, she missed her chance."

Zeno didn't respond. He couldn't think of anything else to say. Carolin shook her head, grabbed her horse by the bridle, and turned her back on the Cloudhorns. With the conversation over, Pearlin and the Riders followed her toward the forest.

They would have kept marching, all the way back to the ocean, if Isolo hadn't spoken up.

"Excuse me, Captain," he said. "Before you go, let me explain why the Alpinees are prepared to fight at your side." Isolo let his ice axe fall to the ground next to Carolin's bow. "Like your friends here, my people have nowhere to go. Our little village is tucked away in the mountains, but we are also under attack. Whoever is choking the Prairie Basin dry is burying us with ice and snow. Young Harper tells us the Philosopher's assistant discovered a device that could cause such damage. But if you walk away, we'll never get our home back." Isolo gestured toward the Prairie Riders. "And those extraordinary creatures will never get theirs."

Carolin, apparently, remained unconvinced; she kept walking toward the woods. Something Isolo said was enough to sway Pearlin, though, and she turned around.

"Tell me about this device," she said. The Riders stopped to listen too.

"It's called a weatherbox," Zeno said quickly, desperate not to miss his opening. "It's a contraption that's capable of controlling the weather. The person who has it can move clouds, make rain, and generate wind. My brother saw a shopkeeper use one. It works."

"This weatherbox can return the Basin back to normal?" Pearlin asked.

"If we find the right one, I think so."

A weatherbox? Is Pearlin buying this? Carolin pulled her horse around and hurried back to the group. She grasped Pearlin by the shoulders and pulled her close. "I want to help the Riders too," she whispered, "but without better weapons, better armor, and a better plan, we won't get past the gate. It's time to turn back. Let's go home."

Pearlin bit her lip and looked at the sky. If they gave up now, the Riders would always be displaced, an outcome that Colonel Orowin would not have accepted. At the same time, Carolin was right: there was no way through the whitefire without risking everything. Returning to the Gorge would be suicide, a sacrifice that the colonel never would have asked of his troops.

That settled it. Pearlin wouldn't ask for that sacrifice either. "Alright, let's get out of here. We'll find somewhere safe for the Prairie Riders near Imperial Bay."

But when Pearlin pivoted to look for the bison, they were gone. The herd was moving across the meadow in the direction of the North Gate, kicking up clods of dirt as they picked up speed.

"Pearl . . . what are they doing?" Carolin asked.

Pearlin couldn't say for sure. After nearly a month of traveling with the Prairie Riders, she had never seen them move like this. Half of the Riders leapt onto the running beasts like warriors, while the other half twisted themselves into wild animal shapes—deer and wolves and bears—racing to keep up with the pack.

"Looks like they're not done fighting," Pearlin said. She mounted her white mare so that her voice would carry across the field to all the remaining soldiers. "And I won't let them fight alone. If anyone else feels the same, I hope you'll join me. But these are not orders—the decision is yours." She rocked forward in her saddle and lifted her reins, directing her horse to follow the stampede.

"Come on, Pearl, come back. They'll never reach the North Gate. Nothing can get past those weapons." Carolin looked for affirmation from the other soldiers, but they weren't listening. In fact, once they saw Pearlin take off after the Riders, the three hundred who remained dropped the gear they had packed for the return trip and rode after them.

See what you started, Colonel? As Carolin watched the Royal Army tear across the meadow, she remembered the orders that Colonel Orowin gave before they left the Basin. "The king has directed us to visit the Silver River Gorge to ensure its protection. We will provide assistance to any Prairie Riders who may need it along the way." *Even when you're gone, sir, they still follow you. Well, I can't let them finish the mission without me.*

Carolin whistled at two archers who were riding by and led them over to Zeno, Isolo, and Esili. "Jump on, Harper. You're coming with me. As for you two," Carolin said to the Alpinees scouts, "you can ride with the archers. Let's hope this run goes better than last time."

⬥

Carolin's group caught up with the rest of the regiment a few hundred yards from the towers. The smoke had mostly settled by then, but the earth surrounding them was blackened and brittle. *How will anything grow here again?* The S&R had fired at this spot during the first assault, but this time Carolin found herself at the back of the formation. For some reason the South Branch soldiers had stopped marching, and Carolin couldn't see far enough ahead to figure out why.

"What's going on up there? Let us through!"

The soldiers separated to make a path for their captain and the two archers escorting the Alpinees scouts. When they reached the front, Carolin had trouble making sense of what she saw: instead of the diagonal formation that Carolin had tried earlier, the Prairie Riders were forming a line perpendicular to the North Gate. Behind them the bison were grunting and smashing the grass with their hooves. *Holy ocean, how is this going to work?* Carolin spotted Pearlin near the bison and rode over.

"What's the plan?" she asked. Zeno, Isolo, and Esili listened in, eager to hear the strategy.

"I'm not sure," Pearlin replied. "I think they're getting ready to lead us in."

"If the Riders want to dodge the flames first, by all means."

"Hold on," Esili interjected. "Do you see the way they're lining up?" She pointed to the front of the formation, where the Riders were assembled not in one row but two. Each side stretched their arms up and across, the branches and vines sprouting and multiplying until they formed an arch, wide enough and tall enough for horses to run two or three abreast.

"They don't want us to run behind them," Pearlin said. "I think we're supposed to run *through*."

Not a second later, the bison confirmed Pearlin's intuition and rushed through the makeshift arch. As they ran, the Prairie Riders extended the tunnel toward the North Gate, the roots of their feet biting into the dirt so that the bison remained protected under the structure.

Pearlin immediately took off after the bison. The other three hundred soldiers remained bunched together in the field, unsure of what to do next.

"What are you waiting for?" Carolin shouted. "Orders from the Colonel? Everyone get inside before the explosions start again!"

Sure enough, the S&R guards launched another round of whitefire from the towers. This time, though, the South Branch didn't split up; the soldiers funneled together under the tunnel, which shielded them from the blasts.

Holy ocean! It's working! Kicking her horse to keep up, Carolin almost forgot that Zeno was riding with her until his arms squeezed tighter around her waist. Something above them was sizzling and popping like firecrackers. Carolin looked up, and the tunnel's roof was burning bright orange and red. Embers leaked down from the lattice as the fire chewed through. *This shelter won't hold up forever, but it should get the archers within range.*

In a matter of minutes the bison cleared the tunnel, bursting out of the opening with the speed of boulders in a rockslide. The brown-and-black beasts crashed into the North Gate, rattling the enormous oak panels, the wood splintering where their horns struck. They backed up and charged again.

Carolin caught up to Pearlin, who was waiting under the tunnel, watching the bison slam into the gate. "Time to send in the archers?" Carolin asked.

Pearlin shook her head.

"What are we waiting for? Those gates are a foot thick. They'll never break all the way through."

"They won't have to."

So how will we . . . Oh, I see what you mean. Once again, the Riders were a step ahead of her—and everyone else, for that matter, including the S&R. Chief Gaffney had not expected the South Branch to come back that night, let alone make it that close to the wall. And now with these beasts ramming into the gate, the S&R guards feared the Royal Army might actually break through. By the time Gaffney realized the true danger, it was too late.

"Stop, hold your fire!" he screamed. "Don't shoot anything close to the gate!"

Despite his warning, a young guard on the tower panicked. She aimed her crossbow at the huge animals directly below and pulled the trigger.

Pearlin cringed as the blast struck down several bison. Although she knew they had charged willingly, that didn't make it any easier to watch: the ring consumed their fur and bones and then roared across the grass. When the whitefire reached the gate, it crawled up the oak boards and devoured the wood like an army of fire ants.

As the red-orange glare grew brighter and hotter, Gaffney realized it was only a matter of time before the North Gate crumbled. At such close range the crossbows were useless, so the S&R had no way to fight back. "Retreat to the Capitol! Retreat!" He ran to the staircase, covering his head, expecting the onslaught of arrows to start any second.

"Alright, archers, it's our turn." Carolin announced. "Take out the guards on the towers and collect any weapons they leave behind. When those gates collapse, meet me inside the city."

Following her orders, the bowmen bolted from the tunnel and fanned out before the two towers. The S&R couldn't escape down the staircase all at once, so most of the gray uniforms were easy targets. *Thud/crunch. Thud/crunch. Thud/crunch.* The royal archers snatched up a handful of crossbows that fell alongside the bodies.

Less than thirty minutes later, the towers were cleared out and the North Gate toppled. Carolin and Pearlin led the South Branch through the three-inch-thick ash into the city. This time not a single soldier was missing, but the captains would later learn they had lost something else in the battle: the Prairie Riders would never leave that meadow.

"Hey, Harper, where's the Capitol?" Carolin shouted as the Royal Army entered the city. She was finally getting her voice back.

"It's over there, past those two bridges. The building with the silver dome."

"Alright, I see it. Let's find that weatherbox. And I guess we can help your Philosopher while we're at it. If there's still time, that is."

◍

You mustn't forget that all of this was new to me—the library, the Grand Fireplace, the Philosopher—so when Sera disappeared, my astonishment was absolute. Instead of her dress bursting into flames, as I expected, the young lady simply vanished, splashed into a waterfall. I had no idea how or why or where she went, but I wasn't alone with those questions.

"Bimo, help me move him," Aris said.

I was still coming to my senses, so it took me a second to realize what he meant. Ozar was lying unconscious on the carpet near the fireplace. Judging by the blood on the mantelpiece, I could see that he had smacked his head against the stone after lunging at Sera. I helped Aris drag his body to the couch and then we stood together before the Grand Fireplace, watching intently for any signs of life. With the fire roaring, six feet away was as close as we could comfortably get. The only sound in the library was the river running beneath us.

"Where did she go?" I asked.

"I don't know," Aris answered.

"How will she get out?"

"I'm not sure that she will."

"Isn't there anything we can do to help?" Considering how little I knew about the Philosopher at the time, it seemed like a fair question.

"Well, we can't go in after her," Aris said. "But maybe we can guide her home. Stay here, I'll be right back."

Aris left the room and returned a minute later with his violin case. He snapped open the clips, removed the instrument from its frame, and tuned up. With his shoulders parallel to the fireplace, he closed his eyes—I closed mine too—and he played "Hymn to the Swallows," the song that he had learned for Vesu's trial. In the expansive library the melody spread out down every aisle, like the music was searching for something. The sound from Aris's strings filled the space so fully that I could no longer hear the fire hissing or Ozar's heavy breathing. It even drowned out the sound of the water flowing beneath us.

When Aris reached the third verse, I heard sounds from behind the fire: gasping, splashing, coughing. I wasn't sure if I should interrupt the song, but I had to speak up.

"Aris, did you hear that?"

He set down his violin, and the sounds became clearer. Someone was definitely inside the flames.

"Sera, we're right here!" Aris called out. "Follow my voice!"

Seconds later, Sera stepped over the candles and emerged from the flames. Her golden hair was drenched, and her blue dress soaked, but otherwise she seemed unscathed. The fact that I barely knew Sera back then didn't diminish the feeling of relief that washed over my body. Although the Four Bridges were still a mystery to me, I knew that wherever she had gone, and whatever she had seen, it would somehow change everything.

"Sera, you made it! We need to get out of here." Aris grabbed her hand, ready to lead us out of the library before the S&R showed up. But Sera didn't register his sense of urgency; her eyes were dazed, her limbs moved in slow motion.

"Are you okay?" Aris asked. "Why are you dripping wet? Where did it take you?"

"I'm not exactly sure," Sera said faintly, like her thoughts were a thousand miles away. "When Ozar pushed me, I fell backwards into the opening, into that hole inside the hearth . . ."

"You fell into the river?" Aris asked.

"I held my breath for as long as I could. I think I saw where it ends."

"Where what ends? What do you mean?"

"I mean the Silver River was *empty*, Aris. Completely dried up. And Sterling was no longer a city, just a collection of abandoned buildings inhabited by ghosts. The Four Bridges had collapsed too. Without anyone to care for them, the wood beams splintered in the sun, cracked into pieces. The flags and banners were strewn about, gnarled into knots, threadbare, colorless . . ."

The looks on our faces must have frightened her because Sera turned away. She stared at the snowy owl in the mantelpiece instead.

"Holding the bridge fragments between my fingers, I felt compelled to find out what happened. So I followed the river north—or the fireplace took me north, however that works—and the Prairie Basin was barren too. Totally deserted. The riverbed was cluttered with skulls and rocks and bones and dust. The hollowness of that place was so haunting that I tried to turn around . . ."

Sera spread out her arms and leaned forward, standing on her tiptoes. "But the wind wouldn't let go. It carried me all the way to Imperial Bay. I had memorized Vesu's stories about the ocean and I always wanted to see it myself. The city that I found, though, was nothing like she described. The downtown was as desolate as the Gorge. The streets were silent, the marketplace falling apart, the stadium in disrepair, and not one soldier was guarding the castle, so I let myself in.

"I climbed the stairs until I reached the bell tower, and from there I could see the royal gardens. I had heard the king's gardens were magnificent—Elerin wrote about them often—but these grounds were beyond beautiful. The landscaping extended for miles in both directions along the bay: curved-trunk coconut trees lined the walking paths, pink coral honeysuckle clung to the trellises, and beach sunflowers blanketed the shoreline. The only thing taller than the orange trees were the fountains, which spouted water fifty feet into the air."

Sera described the royal gardens in such detail that I could picture them perfectly. Despite how radiant they sounded, her description was unnerving. If Imperial Bay was truly empty, who was tending to everything?

"But here's the strangest thing," Sera continued. "I couldn't see *beyond* the gardens. The ocean was covered by clouds. I sensed that whatever killed the Silver River was hiding out there somewhere and it wanted me to come looking for it. The pull was so intense that I nearly took off running toward the beach. In fact, the only reason I stopped was the music. When I heard your song, Aris, I realized that I couldn't solve this on my own. If I kept searching in that dream, I surely would have run out of breath. From there it was too late to change anything anyway. I knew I needed to come back here and search the ocean *before* the Silver River dies."

I was speechless, but Aris had a hundred questions. As he stuttered over where to start, we heard a groan from the other side of the room. Ozar was waking up, and Palo was trying to revive him.

"What in the Gorge happened to you, sir?" Palo asked, dabbing Ozar's forehead with a damp cloth.

I didn't hear Ozar's response. Aris yanked on my arm, and we ran toward the library's southeast exit. As we pushed through those double doors, it was officially the first time that I set foot inside the council chamber.

The first thing I noticed was the dome's stained-glass ceiling, which shimmered in every shade of blue. Then the chandeliers caught my eye, the intricate crystal somehow curved into the graceful shape of raindrops. Next I marveled at the marble floor, which was cut so smoothly that it mirrored the candles glowing above.

I was so absorbed in the architecture that I failed to notice the group at the center of the room: Chief Gaffney and Councilman Taro were standing on stage, surrounded by S&R guards.

"Ms. Avery, we have an emergency," Gaffney said in a shaky voice. "Where's the Philosopher?"

Sera froze. She wasn't expecting anyone to be in the council chamber, let alone so many S&R guards. *Why isn't Chief Gaffney at the North Gate? How are we going to get out of the Capitol?* When Sera didn't respond, Aris took control and led us onstage next to the podium.

"The Philosopher is preoccupied at the moment," he said. "He's conducting critical research to prepare for the next attack."

"The next attack is already here!" Taro shrieked. "Tell the Philosopher that the whitefire failed. The Royal Army has breached the North Gate and they're storming the city."

That's not possible, I thought. *I saw those red-and-white uniforms on fire. I saw the South Branch running away.*

"They'll reach the Capitol any minute," Gaffney confirmed. "We need the Philosopher's instructions for what to do next. Do we surrender and save what we can? Or do we fight back and possibly burn down everything?"

As Chief Gaffney shifted his crossbow from one arm to the other, the hinges on the double doors squeaked open. Ozar hobbled into the room. His ghastly appearance sucked the air out of the council chamber. He needed Palo's support to stay upright as he climbed the stairs onto the circular stage.

"By the owl, what happened to you, sir?" Gaffney asked.

Taro didn't seem to care, let alone notice the bandages wrapped hastily around Ozar's forearm. He tugged nervously at the rings on his fingers. "Mr. Philosopher, what do we do now? If the South Branch doesn't kill us, they'll haul us to Imperial Bay as prisoners."

Ozar gripped Taro's shoulder with his good arm to steady himself. "Let's ask Ms. Avery. I'm sure the Philosopher has an answer."

The chamber became so silent that I could hear the water dripping from Sera's dress, collecting in a puddle at her feet.

"I . . . I don't understand," Taro mumbled.

"I missed it too, Councilman," Ozar continued. "Vesu's treason ran deeper than any of us realized. Ms. Avery conspired with my predecessor to steal the shawl. She must be arrested immediately."

The S&R guards who encircled us raised their crossbows and aimed them at Sera, waiting for the chief's orders. Looking back, I doubt any of them realized the danger: pulling the trigger would have wiped out everyone on stage.

"I didn't steal anything," Sera responded. "I never asked to be the Philosopher. Vesu *chose* me."

As her words echoed up the chamber's walls, the doors on the first balcony burst open. A team of Alpinees scouts rushed in, followed by a stream of South Branch soldiers. They spread out around the rotunda. When everyone was in position, Zeno entered the room with Carolin and Pearlin.

"Let them go," he called out, "and I promise we'll spare your lives."

All eyes were on Chief Gaffney. He removed his cap, tucked it under his arm, and scratched his mustache with his fingernails.

"I don't think you get the message," Carolin warned. "Release the young lady immediately, or we'll put an arrow through your chest and walk her out ourselves."

Her archers pulled back their bows in unison.

"Remember the oath you took to protect the Gorge," Ozar said to Gaffney. "What are you waiting for? Arrest her!"

I'm not sure what Ozar expected Chief Gaffney to do next, but it certainly wasn't this: he dropped to one knee and ripped the four white ribbons from his uniform. Then he slid his crossbow across the floor, where it came to rest at Sera's feet.

"Vesu was right about the armory," he said quietly. "I never should have doubted her. I ask for your forgiveness, Madam Philosopher."

Madam Philosopher. Sera was not expecting to feel the full weight of those words all at once. It was like being at the center of everything and absolutely alone at the same time. *The citizens of Sterling expect me to lead*, she thought, *but I'm the only one who can see what lies ahead.*

A river drained . . .

A lifeless city . . .

An endless desert . . .

Sera tried to swim away, but the visions of the future from inside the Grand Fireplace stalked her like sharks.

A garden maintained by ghosts . . .

A mask over the ocean . . . and whatever was hiding behind it.

I need to know why it's calling me.

"Aris, pick it up!" Zeno shouted.

Sera was lost in thought, so Aris grabbed the crossbow instead. As he set it against his shoulder, it was clear he didn't know what to do with it. Gaffney was down on one knee, but the S&R guards hadn't moved, unwilling to let us leave the stage.

"I don't see a way out, Bimo," Aris whispered.

I didn't see one either. The council chamber was supposed to be where freedom was balanced with fairness, where the search for truth brought us closer to justice, where the vulnerable had a voice, where the low quarters could be lifted up. But that system had been twisted, turned upside down. By inventing enemies and conjuring chaos, we had trapped ourselves inside. I thought we would never leave that stage . . . until Sera spoke up.

"Aris, have you ever wondered how Aldo built this place?" she asked. "How he shaped that stone into a perfect circle?"

We both looked up at the ceiling. I only saw candles, crystal, and glass, but Aris saw the same thing as Sera: a gap in the chandeliers directly above us. *That's enough space to keep us safe*, he thought. *This is our chance to rebuild. Not to start over completely, but to take another path.*

He aimed the crossbow at the ceiling, buried his eyes in the crook of his arm, and blasted the ceiling with a ring of whitefire.

That's how the Capitol dome came crashing down, and how I ended up next to Aris in the rubble.

○

It took us two years to rebuild—not only the Capitol building, but the City Council itself. During that time, Sera presided over the most significant restructuring of the City of Sterling in its long and storied history.

As her first official act, Sera appointed Aris as her Junior Philosopher, which he humbly accepted. Everyone assumed that Zeno would take over the S&R, but he had other plans. Instead, Carolin and Pearlin, who weren't in a hurry to make the arduous trek back north, volunteered to recruit a new class of S&R guards until Chief Gaffney's replacement could be nominated and confirmed. In exchange for room and board, the South Branch soldiers helped to reconstruct the Capitol building and the North Gate, and they finally got their chance to explore the city between the mountains (and every one of its taverns.)

As for the council, Taro was crushed and killed by the dome when it collapsed. The other three council members resigned immediately, and elections for their replacements were held. Once the new governing body was sworn in, Sera set an agenda focused on all the problems that the previous council had ignored, starting with the trillium seeds. With the help of the Grand Fireplace and the Alpinees' mountain medicines, she managed to reverse the epidemic's course and restore much-needed hope to the lower quarters. To live up to Vesu's legacy, however, she had much more to accomplish.

The next order of business was the prosecution of Ozar Wrinn. Although the rescuers found him breathing between shattered chandeliers, the court of public opinion favored swift justice: no one doubted that he deserved to die on that stage. Nevertheless, Sera insisted on a full and fair trial. She wouldn't allow the judicial system to be abused any further. Moreover, she believed that if the council learned the true lengths to which Ozar had gone to unlock the armory—falsifying records, framing the Philosopher, and weaponizing the weather—her other priorities would fall into place.

And it worked. On the first day of fall, over two years after the Capitol caved in, the council returned its verdict. Sera made the announcement on the Low Quarter bridge so that the whole city could listen. Standing under the arch next to Aris, holding Zeno's hand, with long blue banners unfurled behind her, Sera started her speech the same way Vesu always did.

"Fellow countrymen and friends," she said, "although I'm proud to wear the Philosopher's shawl, I'm ashamed of how it fell onto my shoulders. Since my predecessor did not receive the inscription ceremony she deserved, today we will honor her memory."

Sera waited until the bridgekeeper finished carving the full name into the wood panel—*Vesu the Soft-Hearted*—before she continued. "The council has also made its decision regarding the charges against Ozar Wrinn. Despite finding him guilty of his crimes, the council has decided to spare his life." Whispers spread out in waves as the crowd tried to make sense of the verdict. No one had expected Ozar to live another day. Zeno squeezed Sera's hand. *Keep going. They'll listen to you.*

"Rather than perpetuate the brutality that brought us here," Sera announced, "the council will carry on Vesu's work. First, we must destroy the whitefire—we have better ways to defend the Four Bridges." Sera waved her hand, and the S&R guards tossed the crossbows into the river. The white-hot embers that powered the weapons hissed when they hit the water and turned coal-black when they burned out.

"Second, we will no longer let nature be manipulated. As part of our apology to the Alpinees, the weatherbox has been dismantled."

Isolo and Esili stepped forward and bowed before the beam with Amos Harper's name on it. Then they threw the broken pieces of the mahogany table over the railing.

"Third, we must do more to safeguard the Silver River. While my term as Philosopher has been brief, I have seen many things. To ensure the river never runs dry, in one month I will leave for Imperial Bay. I will bring Mr. Wrinn with me so the king may impose the appropriate punishment. I hope my journey will send a message—not only to the crown, but to the entire continent—that the Silver River is our most precious resource. Zeno Harper has agreed to accompany me, and the South Branch is willing to show us the way. In my absence, Aris Harper will serve as the Philosopher—if he's willing to wear the shawl, that is."

Everyone turned to Aris. Although Sera hadn't shared this part of her plan with him, he sensed it was coming. As much as Aris dreaded the spotlight, the responsibility, he knew nothing could stop Sera from going to the ocean after it had called out to her through the Grand Fireplace. He dropped to one knee and let Sera set the speckled shawl on his shoulders.

"Finally, to remember his bravery, Colonel Orowin's name will also be added to this bridge. As for the Prairie Riders, let us honor their sacrifice the only way we have left: to live by their example. To show our gratitude, we will preserve the garden they left for us in perpetuity."

When Sera made this promise, the wind picked up from the northeast, rustling the pine trees of Shoulder Ridge and whooshing through the meadow beyond the North Gate. Even though it was early autumn, the tunnel that the Prairie Riders had formed was bursting into reds, oranges, and golds. While the bison continued to graze peacefully in the field, the breeze blew the leaves right off the branches. Most of the foliage fell into the river, where it floated downstream between the towers, through the upper quarters, and under the Capitol, its silver roof restored. When the leafy blanket finally reached the Low Quarter Bridge where all of us were standing, it truly seemed as though the Silver River was on fire.

I guess that leaves me. After Sera's announcement, Aris invited me to live in the Capitol as the Philosopher's apprentice. Sera and Zeno's journey to Imperial Bay was expected to take a year and Aris needed someone he could rely on to help light the candles in the library. Although I never quite developed his intuition, I must have done well enough because Aris eventually chose me as his successor (which is how I ended up here, of course, writing this journal to you).

But the full story of how I became a Philosopher—the final Philosopher, in fact—is a story for another time. For now, all you need to know is that I followed Aris everywhere, listening to his every word.

I even went with him to Wasko's tavern the night before Sera and Zeno headed north. Technically, I was still too young to get into the pub, but they make exceptions when you show up with the Philosopher.

I sat next to Aris at the bar, shyly observing the conviviality around me. Carolin flirted with Wasko as he poured her another golden ale on the house. Pearlin reclined in the corner, listening to the band with her boots on the table. Sera and Zeno danced awkwardly near the window, mostly laughing at how terrible they were at keeping time.

Everyone was in good spirits, it seemed, except for Aris, who was nervously tapping a beat on the barstool. He was confident that his brother and the South Branch soldiers would keep Sera safe on the road to Imperial Bay, but he wasn't sure how she would reach the king once they got there. And if she was invited into the castle somehow, would the king believe what she saw in the Silver River? Did he know about the Grand Fireplace?

Aris quit drumming when the tavern door swung open, and Mr. Marcel walked in.

"I can't believe he actually came," Aris said to me, his mood immediately improving. "Mr. Marcel, we're over here!"

With a tight grip on his green suspenders, Mr. Marcel pushed through the crowded bar with his head down. Along the way a woman asked the bearded stranger to dance, but he bashfully declined. It was Mr. Marcel's first time inside a tavern, as far as anyone knew, and he was clearly overwhelmed by all the commotion. Zeno and Sera abandoned the dance floor too and joined us at the bar.

"Thanks for coming, Mr. Marcel," Aris said. "Can I buy you a drink?"

The old shopkeeper shook his head.

"Not even one?" Zeno asked. "If you don't drink with me now, you'll have to wait about a year before I'm back in this pub."

"Leave him alone," Sera said, tugging on Zeno's shirt. "We're glad you're here, Mr. Marcel. Any advice for our trip? Considering all those odds and ends in your shop, I'm sure you've seen more of the continent than we have."

Mr. Marcel's bushy eyebrows twitched in excitement, curving upward like a squirrel's tail. He removed a piece of parchment from his pocket and fumbled while trying to unfold it.

"Here, let me help," Aris said. He pushed aside the tin cups on the counter and spread out the parchment. The page was filled with hand-drawn lines and arrows, crisscrossing back and forth, connecting various names and addresses in an intricate web. In the center, where all the scribbles converged, was a crown sketched in green ink. The drawing was clearly a map of some kind, but it didn't show any roads or landmarks, no compass or legend.

"Thank you, Mr. Marcel, but I'm not sure how to use this," Sera said. "I haven't heard of any of these people."

Carolin caught part of our conversation and was curious enough to leave Wasko alone for a minute. She leaned over my shoulder to study Mr. Marcel's map. "I recognize a few of those names," she said. "They're the king's advisors, part of his inner circle."

"Can they help me get inside the castle?" Sera asked.

"I don't know," Carolin said, swallowing the rest of her beer. "But this list is your best bet. From what I remember, the king has more gatekeepers than a shark has teeth. In fact, I never met the man myself, and neither did Colonel Orowin during all his years of service."

"Mr. Marcel, how do you know all this?" Aris asked.

I don't think Mr. Marcel heard the question. He was busy searching his pockets for a pen, which he eventually found clipped to his suspender strap. He grabbed a napkin from the bar, scribbled a short message, and slid the note to Sera.

The light in the tavern was low, but we could all read the green ink clearly enough:

I'll tell my friends you're coming.
Be careful.

About the Author

Brendan J. Dailey writes fiction inspired by his adventures in the wilderness and the songs swirling around in his head. When he's not writing, Brendan practices environmental and natural resources law as an attorney and professor. Brendan graduated from Loyola University Chicago School of Law and from Boston College with a Bachelor of Arts in Political Science and Philosophy. He lives in Chicago with his wife and daughter.

Made in the USA
Monee, IL
18 July 2023